Praise for Sally Nicholls' novels:

All Fall Down

SHORTLISTED
Independent Booksellers' Week ~~P~~
Coventry Inspiration ~~~~

NOM~~~~
CILIP Carneg~~~~
UKLA Book ~~~~ ~~13~~

Children's Books Ireland Recommended Read
We Sat Down Top 20 Books

"Exceptional... A terrific story"
Lorna Bradbury, Telegraph

"Absorbing and utterly chilling...
A welcome return from Nicholls"
Bookseller Children's Buyer's Guide

"A heart-stopping novel... Move over, *The Hunger Games*.
This is the real deal. Writing is a kind of sorcery – and Sally
Nicholls is a true practitioner of the art"
Katy Moran's Book Review Blog

Ways to Live Forever

WINNER
Waterstone's Children's Book Prize
Glen Dimplex New Writer of the Year
Six UK regional awards
Luchs Prize – Best Book of the Year (Germany)
USBBY List of Outstanding International Books (U.S.A.)

SHORTLISTED
Branford Boase Award
UKLA Children's Book Awards
Five UK regional awards
Le Prix des Incorruptibles (France)

NOMINATED
WHSmith Children's Book of the Year
CILIP Carnegie Medal

"I love this book"
Jacqueline Wilson

"Powerful, inspiring and courageous . . . the debut of the year"
Waterstones

"Elegant, intelligent, moving"
Guardian

Season of Secrets

NOMINATED
UKLA Children's Book Awards, 2010

"This is a cracking book"
Jacqueline Wilson

"Nicholls is a writer of enormous power and strength.
Wonderful, evocative, lively"
Literary Review

"Yet another extraordinary story"
Waterstone's Books Quarterly

"Poignant and gripping ... intertwines ancient
myths of pagan gods with an emotive
and touching love story"
Bookseller

"Wonderful, glorious writing...
Odd, strange and wholly convincing"
School Librarian

"Absolutely wonderful"
Bookwitch

Sally Nicholls was born in Stockton, just after midnight, in a thunderstorm. Her father died when she was two, and she and her brother were brought up by her mother. She has always loved reading, and spent most of her childhood trying to make real life work like it did in books.

After school, she worked in Japan for six months and travelled around Australia and New Zealand, then came back and did a degree in Philosophy and Literature at Warwick. In her third year, realizing with some panic that she now had to earn a living, she enrolled in a masters in Writing for Young People at Bath Spa. It was here that she wrote her first novel, *Ways to Live Forever*, which won the Waterstone's Children's Book Prize in 2008, and many other awards, both in the UK and abroad. Sally's second novel, *Season of Secrets*, was published in 2009.

www.sallynicholls.com

ALL FALL DOWN

SALLY NICHOLLS

MARION LLOYD BOOKS

First published in the UK in 2012 by Marion Lloyd Books
This edition published in 2013 by Marion Lloyd Books
An imprint of Scholastic Children's Books
Euston House, 24 Eversholt Street
London, NW1 1DB, UK
A division of Scholastic Ltd

Registered office: Westfield Road, Southam Warwickshire, CV47 0RA
SCHOLASTIC and associated logos are trademarks and/or registered
trademarks of Scholastic Inc.

ISBN 978 1407 13534 2

A CIP catalogue record for this book is
available from the British Library

Printed and bound by CPI Group (UK) Ltd, Croydon, CR0 4YY
Papers used by Scholastic Children's Books are made
from wood grown in sustainable forests.

1 3 5 7 9 10 8 6 4 2

This is a work of fiction. Names, characters, places, incidents
and dialogues are products of the author's imagination or are used
fictitiously. Any resemblance to actual people, living or dead,
events or locales is entirely coincidental

www.scholastic.co.uk/zone

To Zoe Owlett,
who is, I am assured,
very cool.

CONTENTS

BOOK THREE – HOME

BOOK
ONE

INGLEFORN

I buried with my own hands
five of my children in a single grave...
No bells. No tears. This is the end of the world.

Agnolo di Tura
1348

The year I turned thirteen, it rained every day from Midsummer to Christmastide. Sheep, huddled grey and sodden in the fields, caught the murrain and died. What oats and barley and rye we could grow were weak and spindly and covered in strange green mould, which had to be scraped off before the grain could be milled. Everyone was hungry most of the time, and in the villages further up the valley, people died.

Travellers passing through Ingleforn on the road from York told stories of strange happenings in faraway lands. Earthquakes and volcanoes and a new sickness that swept through the people of the cities, leaving not a soul alive. Mostly, the travellers were quite cheerful about these disasters.

"Not a good year to be a Frenchie," they'd say. And, "Paris will be King Edward's for the taking, if he wants it."

Even the wandering holy men, the hermits and friars, the preachers and pardoners, even they seemed to relish all this destruction happening over the seas.

"God sends His angels to wipe the wicked from the earth!" they cried, and the villagers nodded and sighed and agreed that yes, there were a lot of wicked in Castile and Aragon and France indeed, and wasn't it terrible?

But in the summer of the year of grace 1348, the stories changed. The sickness had come to Bristol, some said. At first it was just a rumour; then as more travellers told the same tale, we started to believe it. Then the sickness – the pestilence – was in London. London!

Now the preachers and pardoners and hermits and friars told a new story.

"The end of the world is coming!" they said, eyes blazing with righteousness, hair wild and untamed. "Repent! Repent!"

And the villagers muttered together in little huddles, and some of the richer men – the free men, the franklins and the yeomen – talked about selling their land and moving north, to Duresme maybe, or the wild lands beyond, in Scotland, as though they could somehow hide from the wrath of God. Most of them shook their heads and sucked in their teeth. Most of them don't have the gold to flee. Or we belong to Sir Edmund, and have no choice in the matter anyway.

We knew then that 1349 would be terrible.

But nobody could have imagined quite how terrible it was going to be.

1. *Morning*

It's Sunday morning, early, towards the beginning of June. It's dark still, the pale grey light before dawn, and below the floor of the solar my baby brother Edward is crying. On the mattress beside me, Ned groans and buries his head in the bolster, but I lie and listen to the creak of the bed as Alice climbs out of it below me. A few moments later, I hear her footsteps on the earth floor. I push myself up on my elbows and lift aside the blanket-curtain, peering down. Alice is wearing nothing but a woollen slip and a nightcap, her yellow hair impossibly rumpled as always in the mornings. She lowers herself on to a stool and opens her slip, revealing her heavy, mottled breast. Edward's screams are quietened as he suckles. Alice looks up and smiles as she sees me watching.

"Awake, are you?" she says. "Can you get dressed and get the others up? I'll need someone to go for water."

There are a lot of people in my family. I have four brothers – two older and two younger – and one little sister. The older boys don't live here any more. Richard lives with his wife

Joan in a little house he built himself at the other end of the village. Geoffrey – my favourite brother – comes next. He left when he was eleven. He's at St Mary's Abbey, training to be a priest.

I'm next, then red-haired Ned, who's nine, and little Margaret, still the baby of the family even now we have Edward. They're curled up on the mattress beside me. I shake Ned.

"Nedkin, it's morning. Wake up!"

Ned moans and curls up tighter in his warm little ball of elbows-and-knees.

Margaret is still asleep, a strand of yellow hair falling over her cheek. She wakes easily, blinks her blue eyes and smiles at me.

"Is it morning?"

"Morning. Come on. Get your clothes on."

Father built our solar, a triangular loft space under the roof of our house. It's almost exactly the right size for our mattress, which is made of sacking stuffed with hay. In the corners where the roof slopes down to the floor, grain sacks and tallow candles and lengths of rope are packed. No space is wasted.

"Ned!" I shake my brother again. "Come *on*."

I pull my gown over my head and climb barefoot down the ladder. Maggie follows behind me, carrying her clothes in a bundle. I help her fasten her shoes and tug the comb through her hair. She squeals.

"You're hurting!"

"Here—"

Alice takes the comb and starts teasing out Maggie's tangles. I sit on the bottom rung of our ladder and pull on my hose. It's dark. Alice hasn't started the hearth-fire, and the shutters are still drawn across the narrow windows. The air is cold enough to make me shiver.

The hearth sits in the centre of the room. Alice's pots and flagons and goblets sit round-bellied beside the hams and cheese on the shelves above the table, out of reach of the animals. Other everyday things lean against the walls – buckets and scythes and brooms and sacks of barley and an ale barrel half-full of ale and Alice's loom with a bolt of cloth half-woven. In the low space beneath our solar, a blanket is nailed to the cross-beam to hide the bed where Father and Alice and Edward sleep.

At the other end of the room, behind their wattle wall, the animals are waking up, . Our cow, Beatrice, snorts at me through her nose. We have two oxen for the plough, a cow, a pig, eight chickens and a fine red cockerel. Father is always talking about building a byre to keep the animals apart, but he never does. I don't mind. I like the cosiness of all sleeping together, the funny snorts and breathy noises in the night, their warmth in winter. They add a rich, earthy, animal smell to the other scents in the house – woodsmoke and straw and thyme and rosemary.

My name is Isabel. I am fourteen years old, and I can't imagine ever living another sort of life to this.

– How wrong I am.

"Done?" says Alice, as Mag leans back into her knees. "You look like a girl who wants to fetch some water. Ned! Aren't you up yet? The sun'll be up before you, and we all know what a lay-a-bed she is. Come on!"

But the sun is stirring, turning the frowsy wisps of cloud a pale, early-morning pink. Summer will be here soon. I can

7

feel it as I walk to the well, swinging the empty bucket beside me. Soon there'll be sunshine and harvest and swimming in the river by the church. On a morning like this, the sickness seems very far away.

Our house sits a little apart from the other houses of the village, on the edge of the green, in the shade of two hornbeam trees. It isn't far to the well. As I walk across the grass, I pass other village houses, built in odd clumps around the watermill, the green, and the river, the distances between them growing as you move further away from the church, which sits at the very centre of Ingleforn. Here is the forge, and the oven, and the Manor Oak, where Sir Edmund's steward holds the manor court three times a year. Beyond the churchyard are the archery butts, where every able-bodied man is supposed to work at his archery, though Sir Edmund doesn't mind too much if sometimes they forget, particularly at harvest time and hay-making.

The road from York runs along the river for as many miles as I've travelled it, crossing into the village at the bridge by the watermill and coming along past the church and the front of our gate. The carters come through nearly every day, and the pilgrims in the spring on their way to St William's shrine, and the wandering preachers, the merchants, the lepers, the madmen, and the holy fools.

The two big village fields – Three Oaks and Hilltop – are spread one to the left and one to the right of our door. Father farms nearly a virgate of land divided between the two. Behind the house is a narrow copse of woodland, and behind the woods is Sir Edmund's manor house – we go for the festivities at Christmastide, but mostly we stay away.

Why worry the rich, if you don't want them to worry you? Sir Edmund has another, larger estate in Devon, and a big house in London where he lives for most of the year, God keep him.

Behind the manor house is the village of Great Riding, and behind the furthest edge of Great Riding's fields is the abbey, where my brother Geoffrey lives. Behind the abbey is Riding Edge, and beyond it more farmland – rich, flat ploughland all the way to York, two long days' walking away, where I've never been, but Alice says isn't worth the journey,

"Not when you could be here, Isabel. Not when you could be here!"

There's a line of women and children already waiting by the well. The others nod in my direction, rumpled and sleepy-eyed. Plump, copper-haired Amabel Dyer, who's about my age and sort of a friend, smiles at me.

The women are talking in little huddles.

"They have it in York!"

"York!"

"Fifty dead already, I heard."

"I heard a hundred."

"My man Nicholas said the road from York is full of families fleeing north. Horses and ox-carts and rich men in fancy litters with servants to carry them about so they don't ever need to walk."

Amabel Dyer catches my eye.

"Is it true about York?" she whispers. "Does Geoffrey know?"

My belly tightens.

"Of course it's not," I tell Amabel. "It's just carters' tales."

But all the happiness has gone from the bright morning.

York is less than a day's ride away.

York is nearly here.

2. *The Romance of Father and Alice*

Alice is my stepmother, and one of my favourite people
in the world. It's like a mummer's play, how she and
Father married. My mother died when Maggie was born, and
after that Father didn't want to marry anyone else. He sent
Maggie to Robin's mother to nurse, and my brother Richard,
who was fifteen, had to look after me and Ned and Geoffrey.
He wasn't very good at it, and we got used to living with dirty
clothes, and burnt pottage, and stale ale, and a hearth-fire that
wouldn't light because all the wood was wet.

The women in the village clicked their tongues at this, and
brought us to the manor court, where Sir Edmund's steward
ordered Father to remarry within three weeks, or have another
wife found for him. But Father wouldn't. He just nodded
his head and carried on like he was. So then Sir Edmund's
steward looked at Ned and Geoffrey and me, with our red eyes
and muddy faces and hair all wild, and told Father that he had
to marry Agnes Harelip by Midsummer Day.

Poor Father! And poor us. Agnes Harelip is an old shrew.
She works as a spinster, spinning thread for the yeomen's

wives in Ingleforn and Great Riding, and she lives in this neat little cottage where everything is just so. She looked at Richard and Geoffrey and Ned and me with absolute horror. Father pursed up his lips, but he didn't say anything. The next day, though, he washed his face and hands, and mine too, and combed my hair, and he took me to the house where Agnes's father lived.

Father knocked on the door, and Alice answered. I knew her a little, and I liked her even then. Her yellow hair was coiled in a knot at the back of her neck, but these long strands had escaped and were fuzzing up around her ears. Her big hands were covered in malt, but her eyes were laughing and kind.

"Is your father there?" Father said, and Alice said, "No, but come and take a sup, and bring the child too."

Inside, the house was neat and swept, and Agnes and Alice's little brother and sisters were tumbling about by the hearth. Alice gave us a bowl of pottage, and Father asked about the children, and I sat there eating up my bowl and wishing everything was as nice as this at home.

After a while, Alice's mother said the washing wouldn't do itself, and we must excuse her, and she went out, with a look at Alice. And Alice and Father sat holding their bowls and looking at the fire.

"You've a big family," said Father, and Alice said yes, she had three little brothers and sisters, and one older, who was Agnes.

"But that's what I like," she said. "I'd feel strange in a house that wasn't full of children."

"We've four in our house," said Father. "And the baby. It's a lot to ask a woman to come to."

"I certainly wouldn't ask Agnes!" said Alice, and she laughed. "That fat fool didn't know what he was letting your lot in for, if you ask me."

"Would you have them?" said Father, and Alice looked at him, not at all surprised.

"I'd want my own as well," she said, and Father nodded.

"Of course."

"Well then," she said, and that was that. They were married after mass at the church door. And it wasn't long before we all loved her, apart from Richard, who I think was jealous, being the oldest. But at least he didn't have to look after us any more.

Alice nearly had a baby three times before Edward. Twice the child came too early. Once she had a little girl who only lived a day. But last year, Edward came and stayed.

"Edward's my name!" said Ned, when the baby was introduced to us. Ned's really an Edward, after his godfather, Edward Miller, who is baby Edward's godfather too. Father hopes he'll apprentice them both at the mill when they're older.

Richard doesn't like Alice much, but he *hates* her baby. The more children Father and Alice have, the less land there is for everyone, and without land we'll all go hungry.

"Maybe Edward will marry a lord's daughter and keep us all instead," I say to Richard, but he just scowls at the crib, as though he's working out exactly how many acres baby Edward will take from his inheritance.

3. *Sunday Mass*

The church is full for mass today, but no one is listening to Sir John – our priest – as he drones away in Latin. The news about York runs from body to body, crackling in the air like summer lightning. Nobody can talk of anything but the sickness.

"In London, they don't bury the bodies any more, they just leave them lying in the streets. Anyone who can leave has left."

"What about the ones who can't?" says John Dyer, in a whisper. There's a pause while no one says anything, and then the muttering starts again.

"You can't outrun it. It travels with you. I heard about a man who fled from Lynn. Went to his sister's. He thought he'd escaped . . . didn't have a mark on him. Two weeks later he was dead. So was his sister and all the children."

"In the south there are dead places where nobody lives any more. All these little villages, all the houses empty. . ."

"York!"

Amabel and I stand with Robin and listen.

"Everyone isn't dead in London, are they?" says Amabel.

"They can't be," says Robin. "How many of those men have been to London? They're just telling stories."

"York, though. . ."

When I grow up, I'm going to marry Robin. We've been betrothed all our lives. Mother was friends with his mother, and his father, who died of the quinsy when Robin was small. Robin will inherit his land when he's twenty-one.

The tone of the conversations in the church have changed. William-at-the-Wood is talking in his loud voice to Father. He's leaving the village, selling his land to his eldest son.

"I'll not stay around to watch God destroy my children," he says. "I'm off up north tomorrow."

"Where?" says Father. "Where will you go?" I close my eyes and picture it, William-at-the-Wood off into the wild north where no one can ever find him again. He'll make his fortune selling ribbons or fool's gold, and his daughters will come back princesses and ladies with ermine cloaks and white skin.

William spits and shakes his head. "Up to Newcastle," he says. "Then Scotland. It's a wild land, Scotland – we'll be safe there, I reckon. I wouldn't stay here if I were you, Walt. I'd pack up while you still can."

Now the picture has changed – Robin's family and mine, all our household on the back of our oxen, Stumpy and Gilbert, marching down the wide, grassy roads to the land of the mad Scots. Sleeping in inns, running ahead of the pestilence.

But Father sucks in his teeth.

"Maybe," he says, and I know we won't be going. We can no more leave our land than Geoffrey can leave his abbey. On the road, we'd be beggars, or hired labourers at best.

"Good luck to ye, then," says William, and he turns away.

"Can you really believe," says Amabel, "that the pestilence could come here?"

"No," I say, and I mean it. Plagues and rains of frogs and thunderbolts and sieges where everyone dies happen, I know they do – I've met people who've seen them with their own eyes. But they happen a long way away, in foreign countries where everyone is a heathen and no one has heard of Jesus Christ. I have tried to imagine such a disaster happening here – in Ingleforn! – but my mind cannot hold it.

At the front of the church, the musicians are playing the opening notes of a hymn. The choir – with them my brother Ned – begin to sing. I close my eyes. I believe God punishes the wicked, just as I believe He speaks to his prophets through burning bushes and cures the lame by laying His hand on them. I believe that.

I just don't believe it could happen here.

Afterwards, we stay behind to admire the new painting on the church wall. Sir John hopes that a holy painting might appease God's anger, and we're not about to argue. The young artist has painted Noah, standing in his ark, watching with mild interest as the sinners are swallowed up and drowned. You can't see much of the sinners, just their arms waving about as the waters cover their heads.

"Which is the most pious of God's creatures?" says Sir John.

Emma Baker answers, "The pelican."

"The pelican," says Sir John. "Who tears her own flesh from her breast to feed her young ones.

Pious Pelican, Lord Jesus,
Cleanse me the impure, in your blood,
Of which one drop can save

The whole world of all sin."

Maggie likes this new picture, with the elephant and the chimera poking their heads out of the ark, but Ned prefers the one on the other wall, of the sinners burning in hell and the devils poking them with pitchforks.

"Does the pelican *really* eat its own stomach?" he asks Alice. "*Why?*"

"You do such things for your children," says Alice. She's holding Edward across her chest, his head bobbing out of the top of his swaddling bands. He opens his mouth and dribbles down her shoulder.

"Would you? For Edward?"

"If I had to." Alice isn't like Mrs Noah in the mystery play, who wails and screams when they try to get her onto the ark. If her children were in danger, Alice would be out there chopping down trees and sawing up planks, as fast as the rain fell down around her.

"Would you do it for *me?*" says Mag. Alice laughs and ruffles her hair.

"A big girl like you?" she says. "I'd send you off to get us a pelican for the pot. Pelican stew, how's that for a feast?"

4. The Exiles

Robin and I go up to the woods after church to gather wood.

"Imagine William-at-the-Wood in Scotland!" says Robin. "Do you think Robert the Bruce will chop him up? I told Mother we should go too, but she says she'd never be able to get enough for our land, and she doesn't like to run away and leave Grandmother with the fines."

"You'd leave Ingleforn?" Just the thought makes me dizzy. Ingleforn is all I know – the fells behind us, the wood below the village, the funny little church with the bent spire. I've worked in Father's strips of field since I was smaller than Maggie, stumbling behind the reapers, picking up the fallen stalks of barley. How could Robin think about leaving so lightly?

Robin smiles at me. "You've got your farmer's face on."

"Farmer's face?"

He purses up his mouth and beetles his forehead. "Why don't you care about the oats, Robin? We've got beans, isn't that exciting? Look, Father's bought another four acres, so we can work twice as hard this year, won't that be wonderful?"

I shove him. "Better than your face." Actually, Robin has a lovely face, always moving, always laughing, but I do asleep-Robin, head lolling, tongue out, eyes closed.

"Is there – work—? Can't – Isabel – do that—? It's – so-o-o nice here. . ."

"Sounds right to me," says Robin, but he bends to pick up another branch. My own bag is nearly full. "And yes, I'd leave. I'd rather be poor and alive than here and dead. Did you hear about that convent—"

"Yes, I heard!" The convent story is the worst of all the stories we've heard this year, and it's been a year of horrors, stories of villages empty except for the dead, of corpses lying mouldering in the streets, eaten by ravens and pigs, of children starving surrounded by fields of unharvested grain, of family leaving family to die and no one left to ring the passing-bells or say the mass.

"I don't believe half the things people say," I tell Robin. "And anyway, you can't leave. You belong to Sir Edmund like me, so unless you want to leave your grandmother to pay for your freedom, we're staying here. So what's the point in worrying?"

I push past Robin and start climbing up the rise, the bag of wood bumping against my back, the sticks digging into my spine like unwelcome questions. Maybe the pestilence won't come to us. It might not.

I come out of the edge of the wood. And stop.

There's a caravan of people coming down the road from York. The road isn't too dangerous, except in bad winters, but you do occasionally get highwaymen and outlaws in the woods, so most people travel in convoy. This convoy is bigger than any I've seen before. There are men and animals; voices calling, pigs shrieking, children wailing. There are riders with nothing but what they can fit in their saddlebags, packhorses laden with all of a family's possessions, even what looks like a hay cart piled with bedding and furniture, chickens in boxes and geese skittish with walking, people alone and people in gangs, minstrels and holy men, lepers and beggars next to families with servants and even a canopied litter, drawn between two horses, wobbling precariously as the horses stumble in the potholes and the mud.

Robin's feet sound behind me. His breath catches and wheezes in his throat.

"Where are they going?" I say, without turning my eyes away from the road. Robin leans forward, hands on his knees. He draws in a long breath.

"Duresme. Scotland. Here."

"They can't come here!" They can't. I know how the pestilence is spread. It lives in the houses of the poor and wretched. It's passed by breathing miasmas – bad airs. If you get too close to the miasmas of the sick, you catch it too. That's why if you want to be saved, you have to wear lavender and rosemary and rose petals and other sweet-smelling things, to keep the dead air away.

"They'll bring it here!" I say, and Robin shakes his head.

"They know. Look!"

He points. Two men from our village are talking to the caravan. Even from this distance I can see Gilbert the reeve and Philip de Coverley, the bailiff. They're talking to a little knot of men, pointing down the road.

"They're sending them away," says Robin, but. . .

"They're sending them to the abbey!"

St Mary's Abbey is nearly three miles east of Ingleforn.

The monks won't turn the travellers away. They give shelter to anyone – soldiers, beggars, even one of King Edward's messengers once. But—

"The abbey's where Geoffrey is!"

Robin looks away, back out towards the road. "I'm sure he'll be all right, Isabel."

But he's remembering the convent story. And so am I.

The convent story came from a troop of minstrels, who passed through Great Riding in the spring. They were full of the horror of it – a convent in France, where all but one of the nuns caught the pestilence and died.

"They say the nuns were sleeping with devils," the flautist said, but the drummer shook her head.

"They took in all the sick of the village," she said. "That was what killed them."

"All but one died," said Alice, amazed.

The drummer said, "Just one left to bury the dead, write their names in their big book and drown herself in the river."

That was the story that made us shift and stir uneasily. Nuns – good women – helping the sick and taking in the strangers, like God asked them to. Nuns, killed for their piety, the last nun drowned in the water, with her long hair floating loose around her like a madwoman and her soul pulled down to hell as a suicide.

That was the worst story of all.

5. Boundaries

Will Thatcher is standing with his back to me, watching Gilbert Reeve and Radulf the beadle rustling their bits of parchment. His back is straight, but his helmet is on crooked and there's mud all down the back of his legs. One of Edward Miller's dogs is sniffing at his boots. He looks straight ahead, pretending he can't see.

"He likes you," Amabel Dyer whispers to me.

"Shh! He can hear you," I whisper back, slightly too loudly, and we both giggle.

Will Thatcher is sixteen and one of Sir Edmund's soldiers. He was part of the baggage train in King Edward's army at the battle of Crécy, in France. Now he just guards Sir Edmund's manor, but some of the glamour of Crécy still clings to him. He's one of the best archers in the village and he *is* nice-looking, but whenever he sees me he goes bright red and I just want to giggle. If only he talked more. Or at all.

The whole village is gathered together on the green, under the manor oak. Sir Edmund isn't here, of course – he lives in London. I met him once when I was very small, but I can't remember much about him. He was riding an enormous chestnut palfrey, and he had a fur coat, and he and his steward talked together in a strange language, which Father told me was French.

Someone's taken the table out from the tithing barn and set it up under the manor oak. Gilbert and Radulf are sitting behind it, murmuring to our priest, Sir John. Sir John has the pen and ink from the scriptorium in the tithing barn, and he's playing with the quill, running it between his fingers. Radulf and Gilbert are arguing – Gilbert's hands are waving in the air. I can't see what they're saying, but Radulf is shaking his head and muttering. Alice glares at them.

"Who died and made them King of England?" she mutters, shifting Edward on her hip. Edward holds out his hands, trying to tug at her veil, and she pulls them down irritably.

"Half of Europe," says Father drily.

Ned clutches at his throat and makes choking noises.

"And Gilbert the reeve – is going – to be next—"

We're a smaller gathering than we ought to be. Four or five families have left already, selling their land and heading off north, like the exiles we saw from York.

Can the pestilence really be in York?

Sir John the priest is getting to his feet.

"They say the pestilence is in Felton," he says, and a ripple of fear runs through the crowd. Felton is only a day's walk away. I turn to Alice, and her face is white. She's muttering the Pater Noster under her breath.

"Our only hope is that the Lord spares us," says Sir John, raising his voice above the hubbub. "We must repent of our sins and humbly ask the Lord's forgiveness."

He starts talking about extra masses and prayers and barefoot processions. I try desperately to think of something to repent for. I'm sorry for being rude to Alice. I'm sorry for snapping at Ned and Mag. I'm sorry for being jealous of Alice's yellow hair and for caring so much that mine is limp and orangey-reddish and my nose is covered in freckles and for wondering what it would be like to be kissed by Will Thatcher.

It doesn't sound like very much.

Now Gilbert Reeve is standing up. Gilbert is Sir Edmund's voice and hands in the village – he makes sure we all get to the fields on time and pay our rents and heriot taxes when someone dies, and he buys all the things Sir Edmund needs for the manor – ploughs and yokes and grease and nails, hinges, harnesses, hammers and herrings. Radulf the beadle is his assistant, a tall, waxy-skinned, mournful-looking man, with a long, heavy face and a sticks-and-stones sort of wife, all elbows and nose and pinching fingers. I like Radulf, though. He doesn't say much, but he always has a kind word for Mag and Edward.

Gilbert is stroking his beard as though he doesn't quite know how to begin.

"Ah," he says. "Well. You all know why we're here. Something needs to be done – yes – they say Great Riding is shutting itself off, turning all travellers away. We think – ah – we think we should do the same here."

Radulf's head is down and his mouth is screwed up at the corners. I edge over to Robin.

"Look at Radulf the beadle! What's worrying him?"

"Don't you know?" Amabel isn't listening to Gilbert either. "Radulf's sister lives in York," she says importantly. "He was telling Mother yesterday that we ought to let the exiles stay here. He'd bring the pestilence here and kill us all."

"He couldn't turn his sister away," says Robin, and Amabel bristles.

"He can't let her come to Ingleforn!" she says. "What sort of selfish person would bring the sickness here? She should just stay in York and leave us alone!"

Robin shifts uncomfortably, but it sounds like the other villagers agree with Amabel. The men are talking about organizing work parties to guard the roads into the village.

"They steal animals too, these people," one of the church chaplains says, which is pretty impressive knowledge, given as how we only saw them for the first time yesterday.

"Whatever happened to Christian hospitality?" says Robin. He glances at Alice, but her back is stiff and she doesn't answer. "Those people will die if nobody takes them in."

Alice's arms tighten around baby Edward, who tugs at her veil again with a fat fist. Alice is the most religious person in my family, apart from Geoffrey, but this time she won't meet Robin's eyes.

"Most of those people will die anyway," she says, and I realize that she's afraid.

6. Processional

The abbot leads the procession. He carries a flask of smoking incense which he sways before him as he walks, sending the Latin of the psalms ahead to frighten away the demons and call up the good spirits of the earth. Or the angels. Probably the angels.

The other monks walk behind him in closed ranks, heads bent. I can count thirty-one warty bald heads, which is right because eight of the monks are too old to walk, and the infirmarer and his assistant will stay at the abbey. My brother Geoffrey walks right at the back, neither part of the monks' ranks nor part of the villagers. Poor Geoffrey, not-one-nor-t'other. He's shot up this last year, like a beanstalk, and he has something of the quality of a weed that grows in a dark place, searching for the sun. His thatch of yellow hair spills awkwardly over his ears, the round tonsure in the centre red with sunburn from the hot days last week. Geoffrey isn't a monk. He's too young, for one thing – he's only a year and a half older than I am. He just lives at St Mary's so he can learn Latin and French and Bible stories and all the other things he needs to know to be a priest.

It's a cold day, one of those bleak, windy days which come unexpectedly in the middle of summer, and halfway through the abbot's fourteenth Bible reading, it starts to rain. Mag starts to whine.

"I'm *cold*. Can't I put my *shoes* on?"

I shiver and wrap my mantle tighter around myself.

We're praying to God to take the pestilence away. To spare us. We're asking His forgiveness for whatever crimes we might have committed against Him, we're abasing ourselves before Him, barefooted and repentant, and asking Him, please, to keep His sickness away from our doors. And from the doors of those we love. Just leave us all alone, really, please. Send Your wrath to the really wicked people, in York, and London, and over the seas.

This worked in foreign lands, in Cornwall and Devon. Some villages the pestilence passed right by, like the Plagues of Egypt passed over the houses of the Israelites. But Geoffrey says that the Pope himself led the processions in Avignon, and it didn't save any of his people.

Afterwards, my feet wear heavy boots of black mud, which is probably the only thing which stops them dropping off, they're so cold. Geoffrey and Robin and I go down to the river to wash them clean. Robin doesn't have many friends amongst the village boys – mostly he just has me, and Amabel, and Alison Spinner. But he and Geoffrey were always friendly, right from when we were small.

I'm a little shy of Geoffrey, the way I always am when I see him again after a time apart. I notice all the things I'd forgotten about him. How tall he is! The Norman accent he picked up from five years living with monks. The way his yellow hair falls into his face, and how he keeps shaking his forehead to keep his eyes free.

"Are you well?" I ask, a little nervously. "Are you coming to the Midsummer celebrations? Did you really give a bed to all those people from York?"

Geoffrey's face twists as I ask the last question. "As many as we could. The rest we let sleep in the barn. Don't worry about them, Isabel. Tell me how you are – and Father – and Ned and Maggie—"

"We're well," I say. "Edward has three teeth now! And he can roll over – and clap, and—"

"Clever boy," says Geoffrey, but he doesn't really know Edward, or care much about him. How strange to have a brother that you neither know nor love! I can't really imagine it, any more than I can imagine Alice coming into our family and not loving us, or we not loving her.

"I don't think they'll let me come to the Midsummer Fire," he says. "It's so busy at the abbey, with all those people! I've been working with Galen. Trying to find out if he's ever come across anything like this pestilence."

"Galen?" I say. "Is he the infirmarer?"

Geoffrey laughs. "He's one of the fathers of medicine!" he says. He must see the confusion still in my face. "He lived hundreds of years ago, Isabel."

"Oh." Geoffrey always knows more than I do, about everything. "Are you going to be an infirmarer, then?"

Geoffrey's head is bent over his boot buckle. He says, not looking up, "Can you keep a secret?"

"Of course," I say. Robin nods.

"It's not decided yet – don't tell Father – but there's a chance I might be ordained early."

"Early? But why?"

"Why do you *think*?" says Geoffrey, whose mind always leaps ahead to the answer while mine is still trying to understand the question. Because so many priests have died is why, down south in those places where the pestilence has already reached. Because priests are the ones they send into the houses where pestilence is, to breathe in the foul air and give absolution to the dying. Because now they want to send Geoffrey to some strange parish where the priest is dead and everyone in the village is sick, to do the same.

"Will you do it?" says Robin. "If they ask you?"

"I want to," says Geoffrey, but he still doesn't look up. I don't believe he does want to. Geoffrey went to the monastery for the books and for the words and to learn the names of rocks and stars and saints and bones. He didn't go to sit with the dying. I want to tell him not to do it, not to go. But if you die without a priest to give you absolution and hear your confession, you go to hell. So many people – good people: monks, nuns, Christian folk – so many good people are burning in hell now because their priest died and no new parson came in time. If they ask Geoffrey to serve as a priest, I can't tell him not to go. And I know my brother. If they ask him, he'll say yes.

"And anyway," he says, answering the question I didn't dare ask him, "it's no more dangerous than staying at St Mary's."

There's something in his voice that makes me think he wants us to ask him what he means. I don't want to know what's hidden behind his words, but Robin says, "Why? You don't have the pestilence there, do you?"

Geoffrey's fingers play around the brass buckle on his boot. He doesn't answer.

"You don't, do you?" says Robin. "Geoffrey! You don't!"

Geoffrey's face is white. "You're not to tell anyone!" he says. "The abbot doesn't want anyone in the village to panic. And if Father knew..."

I don't care about Father. I don't really care about the abbot. My heart starts racing, and my head is dull and heavy and full of fear. *The pestilence is at St Mary's. The pestilence is three miles away. The pestilence is in the infirmary where my brother Geoffrey works.*

"Isabel?" says Geoffrey, and I turn to see his pinched, funny, worried-looking face blinking at me. "Isabel—"

I crawl over to him, smearing mud all over my skirts, and put my arms around his neck. He holds me, and I breathe in his ink-and-incense scent, all muddled up with mud and straw and the wet air of the river.

"Don't go back," I say. "Please, don't. Come back home with us and be safe."

Geoffrey's long, bony arms are tight about me. I think of all the things the Bible says, about steadfastness, and faith, and duty, and how I don't care about any of them if they mean my brother has to go back to a place where the sickness is. But all Geoffrey says is, "Isabel, it's coming here too," and I know that even the small protection I can offer him is worth nothing at all.

7. Pestilence

So what is it, exactly, the pestilence? Some say it's a plague, sent by God to destroy the wicked or perhaps the whole world, and that that's why there's no cure. A preacher who came to the village last year said that in the Bible it's written that a third of humanity will be destroyed by plague before the end of the world comes. Which means that God is taking more than His share of death this time around, if the stories we've heard are true.

Some say the pestilence is a disease like any other, caused by bad air, poisoned air, blown on the winds across Europe. That's why it creeps north and north and north, why you can't outrun it, why it never stops. But where did that bad air come from? And what happens to it? If the earth is a ball, like Geoffrey says, will the pestilence roll over the top of the world and come back round to greet us again? Or will it kill us all and go roving over the empty world, forever?

All this last year, travellers from the south have told stories about the sickness. Some call it the *morte bleu*, the blue death, but most say *the pestilence* or just *the sickness*. Some talk of spitting blood, of hard, black buboes the size of pigeon eggs growing under the armpit or in the groin, of God's tokens – red marks, like blood, below the skin. It stinks – everyone who talks about the pestilence talks about the stink.

"Like the devil himself," says one soldier, crossing himself.

"You'd know," says his companion, but nobody laughs.

More sinister are those who talk of a sickness that strikes like an adder, without warning.

"My cousin's child – he took ill in the evening and was dead an hour later."

"My father's pig took a rag that had been used to wipe the blood from a man with the sickness. The pig ate the rag, and fell down dead in the road."

Other folk say that the pestilence brings madness. That folk will leap from their windows, run naked through the streets, babble and cry and fight as though all the king's men are after them.

"Maybe if won't be so bad then," the men say, grinning sideways one to another. "If the young women start taking their clothes off."

How do you keep yourself safe? That's the next question, the one everyone wants an answer to. Surely there are medicaments and spells; surely someone, somewhere has found a way? The preachers hiss.

"By loving God and begging His forgiveness. By turning from the devil and all his works."

"This bone," a wandering preacher told us. "It belonged to St William. Wear it next to your skin and it will save you from harm."

"Chicken bones and glue," Alice muttered. "Either that or he's a grave robber, or a cathedral robber – or worse!"

"Don't look them in the eyes," said the pardoner who came after Christmas selling forgivenesses for any sin you might ever want to commit and a few you never would. "That's how it's passed – through the eyes!"

"I walked through the city of London," said the young man at the Easter Fair, the young man with the weeping sore in the corner of his mouth and the restless eyes that wouldn't settle on any of us. "I walked through the houses of the dying, stepping over the corpses of the dead in the street. I passed through the stinking air of the sickness, and I walked out the other side unharmed. And all I had was this!" And he shook a silken pouch stuffed with rosemary and lavender. "Worn by the skin," he said. "Closer than a lover, and surer on a winter's night."

The silence that followed this was so thick you could lift it with a spoon.

"And you survived?" said Emma Baker.

"And I survived."

The most important question is the one we ask every traveller.

"Once you have it – once you've caught it – can it be cured?"

And the answer is always the same.

"Nothing cures it. Once you have it, you die."

And now it's here, in the house where my brother lives.

And the monks are coming from that house to walk barefoot through Ingleforn, leading us all to pray for the sickness to pass us by. They look so calm and holy, but the sickness clings to their hands and to their eyes and to the underside of their robes. Every time they come, they bring death closer.

And I've promised Geoffrey not to tell.

8. Bone Fire

On St John's Eve, we have the bone fire on the green and the Midsummer revels as usual. All the village gathers around the bone fire and we walk around it in solemn procession, holding hands and chanting the Midsummer rhyme.

"Green is gold.
Fire is wet.
Fortune's told.
Dragon's met."

The rhyme is a riddle that can only be answered at St John's Eve, when the first green leaves are still curled in golden buds, when the water is alight with little wishing-candle-boats, when fortunes are told and St George does battle with the dragon. The answer is Midsummer Eve, of course!

After the chant, the revels begin. At Great Riding, they have a different mummer's play each year, but in Ingleforn we always do St George and the Dragon. Will Thatcher is St George, on Gilbert Reeve's black horse, and Edward Miller stands behind the stocks and is the voice of the Red Dragon.

"I am the Dragon. Here are my claws! I am the Dragon. Here are my jaws!" he calls, and all the children shiver and stare. The Red Dragon itself is the same glorious red and gold kite as it always is, flown by Robin and another boy from the village. Last year my brother Richard's wife, Joan, was the Princess, but this year she's too heavy with the baby that's coming, so Alice's little sister Maude plays her instead.

Will Thatcher is shy as St George – he stutters his lines and blushes when he has to rescue Maude from the Dragon. But when he draws his sword to fight the Dragon, he looks like a real knight from a stained-glass picture window. The Dragon-kite swoops from side to side in the sky, until St George subdues it by waving his sword around and ties a bit of silk around the kite string, to show that the Dragon is now defeated. He and Maude lead the kite by its leash, like a dog, while the audience cheers. But then the silk slips, and the Dragon escapes, and Robin and the other boy roar and bellow and swoop the Dragon-kite up and down to show the Dragon's anger. Two little girls run across the stage trailing a length of red silk to show the Dragon's flames. Will Thatcher collapses in a heap with something like relief, but Maude rolls about and moans most convincingly.

When everyone is dead, Gilbert Reeve saunters in as the Doctor.

"I am the Doctor, and I cure all ills.

Just gulp my potions and swallow my pills.

I can cure the itch, the stitch,

The pox, the palsy, and the gout.

All pains within, all pains without."

He gives a pill to St George and the Princess, who jump back up on to their feet. He gives another pill to the Dragon-kite, which swoops and wails about the sky before plunging down to the earth, dead.

Everyone cheers and claps, and John and Emma Baker come round with St John's dragon-wing biscuits, coloured red with rose petals. Then Gilbert Reeve nods at the musicians and the music starts and the dancing begins.

I love Midsummer Eve. It's the day when you thank God for the old year and look forward to the next. Later, we'll be lighting the candles and setting them afloat on the mill pond with our wishes in them. Now, though, it's time for fortune-telling.

Father gives us some farthings to buy a St John's bread pod each. St John's bread isn't bread at all, but flat, soft brown seed pods coloured like dates and curved like a bow. For St John's bread, you do the how-many, or the *humney*, as in, "Humney children will I have?" or, "Humney years will it be until I'm married?"

Then you bite into the St John's bread and eat it, counting the seeds as you do. The number of seeds is the answer to your question.

I wonder how many people's *humney*s this year are about the pestilence? I think of asking how many days it would be until it reached the village, but decide that since it's coming no matter what I do, it doesn't make much difference *when*.

How many people that I love will die? I ask, instead, but when I open the seed pod and see the seeds, I decide I don't want to count. Any more than none is too many.

I don't believe in fortune-telling, anyway.

Destiny cakes are the other sort of fortune-telling for Midsummer's Eve. John Baker moves amongst the crowd with a tray of cakes covered with a cloth.

"Destiny cakes! Destiny cakes!" he calls. We buy a cake each and put our hands under the cloth to choose our destiny.

Most of the pleasure of destiny cakes comes in trying to work out what they might mean. Robin gets a long, twisted cake like a snake. I tell him it's a hangman's rope and he's going to hang for laziness. He says it's a wave and means he's going to travel over the seas.

"It's a ploughed field, more like," Father says, making a waving motion with his hand. "All that good land you've got to plough!" Robin pulls a face. He's not much interested in ploughing.

Maggie gets a round cake, which Ned says is an egg – "You're going to lay an egg, Mag!" – but Alice says is a nugget of gold, and means she's going to be rich. Alice's is twisted into a shape nobody can work out. Ned says it's a heap of something: "Gold, maybe?"

"Washing, more like," says Alice. "Isn't it, baby Edward? All your washing?"

Mine is square.

"It's a house," says Ned. "A new house."

"Or a book, maybe?" says Alice. "Maybe you're going to be a learned woman, like your brother."

"Maybe," I say, but all I can think is how much that square destiny cake looks like a coffin.

After the destiny cakes, there's dancing. I dance one dance with Father – as usual – where he treads on my toes – as usual – and one with Alice, who really can dance for a woman who's over thirty. Then I dance one with Robin, whose hands are sweaty and who keeps apologizing when he bumps into me.

"Isn't it awful?" he whispers to me.

"What? What's awful?"

"All this fortune-telling," he says. "Midsummer Eve is supposed to be about life – not death."

But maybe it's both. And all this worrying about death is really about wanting to live, isn't it?

Next is a round partner-swapping dance, where I start off with Amabel Dyer and end up with Will Thatcher, who dances much better than Robin does.

The musicians stop to wipe their brows, and then they start up playing a pavane, graceful and slow.

"Do you want to dance another?" I ask Will and he goes red.

"All right."

I love the pavane. I love the slow, stately tread of it. And Will is a good dancer. He holds my hand lightly in his rough palm and I feel something rise in me, something that might be fear or might be joy, or might be neither.

Will's hand rests against the small of my back. My wits are torn between enjoying the dance – all tied up with the music and solemnity and the clear, cold, shivering firelit magic that is St John's Eve – and longing for it to be over. When the music stops, Will holds his hand against my back for a moment longer than he needs to, and I look up at him without speaking for a moment longer than I ought. Then he drops his hand and I bob my head awkwardly and go back to Amabel and Robin, who are waiting by the ale barrel.

"I told you he liked you!" Amabel says, and I turn my head away from Robin's brown eyes full of questions.

The dancing will last until late into the night, but my family won't stay for all of it. Ned is already cross and tired and giddy. Father has had to break up at least one fight with the youngest

Smith boy. And Maggie lolls half-asleep against Alice on one of the benches. But St John's Eve isn't over until we've set the candles on the mill pond.

The candles are set in little parchment boats, one each for every person in the village. I light mine from Father's and drip wax into the bottom of the boat to fix it upright. Now I have to think of a wish. Around me, everyone is talking and laughing, helping the little ones light their candles, launching them into the water. I bet all their wishes are the same. *I wish I may not die this year. I wish my family will come through safe.*

How horrible, I think suddenly. This pestilence is spoiling everything, even Midsummer Eve, my favourite of all the festivals after Christmas.

I wish Will Thatcher would kiss me on the mouth, I wish, and I set my wish-boat on the water before I can change my mind.

If your wish makes it across the mill pond with the candle still alight, it will come true. If the candle blows out or the boat sinks, it won't.

This year, there's a wind rippling across the mill pond, and very few boats make it. Mine does, and so does Father's, but Alice's and Ned's and Maggie's are all blown out.

All of a sudden, I'm ashamed. I bet Alice wished we'd all survive this year. If I'd put my family's safety on the water, would that mean we'd all have come through alive?

Everything is a little flat after St John's Eve. The happy feeling of goodwill doesn't last longer than the next morning, when Ned is sick in the bed and Alice shouts at me for letting him eat too many biscuits.

And the Thursday after Midsummer, I discover something I'd rather not have known.

Radulf the beadle lives at the edge of the village, way over the other side of Hilltop. He has three apple trees, a pear tree, five white geese and three beehives. It's just the sort of house I want to live in when I'm grown.

On Thursday morning, Alice sends me over with a cooking pot that she's promised to Radulf's wife. I'm in a good mood because today is washing-day and I've managed to escape the pounding and scrubbing and rubbing down by the river. I give a little skip as I walk, and think how glad I am to be alive and not in London or York or anywhere else the sickness is.

Radulf's geese make a tremendous honking noise as I come up to the house. They're better than any guard dog. They stick their long white necks out at me, flapping their wings.

"Hey!" I say to them. "Calm down. It's only Isabel."

"Go on!" says someone – not Radulf or his wife. "Go on!"

A little girl is standing on the doorsill making shooing motions at the geese. She looks about eight or nine, with straight fair hair tucked behind her ears and a long green gown. She's leaning on a broomstick that's nearly as tall as she is – she's been sweeping the floor. She smiles at me with her head on one side.

"They make a lot of noise," she says. "But they're friendly really. You don't need to be afraid."

"I'm not afraid," I tell her. "I like geese."

"I didn't mean you were," the little girl says hastily. "Only – if—"

"That's all right." She reminds me a little bit of Edward Miller's little girl, Alison. "What are you doing here? You're not Radulf's new wife, are you?"

"No!" She shakes her head from side to side, taking my question seriously. "He's my uncle," she says. "I'm Edith.

We're just staying with him while the sickness is in York. Mother's here too, but she's gone to sleep because my brother kept her up all night. It's not his fault – he doesn't know any better – he's just a baby. But he does scream! So Mother is sleeping, and I'm minding William and doing the sweeping."

"So I see," I smile at her, but my heart is hammering. This is what Gilbert Reeve was talking about at the meeting. Harbouring fugitives! I ought to report him to – well, to the bailiff, I suppose. But what would happen then? Edith and her mother and the baby would be thrown out of the village, and probably Gilbert and his wife too. And what good would that do? If they've brought the sickness to Ingleforn, it's here already.

I remember all the fugitives coming down the long road from York, the children stumbling behind the carts, the men turning them away from the village. I wonder what happened to them all. Some of them – the wealthy ones – perhaps had manors and relatives to go to. But those that didn't? We didn't let them into Ingleforn, and I can't see that any other village would let them stay either. Perhaps they died of starvation, further down the long road. Perhaps the sickness caught up with them, and they died in a ditch somewhere. I look at this fair-haired child, and I know I'm not going to tell anyone that she's here.

"Where's Radulf?" I say to Edith.

"They went to the village. Oh!" And she claps her hand over her mouth, her blue eyes round and horrified. "I wasn't supposed to talk to anyone!" she says. "No one's supposed to know we're here! It's supposed to be a secret!"

"It's all right," I say. Partly I just want to reassure her, but partly … I'm not really going to let them turn her mother away. Not with a baby. "I won't tell anyone," I say.

"You mustn't," says Edith, her fingers gripping the broomstick so tightly that the knuckles turn white.

"I won't," I say, and I wonder what I've done.

9. Free Men and Bond Men

There are two sorts of people in our village – free men and villeins. If you're free, you can go where you want and do what you want and marry who you want, and so long as you don't break the law no one can stop you.

If you're villeins like we are, you can't.

Being a villein means you belong to Sir Edmund and Lady Juliana. Mostly what it's about is money. We have to pay fines to Sir Edmund if we want to leave the village, fines if we want to marry someone outside the manor, fines if we don't go and work on his land when he asks us. Everything we grow on his manor belongs to him, so if he got really hungry he could take that too. He never has, though.

There are some lords who don't ask much of their villeins. Some ask for no work at all, others maybe for a few days at harvest. Sir Edmund is harder than most. We have to work two days a week on his land, and five at harvest time, which is when we have the most work on our own land. Father usually hires labourers to work for us, but it's still a long, weary, aching business, working until five on Sir Edmund's land, then coming back to our own to start the harvesting again.

Robin's mother is a villein too, but she never does her days in the fields.

"I've got enough work of my own," she says, "without doing some old windbag's weeding for him. Let him come after me if he wants!" Sir Edmund's steward doesn't fight, though. He fines her a couple of pence every manor court, which she never pays, and leaves it at that.

There are three ways to stop being a villein. You can be given your freedom, you can buy it, or you can run away and live in a town for a year and a day. Most people don't. My father actually had enough money to buy his freedom last year, but he used it to buy John Adamson's plough land in Three Oaks instead.

"But you could have been *free*," I wailed.

"But you could have been *fed*," he wailed back, and that was that.

I care about land as much as Father does, but I hate belonging to another person. I've always hated it, as far back as I can remember; it's like an itch that won't go away, no matter how hard you scratch it. Robin hates it too. When we're grown and married, we're going to work and work until we've saved enough money to buy our freedom. And then our children will be free, and they'll be able to go where they want and live how they want, without caring about Sir Edmund or the law or any of those things we have to worry about.

And that's a promise.

10. *Little Edith*

"**D**o you think I should have told someone?" I say to Robin. It's a few days later, and we're bringing the animals home from the pasture, me with our cow and the two oxen, Robin with their old milk cow with the crumpled horn. The sun is setting warm and hazy behind us.

"No..." says Robin, but his voice is puzzled. "But why do you care so much?"

Why do I care? I don't know. Yes, I do. It's because if I can keep little Edith – flaxen-haired Edith, small-boned and frail as a baby chick – if I can keep her alive, then there's hope for the rest of us: Ned and Maggie and Edward and all the muddle of people that I love. Except that by keeping her alive, I may be bringing this sickness closer to my family. It makes my head ache, trying to make sense of it. Am I being a good Christian by helping Radulf take in the homeless? Or am I stupid and careless and dangerous? If the sickness comes here – *Isabel, it's coming here too* – will it be my fault?

"Wouldn't you care?" I say, instead. "A little girl Ned's age?"

45

"Of course..." says Robin. "But plenty of little girls Ned's age have died of this thing already.

"Well..." I say. "If she's brought the miasma, it's already here."

In the last few days the number of refugees coming down our road has shrunk to almost none. Very few people have come north at all, in fact. No carters, no traders, no pardoners or pilgrims or any of the ordinary people travelling through the village on their way to Duresme or York. It's eerie.

At the forge, Robert the smith is shoeing a horse. His son holds the horse's head, while Robert hammers the nails into the foot. There are a few women talking by the well and a little gaggle of children playing with a kitten at the side of the road. Tolly Hogg the swineherd is bringing the pigs back to the village and a few chickens are pecking in the dirt. Everything is ordinary, and happy, and safe.

Back at the house, Alice is scolding Ned.

"I told you to mind the fire, not go and play dice on the green! Now look what's happened!" There's a burnt, smoky smell in the house, and a black hole in the bottom of the cooking pot. "How are we supposed to eat now?"

Maggie is sitting on the floor playing with baby Edward. She's fluttering her chubby fingers over Edward's face, while Edward stretches for them. Edward likes to grab at anything – flames, patterns on cloth, marbles, dice. Then he tries to eat them. Maggie runs up to us as we come in the door, calling, "Robin! Robin!"

Robin swoops her up in his arms and spins her round until she screams. Then he tips her upside down. She squeals and grabs at his legs, but when he puts her down she says, "Again! Again!"

All little children love Robin.

Alice is in a fine fury.

"Don't just stand there!" she says to Ned. "You'll have to go fetch back that pot I lent to Muriel, if you want any supper tonight."

"No," I say quickly, thinking of that little girl and Ned's busy tongue. "Don't send Ned. I'll go."

The light is fading as I walk through the village to Radulf's house. The birds are singing in the trees over my head and the gnats are out over the pools under the trees.

The house sits quiet in its hollow. Smoke curls out of the thatch and the chickens are pecking at the grass, but otherwise it could be deserted.

I knock on the door, and after the longest time, Radulf answers.

"Isabel!" he says. "Oh – Isabel. Now's not—"

"I came for Alice's cooking pot," I say quickly. I don't want to get Edith into trouble. "I don't want to stay."

"Oh," says Radulf. "Well—" He dithers a little on the doorsill, but at that moment I hear a child's cry from inside the house, a high, fretful wail.

"If—" says Radulf. "Just – wait there."

He shuts the door in my face and goes back into the house. I hear banging about inside, and Radulf swearing, and then the child crying again, louder.

The door swings inward.

Edith is sitting upright in a low bed by the hearth. Even from the doorway I can see her little face is red. Even from here, I can smell a sweet, slightly rotten scent, like old apples. Even from here, I can see the black, swollen lump

on her neck, so large that it pushes her whole face sideways.
I don't know much, but I know what that means.
The sickness has come to us.

ii. *Rites and Wrongs*

It's growing dark by the time I come back to the green. Alice's cooking pot bangs against my leg. They'll be getting hungry at home, waiting for me.

The pestilence is here. Here in Ingleforn.

Sir John's house is next to the church. I bang on his door. From inside I hear murmuring voices, getting louder as he comes closer. The door opens, and there he is, clutching his ale mug, his big belly straining against his cote. Gilbert Reeve is there too, sitting on a stool by the hearth. They've been eating supper – I can see the half-eaten pottage in their bowls.

"Isabel." Sir John frowns. I must look a sight. My face is red and my hood has half-fallen down around my shoulders and I'm still clutching the big cooking pot. "Is anything wrong?"

I take a deep breath of air, trying to breathe, trying to breathe, trying to breathe.

"It's here, sir. It's here. They have it at Radulf's house."

Sir John draws back so quickly it's almost funny. The ale slops out of his mug.

"The sickness?"

I nod. "His sister brought it from York. Her little girl has it." I see her again in my mind, little Edith, her face red, her mouth open and crying, the horrible swelling on her neck. "Please, sir," I say to Sir John. "Muriel says can you go and see her? I don't—" I trail off. Radulf didn't want me to tell anyone, but this is a bigger secret than just strangers in the village, isn't it? And what will happen to that little girl if – when – she dies? You can't keep a priest from a dying child, can you?

Sir John is backing away from me.

"Ah," he says. "Well. I don't know. I can't – I mean, I don't know if there's anything—"

Gilbert Reeve is staring at him.

"You can't refuse to visit the sick," he says, which is just what I'm thinking. Is he going to send us all to hell unshriven? That miserable old coward!

"Ah," says Sir John. He looks about him as though expecting to find an escape somewhere. There isn't one. "Ah. Of course. I'll just – if you just—" But he doesn't move. Gilbert Reeve is looking at me.

"Are Radulf and Muriel sick?" he asks. I shake my head.

"No. Not yet," I say. And then, catching his expression, "You aren't going to do anything to them, are you?"

"If he's brought the pestilence here," says Gilbert grimly, "he'll have the safety of the village to answer for. What happens to him isn't up to me."

The safety of the village. The hair prickles on the back of my arms. The safety of a little yellow-haired girl against the safety of us all. The love of a brother for his sister and her children against the safety of Alice and Ned and Father and Robin and Amabel and Mag.

The importance of caring for the sick against Geoffrey's life. The safety of the village against the promise of eternal life. Life against death. Virtue against despair.

News spreads fast here. The next morning, at mass, everyone knows. You can hear the fear passing between them, the rustles and glances and murmurs.

There's no sign of Radulf or his wife, Muriel.

"Have you heard?" says Emma Baker.

"We've heard," says Alice. "That poor child."

"But did you hear about Sir John?" Emma's eyes are bright with excitement. Alice looks away and draws in the air through her nostrils. She hates gossiping about holy men. She walloped Ned hard across the back of his legs once for calling Sir John an old windbag.

"It's not our place to speak ill of a priest," she says, but she doesn't know what's coming next.

"Wait until you hear," says Emma, and she lowers her voice. "He's gone!"

"Gone?"

"Run away and left us. He was supposed to be visiting that child, but he never came. So Muriel went up to his house, and he'd gone. Taken all his clothes, and the good plate and—" Her voice drops. "The candlesticks from the church too, they say."

Our church has two silver candlesticks, which sit on the altar at mass. They're sitting there now.

"The candlesticks are still there," I say. "Emma. Look."

Emma glares at me, then carries on as though I haven't spoken.

"That little girl," she says. "What will happen to her when she dies? Without a priest to hear her confession." I shiver. If you die without confessing your sins, and without receiving absolution, you carry your sins into the next life, where you have to pay for them with years and years of burning in hell. Receiving absolution is one of the most important things you can do, if you want to get to heaven. "What's going to happen to us all?" says Emma, and her voice rises. "What's going to happen to us without a priest?"

Father presses his lips tight together, the way he always does when he's angry or upset, but before he can say anything, there's a movement up at the front of the church. One of Sir John's chaplains is calling, "Hello? Hello!"

There are some nudgings and shufflings and everyone quietens right down, which almost never happens in church. Usually it's just Sir John mumbling to himself in Latin while we all carry on talking about the weather or the harvest or how ill Agnes Harelip's new kerchief suits her, and how Edward Miller shamed Emma Baker by taking his new wife up to the altar before her to take the communion wafer.

"As some of you may have heard," the chaplain says, "Sir John is unfortunately no longer able to perform his duties as priest of this parish." There's some grumbling at that, and a little laughter. "We'll be sending a messenger to the bishop asking for a replacement to be sent. In these difficult times, we can't know how long that will take" – the voices rise, then sink into silence again as the chaplain continues speaking – "so in the meantime, the monks from St Mary's have agreed to come and help with the services."

The murmuring grows louder. *In these difficult times*. Priests are dying, that's what he means.

The chaplain hasn't finished speaking yet. He's only Alice's cousin from Great Riding, but he knows how to read, and he's holding a piece of vellum with writing on it.

"The Archbishop of York," he says, "has asked us to tell you that any member of the laity – man or woman" – there's a little ruffle of sound at that – "will have the power to hear confessions and grant absolution *so long as this disaster is visited upon us.*"

Now no one is even pretending to be quiet. Women, allowed to hear confessions! Alice looks like somebody has slapped her. I'm filled with this odd mixture of shock and excitement, like the world is shifting and moving below my feet and I'm not sure where we're all going to end up when it settles. I like it and I don't at the same time. What sort of a world will it be, if people like me and Alice can do all the things that priests can?

"For *shame*," Alice is saying.

"*Listen.*" The chaplain is shouting over the hubbub. He has to shout twice to get everyone to calm down. "*Listen.* As you know, many of the monks at St Mary's are ordained priests. After speaking to us, they have agreed to help in our time of need. Any of you needing the services of a priest should come to the abbey, where they'll do all that they can to help you."

Quiet. If anyone needs the last sacraments, that's what he means. Like that poor little girl in Radulf's house. The fear churns at my stomach. There are a few mutterings and shuffling of feet, and then Emma Baker calls out, "So you don't support this abomination, then?"

"We hope that no one here will have need of it," says the chaplain evasively.

"Those foreigners in York can do what they want!" Edward Miller shouts. "It's turning the world upside down, it is, and we're not having it here!"

I see Father shaking his head in frustration and I edge over to him.

"What do you think?"

Father sighs.

"I think the world is turned upside down," he says. "And no matter what Edward Miller thinks, we are going to have it here."

For the first time I can remember, there's something almost like quiet while the chaplain gives the service. Afterwards, he says we can all take communion. There's a ripple of excitement through the church at that, and Alice starts muttering the Pater Noster to herself very fast in Latin.

I know it's horrible, but some evil part of me hopes I *will* have to hear someone's confession. Not anyone in my family, but a stranger, maybe – a traveller from York, dying on the road. Geoffrey says you serve God by making the bread and bringing in the harvest, but giving absolution through God – what would that feel like? I might never get another chance again.

When it's my turn to receive the host, I shut my eyes and try to think holy thoughts, but it just tastes like dried-up paper, like always. I don't think I'm really holy inside, like Geoffrey, that's my problem. I try to be, but then I start thinking about something else, like my vegetable patch, or Robin, or whether I really like Will Thatcher or just pretend I do to annoy Robin, and suddenly prayers are over and I haven't said anything to God at all.

Afterwards, everyone stays outside the church for ages, talking. The pestilence in Ingleforn – Sir John – women to hear confession – Radulf! – Sir John – the pestilence in Ingleforn.

"They should be banished!" says Agnes. "Bringing the

sickness here! We should turn them out of the village like lepers and let them rot." She spits a chewed-up clove on the dry earth. The spittle sits there in a wet mound, bubbled and foul.

"We should hang them," says Dirty Nick. Dirty Nick is lank and long and ragged, and filthy around the edges. He lives by idling and drinking, paying for his bread by begging and by pieces of day and half-day work here and there. I hate him.

"Hang them!" says Alice. "Lord, where would you find men in this village willing to hang Radulf and Muriel? And what purpose would it serve?"

I hope Alice is right, but I see the dark expressions on the faces of one or two men, and I wonder.

"What is going to happen to Radulf and Muriel?" I ask Margaret, Robin's mother. I tried asking Father, but he told me to keep my nose out of other people's business. Margaret sighs.

"Gilbert Reeve wanted to banish them," she says. "But I expect they'll stay. People will have more things to worry about soon anyway."

Radulf – Edith – the church candlesticks – the monks. The pestilence in Ingleforn.

I grab Robin by the arm and drag him to the side of the church.

"I saw her," I whisper. "It was me who found her. I went and asked Sir John to go and see her, and that must have been when he ran away!"

Robin's face is serious.

"What did she look like?" he whispers back.

I think back to Edith. All I can think of is her red face and her tears.

"She smelt," I remember at last. "That part's true. A horrible sort of rotten smell. Robin, what are we going to do? It's here! In Ingleforn!"

"I think we should run away," says Robin. He sees the look on my face and sighs. "I knew you'd look like that. Mother pulled exactly the same face when I told her. I don't care. If I was a man, I'd go tomorrow."

"But how—?" I begin.

"I don't know how I'd live!" says Robin. "Maybe I wouldn't. But it would be better than staying here, wouldn't it?"

I'm silent. Alice wanted to leave, I know. But every part of me screams that if we leave our land, if we leave our fields, it wouldn't matter if we survived the pestilence. We'd have stopped being ourselves already.

I turn away from Robin and look over the churchyard. Ned and Maggie are running through the graves with the other children. They run up to us, Ned charging straight into my stomach, making me gasp.

"Ned! Behave yourself!"

Ned pulls himself away.

"Why is everyone so angry?" he says.

"Because of what that chaplain said," I tell him. "He said that anyone could hear confession – like the priest does. You could, or Magsy."

Ned sputters. "Not Mag!"

"I could!" Mag bounces up on to her toes. "I could, couldn't I, Isabel?"

"That's what the chaplain said," I tell her. "And so can I, and so can Alice."

Ned splutters again into his hands. You can see his mouth stretched wide with laughter behind his fingers.

"Alice might be able to talk to God," he says. "But Mag – never!"

12. *Miracles and Magic*

Ned and Maggie are finding it hard to take the pestilence seriously. When Father and Alice go over to one of the alewives' houses to argue and whisper about Sir John with the rest of the village, they decide to prepare our house for its coming. I'm working in my garden, but they come and grab my hands and insist on showing me all the things they've done.

"We've got a cross on the door, look—" So they have – a wobbly crucifix drawn with a burnt stick, Jesus with a downturned mouth instead of his usual patient expression.

"He's upset because he's been nailed to a cross," Maggie explains. "And look—" They've put a bucket half full of piss on the doorstep.

"Don't tread in it!" says Ned.

I step over the bucket. It stinks.

"Why...?"

"It's to stop the miasma. You get sick because you smell the pestilence smell, don't you? That's why Alice has all that rosemary and juniper to burn. But *we* thought piss smells much stronger than juniper, so it's double the protection."

"You have to sniff it," Mags explains. She bends over the bucket, takes a deep breath and immediately starts coughing. "Eugh!"

"I think I'll avoid that one," I say. "What else have you got?"

"Old beardy-Bede."

Alice's little pewter St Bede stands by the loom. Alice bought it on a pilgrimage to Duresme Cathedral. She lights candles by it and prays to it, and once, when Mags took it and dressed it up in a bit of fleece and took it for a walk all round the croft, she was so angry that she boxed Mag's ears and called her an imp of Satan and not worth the breath she'd wasted in prayers for her. St Bede is still standing on his shelf, but he's got an extra candle and he's knee-deep in daisies and dandelions and forget-me-nots. Ned and Mag have added a pile of clumsy little figures as offerings, made from the slimy riverbank clay that Mag likes to play with when Alice and I are washing. "Father, Alice, you, me, Maggie, Edward, Geoffrey and Richard." Ned points to the clay people in turn. I see that the bulge in one of the figure's arms is supposed to be a baby. Alice often gives St Bede offerings – a clay arm when I sliced mine open on a scythe, a clay eye to cure her father's blindness – but this set looks ominously like a pile of corpses on a battlefield. One of Father's feet has already fallen off.

"More crosses—"They've drawn wonky black crosses on all of the beams, and at the head of Father and Alice's bed. Alice isn't going to be happy. "And this is for you."

Maggie hands me a bit of cloth – one of the leftover pieces of Alice's dressmaking. It's tied into a bundle with a bit of string.

"Smell!" Ned commands.

I sniff. It smells of dried lavender and woodsmoke, the

scent of home.

"It's got lavender in it," Mag explains. "You're supposed to tie it round your neck."

"We've thought of everything," says Ned, and suddenly my eyes fill up with tears. Because foolish though Ned and Mag are, do any of us have anything better?

And then Father comes in at the front door with Alice behind him, and steps straight into the bucket of piss, proving that Ned and Mags haven't thought of everything after all.

13. *Those We Remember and Those We Forget*

When I thought about the sickness coming here – which I've thought about a lot, this past year – I'd thought of it coming like the styche, or the flux – maybe a child catches it, and then perhaps another child in the family, and then the mother, and then after a few days, it moves to another family in the road, or then to the mother's sister, and so is passed like a rumour or a secret from one house to the next.

When I go down to the well on Monday morning, Amabel Dyer is there. She's got a full bucket of water already, but she's not going anywhere. She waves at me as I come over.

"Did you hear?" she says, in a half-whisper.

"Did I hear what?"

"Radulf and Muriel both have it! Gilbert Reeve went over there yesterday and he found them. And now Gilbert has it too, my sister says."

"Pssh." The woman next to Amabel – it's Agnes Harelip, Alice's sister – blows the air out of her mouth with a disgusted noise. "Gilbert Reeve doesn't have anything! I saw him this morning going off to the market. Your sister's talking nonsense, girl."

Amabel looks abashed, but only for about half a moment.

"Little Joanie Fisher has it too. Her mother bought some of Muriel's honey from them only last week. She'll get it next, I reckon."

Joanie Fisher is three years old. Her mother, Sarah, is a friend of Richard's Joan. I feel the ice sliding down my back.

"You can't go near someone who has it," says Alison Spinner, who's half a year older than me, "or you'll get it. They pass it through the eyes – look in their eyes and you're dead for sure."

"How can you not go near people? You have to! How can you not go to the well – or to the fields – or to *church*?" I wouldn't mind so much missing church, but I'm trying very hard not to annoy God at the moment. "You'd starve!" I say.

Alison Spinner shrugs. "Then you die," she says.

I'm quiet. So are Amabel and Alison. This is happening too quickly. What I need is something like the pause after the minstrels have finished playing, the space where everyone breathes in and comes back from whatever place the music has sent them. This is too much.

Alison Spinner passes her pail of water from one hand to the other with a look of unconcern.

"Mother heard," she says. "They're going to send us a new priest. By the end of the week, Sir Edmund's steward told Gilbert Reeve. They'd better be quick, he said to the messenger. Or we'll be all be dead by the time he gets here."

"Alison!" Amabel looks shocked, and a little bit like she wants to giggle, like Alison has made a rude joke or something.

"He didn't say anything of the sort," I say to Alison, cross suddenly: with Alison for not taking this seriously, even – yes,

I admit it – with Muriel and Radulf and little Joanie Fisher for falling sick, and me with nothing I can do about it. I'm like Alice – I like making things better: scolding the children, bandaging the cut, cleaning up the spilt ale. But this? There's nothing you can do about this.

We have our first death the next day – little fair-haired Edith, Radulf's niece. One of the monks from the abbey performs the mass, but only her mother and her baby brother come to pray for her soul. And then we hear that the mother is sick too.

"But who's looking after the baby?" I'm on the floor playing with Edward, walking my fingers across his belly, then tickling him until he squirms, and the thought of this other baby – alone, hungry, crying to itself in an house full of the dying – is too horrible to think of.

Alice is chopping leeks at the table. She won't meet my eyes.

"People have their own families to think of, Isabel. They don't want to bring the sickness into their houses. And it's not a baby anyone knows. . ."

Alice, with all her talk of Christian charity! I stare at her, horrified. She fusses with her kerchief, then says, defensively, "It's bound to catch the sickness soon, anyway, Isabel."

But somehow that baby is the most horrible thing that's happened yet, more horrible than Edith and her mother, who at least nobody could have helped anyway. I can't stop thinking about him – crying and lying in his own filth while his mother lies dying. Something tugs at me – should I go and help him? But what would I do with him, if Alice won't let him here? Would the monks take a baby?

I'm so angry with Alice about it, angry with myself for not going. I rage about it to Amabel as we go down to the archery butts with Robin and Ned, to watch their shooting practice.

"They just left it . . . left it to die. A baby! It's probably there now, with no one looking after it, everyone too scared to go into the house with them all sick."

"I wouldn't go," says Amabel. "And I don't think your Alice should either. People have their own children to think of. They can't bring the sickness into their own houses."

"You don't think that, Robin, do you?" I beg.

"I think it's terrible," says Robin, and my heart lifts. Dear, kind, Robin, friend to small children and lame puppies. "I'll go there now with you, Isabel, if you want," he says, seriously. "I'll go and see, if you want me to."

"Are you mad?" Amabel screeches. "You can't just take someone else's *baby* home! You'll catch the pestilence!"

"I know," says Robin. His dark eyes watch mine, under his thatch of dark hair. "I'll still go, Isabel, if you want to."

I hesitate. My heart starts beating faster.

"Would your mother take a baby, if it wasn't sick?" I ask. Robin shrugs.

We're walking past the mill. The waterwheel is turning in the millstream, flecks of bright water splashing us as we pass. Birds are singing in the trees above our heads. We're alive. We might not be soon. Probably that baby is sick already anyway.

"Oh, I don't know," I say. "I don't know what I want." And I run forward, before Robin can answer.

Three days later, they ring the passing-bells for Radulf and Muriel, and for Edith's mother. We hear them as we're taking the oxen out to pasture, and we grit our teeth. There are twelve more cases in the village now, and still no priest has come.

No one mentions a baby.

People start behaving differently now that sickness is here. They keep to themselves. If they see someone coming from a house of sickness, they step aside and look away. The Sunday after Sir John leaves the church is full – unusually so – but everyone stands as far away from everyone else as they can get. The brother who's leading the mass has nearly six feet between him and the front of the crowd. At the well, people mutter, "God keep you" and keep their eyes down. Everyone is frightened. When Joanie Fisher died, hardly anybody went to her mass. The brothers wouldn't let her body lie in the church, for fear of the miasmas gathering, but they held a funeral procession through the village and a mass at the graveside. Joan went, and she said the only people following the coffin were Sarah, Sarah's sister, the monk who led the service and a beggar she'd never seen before, who asked for 2d just for ringing a hand bell.

"Godspeed they send us a priest soon," grumbles Alice, standing in the doorway with Edward, who's wailing fit to bring down the thatch. "Isabel and Ned, I told you, we're brewing ale today. How are we going to do that without some water? And Isabel, you come straight back and don't stand there gossiping to Amabel Dyer. I won't have you bringing the sickness here, you hear me?"

Ale means a lot of water – two buckets each and a pole across our shoulders to carry them home. Ned scuffs his shoes along in the earth. He's worried, you can tell.

"Isabel?" he says. "If you catch the pestilence – can you get better?"

"No," I say. "You always die."

Ned hunches his shoulders. I wonder who he's anxious about – Philip-at-the-brook, who he plays with sometimes on the green, or old John Adamson, or ourselves, when this thing comes to us.

"Ned?" I say, but he pulls away.

"I don't care," he says. "I don't care about you or Alice or any stupid pestilence." And he runs off to the well with his buckets swinging.

The women by the well are swapping bad news. Stupid old besoms. As we come down towards them, they stop their talking and look at us over their shoulders. Bad news coming to us. I feel something cold settle in my stomach. The pestilence coming to someone I love. Robin. Richard. Geoffrey. Amabel Dyer. There are so many possibilities.

"Isabel, did you hear?" one of them calls. "The new priest has come. Arrived late last night. Just a boy, Beatrice Reeve says."

"That's good," I say, and some of the tangle of fear in my stomach loosens itself. The woman looks as though she's about to say something else, and I tug on Ned's arm before she can work herself up to it.

"Come on, Ned. Alice is waiting."

I drag him over to the well. The women watch. I move restlessly as we wait in the line, stretching the muscles in my arms. The women talk, their wimples nodding, their shoulders moving restlessly. No one says anything to us. It's only as we're done filling our buckets that a woman calls to me.

"Isabel, wait a moment."

It's Emma Baker.

"Does your father know?"

Ned answers before I can stop him. "Know what? About the priest?"

"Margaret is sick," says Emma.

Margaret. Robin's mother. My belly tips, as though I'm standing at the edge of a cliff, about to plunge over the edge into nothingness. Robin. My Robin, with his black hair falling in his eyes and his wide mouth open and laughing. The sickness in Robin's house.

"Brother Simon from St Mary's was there this morning. It's the sickness all right. If you know what's good for you, you'll stay away from there, you hear?"

"We've got to go," I say. "Alice is waiting!" And I'm almost running, fast as I can with the buckets on my shoulders, Ned running after me.

"What did you do that for? Why are we running? Isabel – wait for me!"

"How dare she?" I say. I'm shaking. "How dare she tell me what to do? What's it got to do with her?"

"Are you going to see Margaret?" says Ned. "Isabel?"

"I'm not going to do what those old hags tell me," I say, and I stamp off back home before he can ask me any more questions I don't have the answers for.

Alice is crushing the malt at the table when we come back. Ned is full of the news.

"Margaret at Brook has the pestilence!"

Alice lowers the pestle and stares at him. Her face is red, and a strand of hair has escaped her wimple and is stuck to her cheek.

"Oh, Ned," she says.

"Can we have Robin here?" I say. "While his mother's sick?"

Maggie, who is rolling Alice's spindle across the floor, looks up.

"Yes!" she says. "Can he? Can he sleep in our bed?"

"I'm sorry, Isabel," says Alice. She looks tired. She brushes the stray strand of hair off her forehead with the fleshy back of her hand. "I've got Edward and you children to think of. What if he brought the sickness here?"

"Will Thatcher says we oughtn't to speak to anyone who's sick," Ned pipes up. "He says we ought to stay at home and just lock our doors and—"

I remember all the people who have come down the road from York – the preachers, the carters, the beggars and lepers and holy men and refugees. There is nothing to be done. I remember that baby – what did happen to him? I remember Robin, my kind, anxious Robin. Locked in with the miasma and no one coming.

"I don't care what Will Thatcher says!" I shout, so suddenly that Maggie looks up, startled. "I don't care what anyone says! You can't stop me!"

I push past Ned blindly and run outside. Alice calls after me, "Isabel! You come back here!" but I don't answer.

Robin lives across the green from us, the middle house of a row of three with John Baker and the oven at one end and the forge at the other. The two little Smith girls are playing in the garden as I come up to the house – they stop to stare at me over the fence. I ignore them. I'm trying not to listen to the voice – Alice's voice – in my head telling me to walk away and not bring the sickness on our family. The voice that tells me that these people are in God's hands now, and there's nothing I can do for them.

"Robin," I call, and I rap on the closed door with the back of my hand. Then, when no one answers, "Robin!"

No one comes. The chickens carry on pecking at the earth around my feet.

There are noises inside the house, scuffles, then the door opens, and Robin appears. He looks smaller than I remember, and paler. He's got a posset of something – herbs, probably – in a little sack pressed up against his nose to protect him from the pestilence scent.

"Isabel!" he says, alarmed. "What are you doing here?" I come closer, and he retreats into the house. "No, get back! Don't come any nearer!"

"I wanted to see you," I say. "Don't go away! Otherwise I'll come right inside the house and kiss you. And you won't be able to stop me, so don't try. How could I not come and see you?"

"You oughtn't to have come," says Robin, but he's smiling a little, and I know he's pleased to see me. Robin doesn't have any family left in the village except us, and his mother, and an old, blind, addled grandmother who is no use to anyone.

"Listen, Robin," I say. "You're going to need food. And water. I don't think you want to go to the well, do you?"

"Oh..." Robin clearly hasn't thought about food. But I've seen how the villagers gathered their skirts up away from Sarah Fisher when she tried to go for her water, and wouldn't speak to her, and I couldn't bear it if they turned away from Robin too.

"Perhaps..." he says.

"I can get you whatever you need," I say. "If you need

anything, just ask me." Then, all in a rush: "Robin, be careful, won't you, please. Don't—"

Don't die, is what I want to say. But how can he avoid it, living in that miasma?

"Don't look in her eyes," I say, instead, and he gives a hiccuppy laugh.

"I'll be fine, Isabel," he says. "Don't worry about me. Please." And I want to weep. What right has Robin got to be worrying about me, when he's stuck in a pestilence house with a mother who is almost certainly going to die? "I'll stick my head in the pig dung," he says. "I won't wash!"

I try to smile. "They should send you up to the infirmary at the abbey," I say, trying to play along. "You'll give them all Robin Fever instead of the pestilence."

Robin smiles, but half-heartedly.

"Is it—" I say. *Is it terrible?* is what I want to ask. *Your mother, has she gone mad? Does she piss herself? Does she stink? Is her flesh rotting on her bones? Are you all right, cleaning up the blood and the vomit and worse?* But how can I say these things? And what would Robin answer if I did?

He doesn't let me finish.

"Listen," he says. "You mustn't come here again. Promise me. Behind the fence is fine, but not like this again – not so close that you can smell the miasma. If anything happened to you – if anything happened because of me – I couldn't bear it. I mean it, Isabel."

I nod, the tears rising in my eyes.

"Take care," I say. "Please, please, Robin, take care."

"You too," says Robin, and he shuts the door, so suddenly that I don't even get a chance to say goodbye.

14. The Boy-Priest

It begins to rain as I'm coming back home – a greyish drizzle that soaks into my mantle and reminds me of last year, when it rained without ending and all the harvest was ruined. I wonder gloomily if the world really is ending. Sometimes it absolutely feels like it.

I feel like I'm trapped in a cage, a cage which is closing tighter and tighter around me, until I'll have nowhere left to turn, and then the black thing, the miasma – in my dreams, the miasma is black, like a cloud, and it seeps under the door and coils up over the fireplace and into our solar – then the miasma will come and find me, and I won't have anywhere to hide.

My head is full of . . . what? Rotten corpses, that stench in Radulf's house, the taste of blood and the thought of Robin alone with . . . all that . . . the pus and the blood and the vomit. What can I do with that? I want to scream, to smash something, to get as far away from this place as I can.

I like *fixing* things. *Mending* things. Most of the things in my life get better if you work at them. This doesn't. How can I help Robin if I'm not even allowed to visit him?

It's only as I'm at the gate that I remember the new priest is supposed to have arrived. Priests visit the sick, even those who are sick with the pestilence – this priest can visit Margaret and Robin even if I can't. I'm so pleased with this thought that I turn straight around and head back towards Sir John's house. No priest would leave Robin to look after his mother on his own, would he? Apart from Sir John.

Nobody comes when I knock on the door. I bang on it with both fists. What will I do if he doesn't answer?

I'll go to the abbey and find a monk is what I'll do. I don't care if he's praying, or in church, or writing in his scriptorium, I'll make him come to Margaret. I'll go to one of the chaplain's houses and make him find the new priest.

"Yes? Can I help you?"

The man standing on the doorsill is younger than Richard. For a brief, dizzying moment, I think it's my brother Geoffrey; then as he steps out of the shadow, I see that he's older than Geoffrey, maybe eighteen or nineteen. He's tall and gangly, with long, white fingers twisting anxiously around themselves. It's his hair that made me think it was Geoffrey – a shaggy blond mop – that and the slightly Frenchified English that Geoffrey picked up after a couple of years speaking French with the monks of St Mary's. This man's hair is darker than Geoffrey's, though, and he's thinner. He looks like a string bean with all of the colour bleached out of it.

"Yes?" he says again. He's got a high, rather nervous voice.

"Please," I say. "My friend's mother – Margaret – she's dying, I think. I mean, she's sick. So could you come and – and—"

"Oh." The priest jumps. "Wait there." He disappears into

his house. I wait on the path. There's a clunk from inside, and the sound of something falling.

"Are you all right?" I ask, peering around the open door.

Sir John's house is small, cluttered and dark. It's bigger than ours, but there's no solar. There's only one candle burning beside the little hearth-fire, which is sputtering in the wind from the door. Several bags sit open on the earth floor, clothes and books and other interesting-looking objects spilling out of them. The boy-priest is tumbled on to the floor, under Sir John's ale barrel, which is spilling ale out on to the floor and over his hose.

"*Benedicte!*" he says, then he sees me there in the doorway. "I mean—"

"It's all right," I tell him. "I don't mind you swearing. Here—" And I go and help him heave the ale barrel up and off him. He's a man nearly grown, but I'm stronger than he is.

"I'm sorry," he says. "I only arrived last night, and there's so much to do. There are so many people who need visiting. And I don't know where anything is. I'm still studying, really, but so many priests are dying. I mean—" He stops and looks confused.

"It's fine," I tell him. "I know there aren't many priests left. And I wouldn't bring the oil and candles if I were you; I'd save them for people who are actually dying." He looks at me so gratefully that I stand up a little straighter. "I'm Isabel," I tell him. "And don't worry. I'll look after you."

"Thank you," he says, very seriously, though I can see a smile puckering at his lips. "I'm Simon de Marcham. And I'd be very grateful if you'd show me where your friend's mother lives."

*

Robin's little house sits closed like a treasure chest between the baker's and the forge. Next door, Robert Smith is leading a horse around the forge-yard, trying to calm it down. The horse snorts and tosses its head, perhaps sensing the disquiet around it.

The young priest – Simon – fumbles with the catch of the gate. I lean over and open it for him.

"You can go home now," he says. "Don't stay."

"All right," I say, but I wait at the gate as he goes up to the house. The door opens a crack, but I'm too far away to see anything but darkness inside. Simon the priest goes into the house, and the door shuts behind him.

15. *Kisses Against the Night*

F our more people fell sick yesterday, and eight today. One of John Dyer's oxen fell down dead on the green, and no one would go near it to bury it. One of Agnes's chickens was stolen in the night by one of the exiles from York, or some other village in the south. The bell rang out twice for the dead this morning, and once this evening. I don't even know who the last bell was for.

It's worse at the abbey. Amabel Dyer says she heard ten monks died. Emma Baker says eighteen, and thirteen of the exiles. Agnes says, if God is punishing those monks, they must have done something terribly wicked.

"I heard they were sleeping with *devils*," she whispers, at the well, and I clench my fists to stop myself from answering. Father says she's talking nonsense.

"All those sick folk in the infirmary, no wonder they're dying."

I worry that Geoffrey is dead. I want to go up to the abbey and see, but Father won't let me.

"Not while the sickness is there," he says. "I'm serious,

Isabel! There's time enough to worry about Geoffrey when this is over."

I don't understand how he can bear not to know, but I know he means it.

We don't hear anything more from Robin. I go and leave food and water on his doorstep every day. The second evening, Alice catches me with the bread under my arm.

"So it's you who's taking it! I didn't think it was Ned. Where's it going, then?"

"Robin's house." I brace myself for anger, for Alice to tell me how stupid I'm being. But she just stands there, biting her lip.

Then she says, "They'll need ale as well—" And she goes and fills me up her favourite green flagon. "There," she says, and, seeing my surprised look, "You're a good girl, Isabel. But don't tell your father now."

I never see Margaret or Robin, but the food always goes from the doorsill, and after the second evening the green flagon is always left just behind the gate, so someone must be alive in there. After the first day, I don't knock again, although I always want to. I look over the fence to see if I can catch sight of Robin – perhaps he'll be bringing in firewood or cleaning out the pig or something – but I never see him. I don't even know if he's ill, though I guess not, as someone is fetching the food each day.

Three people buried today. Two yesterday. There are more bells from St Paul's Church in Great Riding – they have the sickness there too, worse than we do, I think, from the ringing.

Simon gives his first service to a church that is already emptier than usual. I'm not sure who is dead, who has family sick, who's left the village and who is simply frightened of coming. The service is received in near-silence, which is stranger than almost anything else. Simon trips and stumbles over the Latin, but as far as I can tell he doesn't get anything wrong.

Afterwards, he tells us that bodies will no longer be allowed to lie in state in the church, and that instead of a funeral mass, the dead must be satisfied with a placebo read at the mouth of their grave. There's some muttering at this – if no one prays for your soul, how will God know to send it up to heaven? – but no one argues. Everyone looks too tired and cowed to protest. Afterwards, only Gilbert and Emma Baker stay to talk to Simon. The rest of us hurry back home.

There's another procession through the village. Alice goes, but she leaves Edward behind, and Father won't let any of us go with her. We hear them chanting and ringing hand bells as they walk past our door, but we don't look out.

And every day this sickness lasts the more trapped I feel. I want to kick a hole in the wall of the house, or fight somebody, or run and run and never come back.

"I don't see what difference staying at home makes," I say to Alice, when she comes home from the procession. "If the miasma is here, it's here, isn't it? It's in this house – in the air – everywhere. The only way to escape is to run away, and we aren't even going to do that!"

"It clings to the sick," says Alice. "Or those who are about to fall ill." She's working at her loom, weaving a new bolt of cloth.

"Why are you even bothering with weaving anyway?" I say. "If we're all going to die!"

"We all have to die some day," says Alice calmly. "And those who survive the summer will need warm clothes for the winter."

"The Day of Judgement is coming!" I shout at her. "And you're sitting there weaving!"

"If the Day of Judgement really is coming," Father says, "I'd rather wait for it in the warm. Go and fetch me some firewood and stop making a nuisance of yourself in here."

He doesn't sound really angry, but there's an edge to his voice that I don't want to cut myself on. I pick up the basket and stamp outside. They *are* idiots. Carrying on as usual, when anyone can see that everything is as far from normal as it's possible to be.

It's nice to be outside. We've been staying indoors as much as possible since the first case came to the village, and coming outside I feel like my soul is breathing out at last, after all day in our dark and smoky and stuffy little house. Outside, the air is cold and fresh, and there's this achingly pale sky high above my head. I swing the basket from my arm and take my bad mood down the muddy track towards the woods, where at least it can't crash into anyone else.

The woods cluster around the back of the church. Tolly Hogg brings the pigs here to root for truffles, and Ned and I pick mushrooms and rosehips and wild garlic here in the summer. It's dark and safe and rich with the scent of pine needles and old wood.

There are people here already. A little cluster of boys and girls about my own age perched on a fallen tree trunk. Amabel Dyer and Will Thatcher and Roger Duresme and Alison Spinner and a few others. They've got a flagon of ale and they're passing it between themselves. Amabel waves when she sees me.

"Isabel! Over here!"

I come willingly enough. "What are you doing?"

"We're drinking to the spirit of cheerfulness." Roger holds up the ale flagon. "Squashed by dull old priests and miserable crones. I don't know what they're worried about – they'll all die soon enough anyway. Drink?"

"Thank you." I take the flagon from him. His ale is stronger than Alice's, but not so sweet.

"Is everyone in your house weeping and wailing?" says Amabel. "Mine is terrible. 'The world is ending! We're all going to die!' If we're all going to die, then why do I have to do the spinning? We might as well have a good time while we can and not worry about it."

"Mine aren't moaning," I pass the flagon up to Will. "They're just ... worrying. And then trying to pretend that nothing is wrong."

"Fools," says Will. He smiles at me, shyly, and I smile back. He's got a dimple in his right cheek when he smiles. I've never noticed it before.

"Don't you sometimes want to just run away?" says Amabel. "My sister is a maid to a lady in York. She lives in a big house and eats meat three times a week. That's what I'm going to do, after all this is over."

"All right if you're free," I say bitterly, but Amabel shrugs.

"When the pestilence is gone, everything will be different. You'll see."

We pass the ale around as the sky grows darker. Nobody wants to go home. After a while, Alison Spinner produces a whistle and tries to play some of the songs the jongleurs played at Easter. She muffs the high notes, and the boys cuff her good-naturedly across the head while she shrieks and hides her face in her skirts. Roger and Will dance drunkenly, then Will headbutts Roger and Roger charges back at him, mock-angry, and suddenly they're wrestling, rolling about on the grass, with Amabel and Alison and me cheering them on. It's like the wrestling matches they have in the churchyard, only neither Roger nor Will really want to hurt the other. They scuffle half-heartedly, until Will manages to climb on top of Roger and pin his arms down. The girls on the tree trunk all cheer.

"A drink for Will!" says Amabel, passing him the flagon. "If you can't have a drink when the world is ending, when can you?"

"Can we have whatever we want now then?" says Will, laughing a little.

"Why?" I kick moss down at him from my place on the tree trunk. "What do you want?"

Will stands with his feet apart, looking up at me. He's more handsome than Robin, and nearly as familiar – I've known him for as long as I can remember, though for most of my childhood he was busy with the older boys, and for some of it he was away in France. His eyes are lighter than Robin's, but Robin's crooked smile is wider. Usually he's so shy – he must be a little drunk to speak to me so boldly.

"I want a kiss," he says.

The girls whoop and cheer. I force myself not to look away. Will is still standing there watching me with that serious look on his face. He means it. I remember my wish-boat, and I feel myself blushing. I didn't believe a paper boat had the power to grant your wishes, but maybe I should have wished for the lives of the people I love, if my wish-boat could do this.

Perhaps this is God's punishment for my selfishness. To give me everything I asked for, and to take Robin away.

"Don't kiss him if you don't want to!" says Alison. "Why should she kiss you?"

"Because the world is ending," says Will.

He's right. And even if the world doesn't end, I might be dead tomorrow and so might he. And his eyes are very light, and his hair is wavy and thick, and I've always liked him, just a little bit. And if God is going to take everything from me, the least He can do is let me kiss a young man on the mouth before I die.

"All right," I say.

I slide off the tree trunk and come and stand before him. The others applaud.

"Go on, Will!"

"Get on with it!"

"Alison's turn next!"

Will smiles at me a little awkwardly. I like his eyes. I like the freckles underneath his mouth. I like the scar that he got in France, who knows how. I lean forward and kiss him, dry lips against dry lips, tongue against tongue.

"Woo!"

"Isabel likes Wi-i-ill."

I surface, bright red, pleased and embarrassed, proud and ashamed. Will looks equally red-faced and confused.

"Now then," he says, taking the ale from Roger. I climb back onto the tree, trying not to smile.

It's late when I get back, and the hearth-fire is nearly out. Father is about to be angry, but Alice purses her lips at him to stop.

"What have you been doing all this time?" he says.

"Living," I say. "Which is more than you have."

I glare at them, but Alice holds out her hand to me and my anger smacks into the wall of her kindness. I stop, confused. Her lap is full of wool, her spindle between her legs.

"Isabel—" she says, and there's something in her voice which stays my angry words in my throat.

"What?"

"Robin came while you were gone. His mother died this afternoon."

16. A Bad Death

I know what a good death looks like. I know from when Mother died. A good death is the priest in his vestments coming to the house, and the village behind him with candles and bells and prayers. A good death is the Seven Interrogations, holy water sprinkled into the corners of the chamber, the anointing with oil, the communion wafer and the wine to keep away the demons who hover around the heads of the dying, waiting to drag them into hell.

Margaret didn't have the last rites. Robin and my father went for Simon the priest, but nobody answered when they knocked at his door. Father went to St Mary's, but by then it was too late. I don't know if Robin heard her confession, like the priest said he could. I didn't dare ask. I asked Father and he said, "She wasn't really in any state to take confession," which could mean anything.

Mother's body was pulled through the village on the funeral cart, with mourners walking behind her carrying candles and crosses and singing prayers, while the church bells rang out all around us. She lay in the church for a full day and night with candles at her hands and feet. In the evening, Sir John gave the service of the Office of the Dead, and in the morning a requiem mass was said for her soul. Most of the village came to her mass, and afterwards there was a tea with ale and salt pork and roast chicken, and we gave pennies to the beggars who followed the cart and her name was remembered in the prayers at church for months afterwards. I used to watch out for it at mass. I can still remember the day when they stopped praying for her soul, and how much I minded.

This isn't the funeral cart. This is Robin's mother's cart, with our ox Stumpy. Margaret is wrapped in a sheet and lying on the hay. We've got candles, but no crosses – only our little pewter St Bede, which Robin is carrying. And there are so few of us in the funeral procession. There isn't even a priest – he has another burial to watch. There's just Robin and Father and Alice and me, one of the church chaplains, Robin's blind grandmother and a few beggars who I think are foreigners because I don't recognize their faces, but who demand two pence each for following the coffin. I expect Alice to be angry, but she pays without a word.

The bells in the church are ringing, but I can't be sure if they're for Margaret or for someone else. They were ringing last night as well. When Mother died, the bells were solemn and sacred and full of holy sadness, but now Alice twitches her head and says,

"Lord, those bells! Will they never stop?"

We follow behind the cart. Robin's face is pale and stiff, and somehow softer-looking. When Father is unhappy, all his muscles tense and he stiffens – it's almost frightening – but when Robin is sad, his whole face relaxes and all his features seem to sink into each other. All of the animation, the energy, goes out of them. He cries sometimes too, though he's not crying now. He's gripping the pewter St Bede and looking down at the ground.

I wonder what's going to happen to him. No one's said. I remember how Alice wouldn't take that baby for fear it would bring the pestilence into our house. Robin's as sopped in pestilential miasma as that baby ever was. I think about Maggie and Ned and baby Edward, who Alice wouldn't let come to the church today. Part of me wishes she hadn't let me come either. That thing in the cart is thick with the smell of death. I press my posset of herbs to my nose. They seem such a small thing between me and the sickness.

But I don't know how Robin will live if we don't help him. He can't weave like his mother could. He can brew ale, but I wouldn't pay to drink it. He gets some money from his land, but John Phillip's son who rents most of it is sick himself, and what will happen when he dies?

There's a small, scared part of me that almost hopes Alice *won't* let him come to us. I try and push it down so God won't hear it and send the pestilence to punish me, but it won't go away. There's only one bed in our house, and our straw mattress in the solar. Would we have to share a bed with him if he caught the sickness?

The dead ox on the green is still there, stinking and mauled by the pigs. It's disgusting. There's a dead sheep there too, now. Right in the middle of the village!

When Mother died, people came out of their cottages to join the procession as we passed them. Today, no one comes. Smoke blows out of the thatches of a few of the houses as we pass by them, but no one comes out. I don't blame them. I wouldn't go to their funeral either.

When we reach the churchyard, Adam Goodenough the sexton and another man I don't recognize are climbing out of a grave pit. There's a small gathering around the grave – Simon the priest with Lucy Hogg and her son Nicholas, who's a year or two younger than Mag. There's a husband as well, and an older son, Jankin, who's Ned's age.

The gravediggers come over to us.

"One more, is it?" says the one I don't recognize. "It can go in with this one then, if you'll wait a moment. That'll save you some time?"

Robin stirs beside me, but he won't speak, I know. I can feel his unhappiness, but I don't know if there's anything we can do about it. The churchyard is lumpy with fresh graves, like a field after a family of moles have been through it, digging up all the smooth grass into messy hills of earth.

"Whose grave is it?" Alice says. She's friendly with Lucy. Alice is friendly with everyone.

"It's Jankin," Adam says. He lowers his voice. "And I wouldn't get too close to Lucy either – I hear the husband's sick too."

Alice sighs, but I realize with a dull shock how little I mind. One more death. I'm just grateful it's not someone I know better.

I touch Robin's arm. He's shaking.

"She doesn't even get her own grave! They're just going to throw her in on top of him!"

"I know," I say. "I'm sorry." I can't see what we can do about it, short of digging our own hole.

Robin turns away.

"One day," he says, and his voice quavers. I don't ask him one day what.

As the family moves away and Adam Goodenough starts filling in the grave, Simon comes over to us. He's wearing Sir John's robes, which are too big for him and keep slopping off his shoulders. His cheeks are still pocked with spots, like a boy, and there's a smudge of something – ash maybe – down one cheek.

"God keep you, Isabel," he says to me, and he smiles at Robin.

"And God keep you, Robin."

Robin jerks his head.

"This is a sorry sort of parish for a boy like you," Father says to Simon, and Simon blinks and nods and looks at the earth.

"I – well, I'm still learning, sir, but I'll do the best I can," he says. "Really I will."

"I would expect nothing less," says Father gravely.

Simon says the placebo clearer than he reads the mass. Perhaps he's had more practice over the last few days. Father and Adam Goodenough lower Margaret into the grave, all wrapped up in her winding sheets. Simon drops a speck of holy water on her head and feet and blesses her.

"God rest their souls," he says, and turns away Adam shovels quicklime over the open grave.

Afterwards, we stand outside the church, rubbing our arms and looking at the grass and the sky. It's a mild day, a light breeze blowing the flower scent from Sir John's garden over the churchyard wall. If the end of the world really is coming, no one seems to have told the wind or the sky.

Robin shifts his feet.

"I'll be getting home then," he says.

"No, you won't," says Alice. "You're coming back with us."

And that's that.

17. *Loving-Kindness*

Father takes Robin back to his house to pick up his things, and to bring back the chickens, and Margaret's cow. There are all sorts of useful things in Margaret's house – bags of grain, pots and pans, a fine woven blanket that came from France. But Alice won't let Robin bring anything except what's absolutely necessary, for fear that the miasma might cling to it.

When Father brings him back home, Robin has his arms clenched tight around a bundle of things wrapped in a blanket. All of his things. He looks very small, though he's taller than me. He doesn't greet us, and he ignores Maggie, who's watching him round-eyed with her head tipped sideways against her shoulder. He just stands by Father with his eyes big and dark in his white face. I want to go and say something to him, but I'm frightened and weirdly shy. Alice would know what to do – she's better at loving than anyone I know. But I'm not Alice. I'm just clumsy Isabel and I don't know anything.

Alice's sister Agnes is here with her spindle. She's sitting by the hearth with Alice, who is stirring the pottage with one hand and rocking Edward's cradle with the other. Agnes's eyes widen when she sees Robin, though she must have known Father was bringing him here.

"You're letting him keep that child in your house, sister, are you?" she says, her voice all high-pitched and disapproving.

"Of course I am," says Alice, and her voice tightens. "Robin is welcome here as long as he needs to stay."

"Well!" says Agnes. "I think you're making a mistake, sister, I do. Bringing a brat with the pestilence on him into your house! Why, he might kill you all, if you're not careful."

Margaret stirs uneasily by the fire. Her blue eyes move from Alice to Robin to me. I shrug. Ned says, "Robin's coming to live with us, isn't he, Father?"

"Of course he is," Father says, just like Alice. He puts his hand on Robin's shoulder. Robin wriggles and grips his bundle tighter. "Robin was my wife's godson and his mother was our oldest friend. I'll not throw Margaret's son out of doors when I have a home of my own. And if you want to share our hearth, sister, I'll ask you to remember that."

Agnes draws herself up.

"Well!" she says. "I won't stay here to be spoken to like this. I hope the good Lord doesn't bring His displeasure down on you and on these poor children. But I won't be coming here until I'm sure He's spared you."

My father's face is set stiff.

But, "You'll be welcome, sister, when you do come back," is all he says.

Agnes is gathering up her things, pulling her hood over her head. She kisses Mag's head and says, "I hope you survive this, little cousin." Mag just blinks at her. You can tell she doesn't really understand what's going on. Agnes draws herself up to go. But she's got a problem. To get out of the door, she has to get past my father and Robin. She glares at Father, who stares back without speaking. In the end, she draws herself up, stuffs her hood over her nose and marches past them, stretching as far away from Robin as she can get. We all wait tense in the candlelight until the door bangs shut behind her.

It's like the air goes out of all of us. Alice says, "Well!" and bursts out laughing. "Come here," she says, and she goes up to Robin and takes his hands in hers. "You're welcome here as long as you need a home," she says. And she leads Robin over to the fire and sits him down between herself and me, and I rub my hand against his leg to show that I want him here too.

"She's an old toad, Agnes, don't listen to her," I whisper, and he gives me a tight smile and shakes his head slightly.

I think of all the people I know, Alice is the closest to being a saint, even with her big feet and her red hands, even if she did leave that baby in Radulf's house. She's looked after five stepchildren who don't belong to her, and one baby of her own, and now she's taken Robin in too, without even blinking.

"Why didn't Auntie Agnes want Robin to live with us?" says Margaret.

"Oh!" Alice rubs her hand backwards through Margaret's hair. "Because she's a sour old besom, who never did lift a hand to help her neighbour. Don't listen to her, bunting."

"Robin's staying with us for always, isn't he?" says Mags.

"That's right, bunting. And he's going to sleep in your solar with you, isn't he?"

Mags nods. "Because his mammy and daddy are dead."

"Listen, Mags," says Father hastily. "Why don't you and

Ned and Isabel go and fetch some water? Poor Robin needs a bath before we do anything else with him."

Ned groans, but I cosh him over the head.

"Come on, Maggie." I haul her up by the back of her gown. She shrieks and slaps at me, but when Ned and I head out the door, she runs after us, her leather shoes slapping on the earth floor.

It's a clear evening, with a slender thumbnail moon hanging in the pale sky over the trees. Sound travels on an evening like this: a dog barking, the creak of the waterwheel from the mill, someone hammering nails, a pig snorting in one of the gardens, men's voices at the forge.

"Do you think Father's stupid for letting Robin stay here?" says Ned.

"Maybe. But we couldn't have left him on his own, could we?"

"No-o," says Ned, but he doesn't look sure. "Do you think we'll catch the pestilence off him, though?"

"Oh, Ned, how should I know?" I run a little way forward, to get away from his questions. "I'd rather die than turn Robin out!" I call over my shoulder, but I'm not sure if I'm telling the truth.

Back in the house, Alice has Robin sitting on a stool by the fire, with a bowl of bean pottage and a hunk of bread. He still hasn't said anything. His face is very white in the dimness.

"Come in and get something to eat!" she says, when we appear. She stands up and takes my buckets of water from me. As she tips the first bucket over the cauldron, the cauldron swings, casting high shadows over Edward, who starts to wail in his crib. Alice drops the bucket down on the earth.

"Whist, child, can't you, for once in your blessed life? Here –

Isabel, take him for me. It's just wind," she says, thrusting him into my arms as his screams grow louder. So maybe she's more fussed about Robin coming to us than she pretends.

We give Robin the warm place in the middle of our mattress, next to Mag. Mag wants to whisper and show him all her things – "This is my dolly – look, Robin! – and those are the bags where Father keeps the barley, so the rats don't eat it. And that's—"

"Hush *up*, Mag." I reach over Robin and shove her. "Robin doesn't care about Father's barley."

Mag's face crumbles.

"Don't be so cruel, Isabel! I'll tell Alice!"

"Oh, be quiet." Ned is in bed already, curled up in a ball with far more than his share of the blankets. "It's time to *sleep*." Ned would sleep all day if you let him.

He and Mag fall asleep almost immediately – you can tell from the slow in-and-out of their breath. I'm not used to sleeping by Robin, so I'm not sure if he's sleeping or not. I've been this close to him before, but I've never been so aware of the warm, dark shape of him, lying on his side beside me. It makes me feel bigger and clumsier than usual, and I'm very aware every time I turn over or tug on the blankets. I lie awake for what seems like hours. Father and Alice are awake too – I can hear them mumbling to each other through the solar floor, the old, quiet, comforting sound of their voices. It reminds me of being small, listening to Mother clattering around the house, putting the cover over the hearth, washing out the pans, tidying things away or working at her loom, me up here between Geoffrey and Ned, too awake to sleep, watching by the orange candlelight from the chink between the blanket-curtains.

At last, Father and Alice's voices stop. The house is silent except for the occasional sigh from the oxen, and the others' snuffly breathing in the dark. I lie on my side with my eyes open and this bedfellow fear, the fear that kept Father and Alice awake beneath me, which made Agnes tell us to leave a fourteen-year-old alone in an empty house. What will happen when this thing comes to us? I think, and I don't have an answer.

I roll over on to my stomach, and see Robin's eyes, open and white and watching in the darkness.

"You're awake."

"Yeh."

"Robin..."

"What?" I reach out my hand and touch his arm, but I don't answer. "What, Isabel?"

"I thought you were going to die," I say.

"So did I."

I lie there on my stomach beside him in the dark, very still, and after the longest time I hear his voice catch in the darkness, so I know he's crying, and I shuffle closer to him on the mattress and bump my forehead against his, but he doesn't respond, and he hardly feels like my Robin any more, and I don't know what I'm supposed to do.

"Shh," I say, as though he's as small as Edward. "Shh. I'm here."

Robin doesn't answer, but he rubs his head against mine, to show me that he loves me. I put my arms around him and he lies against me, with his head against my shoulder and his arms around my neck. I hold him close, like Noah and Mrs Noah, sitting on the roof of the ark and watching the waters rise around them. In the mystery play, God promises never to send another flood again. He doesn't promise anything about a pestilence. I hold him tight, like I used to when we were smaller than Mag and played weddings with Geoffrey wrapped in a blanket as the priest. I think how often Robin looks after me, how often he tells me not to worry, or listens to me rage about Richard or Alice or the little ones. Now it's my turn to look after him, and I don't know how.

I'm almost asleep when Robin lifts his head.

"Isabel," he whispers. "Let's run away."

"What?"

"Just you and me. And Geoffrey, if he'll come. We could go and live in the woods like the hermits. We could have chickens and bees and a garden, and stay there until I'm old enough to inherit, and then we could come back as a freeman and a freewoman, and by then the pestilence would be gone and nobody could tell us what to do."

It sounds so lovely . . . like something in a minstrel's tale. For a moment I am dizzy with the possibility of it.

"Would Geoffrey come, though?" I whisper. "What would he do?"

"Well. . ." Robin obviously hadn't thought of this. "He could go back to being a priest if he wanted, after the pestilence was gone. Or he could live with us. Think of it, Isabel. Nothing could hurt us."

His voice is fierce in the darkness. On the mattress beside me, Maggie turns, mumbling to herself. Of course I couldn't go. How could I leave these people? Father and Alice and my brothers and sister? And my land? How could I do such a thing?

Robin must have heard my answer in my silence, because he sighs and rolls on to his back. I reach over and twine my fingers through his, and we fall asleep together like that, his fingers locked tight between mine.

Later, much later, I'm woken by the sound of Edward crying. Robin shifts beside me, but doesn't wake. Below, I hear Alice fumbling to light a candle, talking softly to Edward so as not to wake Father.

I prop myself up on my elbows and lift the blanket-curtain aside, so as to see into the room below. Alice comes through from her chamber. She's holding the candle in one hand and Edward in the crook of her other arm. Her hair is wild and dishevelled under her nightcap and her woollen slip is open at the breast. She settles herself at her stool, and lets Edward find her breast and start suckling. I watch from the solar, expecting Edward to finish and Alice to go back into bed with Father, but she stays there in the dark chamber, murmuring to Edward or perhaps to herself. In the yellow candlelight, there's something beautiful about the two of them – a little like the painting of the Virgin Mary in the church, but more earthy, more solid.

From the safety of my hiding place, I watch the two of them. After Edward has finished suckling he falls back quickly into sleep, but Alice stays awake for a long time, sitting at the stool by her loom, her rough head bent over her sleeping son. I wonder what she thinks, really, about having Robin living with us. I wonder what Father thinks about him sleeping in the same bed as me and Ned and Mags. I wonder, watching Alice holding her child, if somewhere inside her she regrets bringing him here. And I know that I will never, ever know.

18. *Emma Baker*

It's very strange having Robin living with us. At first, I'm awkward and a little shy – not sure how to treat someone who's watched his mother die of the pestilence. But in the end I just watch what Alice does; brisk, loving, practical Alice, scolding the little ones when they pester him, softening Father when he asks too much, sending him away – "Go and fetch me some wood, Robin, won't you?" when it's obvious that our crowded little house is too much for him.

He's quiet and withdrawn those first few days, brushing aside my attempts to comfort him – "Not *now*, Isabel" – and going off alone to the archery butts, or the well, or the wood. Mag follows him around like a friendly puppy, curious about this strange, subdued version of her old friend. She brings him things to interest him – "Look, Robin, here's the cheese that I helped Alice make. Look – these are our hens. Father made this hoe – look." Robin tolerates her, which is more than Alice or I do.

"Send her to me if she bothers you," says Alice, but Robin shakes his head.

"I don't mind. She's nice, Mag."

Father manages to sell Margaret's cow to Edward Miller, whose cow and all his sheep died of the pestilence. We keep their chickens, but we put Margaret's cockerel in the pot. No one wants a cockfight every day in their yard.

Mostly, Robin's out all day in the fields with Father and Ned. When he comes back, we don't talk much. We just sit by the fire; me with my spinning, or my weaving, or my mending, him watching my fingers, watching the fireside, resting his head on my knee or my shoulder, quiet.

"Was it awful?" I ask him, one day when he's been living with us for nearly a week, and he gives a sort of shudder.

"Tell me," I say, but he won't.

All he says is, "They go mad, Isabel. After a while. They don't know who they are, or who you are. They don't care that they're lying there in their own blood and shit. It's better, probably, that they don't. . ."

Five hundred and fifty people live in our village, including Sir Edmund's soldiers, and more – like the pedlars and the carters and the man who brands the sheep – who come through, stay a few days, and then leave.

Today, as we stand at the back of the church, Father's eyes look down, but Alice's head is turning, counting the missing and the dead. Twenty-three dead this week. More missing. Edward Miller stands against a pillar with his arms crossed and his eyes closed. He lost his mother and his two children in the last week. The eldest was sitting by the fire, with her spindle. They didn't even know she was sick. Her mother went out to bring in the chickens, and when she came back, she was dead. Amabel's grandmother died just the same way.

This sort of death is the worst of all. Every morning when I wake up, I lie in our solar and wonder, *Who died tonight?* I touch Robin and Mag with the back of my hands, to see if their bodies are still warm. If Father and Robin are late home from the fields, I think, *Perhaps they've fallen down dead.* I feel all the time – every day, every moment – like I'm sitting under an axe, waiting for it to fall. I start at unexpected noises, at the sound of crying. I'm frightened, every minute of every day.

I look around the church like Alice, seeking out bad news. Emma Baker is missing too. She's not sick, but her husband is. The oven's been out since he fell ill. One of his apprentices ran away when the pestilence began and the other's mother is sick in Great Riding and he's needed at home. I can't think what will happen when John Baker dies. How can you have a village without an oven? What will we do without bread?

The two smallest Smith children from the forge are here, but their parents aren't. Their father is dead and their mother is home with the oldest boy, who's sick. Alice turns her head when she sees them, and nudges me.

"Go and tell Alice Smith they can come and eat with us after church. Poor little mites – their mother's got enough to do without putting on a meal."

I push my way through the people to the back of the church. Alice Smith is about Ned's age, with straight, lank black hair. Her little sister is smaller than Mag.

"Alice says you're to come and eat with us after church," I tell her. She stares at me.

"We can't. We have to go home and see our brother."

I shift Edward on my hip and scowl at her.

"Alice says you're poor little mites. She says your mother's got enough to do without feeding you."

Alice Smith's little sister sticks her fist in her mouth and turns her face from me to her sister. Alice Smith's white face goes pink at the cheeks.

"Our mother can cook better than your Alice can!" she says. The people in front of us turn and make *shh*ing faces. "We don't need food from you!"

Her sister's hair is wild and uncombed, and there's a grubby look to their faces, but I bite my tongue. I make my way back to Alice and Father.

"She says their mother can cook better than you can," I tell Alice, and she sighs.

"Really, Isabel! I don't know what's got into you lately. What did you say to them?"

What's got into me lately? The end of the world is what's got into me lately! All the empty spaces in the church – all the fresh-dug earth in the churchyard. Alice is a lunatic. If it was the Last Judgement and the dead were rising up from their graves around us, she'd say, "Comb your hair, Isabel, wash your face and don't pick your nose. What will Jesus and St Michael think of you, looking like that?"

On Tuesday morning, John the baker dies. There are mutterings about sending to Great Riding for another baker – but what baker would come to a pestilence village? – or for John Baker's brother, who lives in Felton and might remember how to work an oven. By Tuesday evening, though, smoke is rising from the oven again. Alice's head turns.

"Who's got that going?"

"One of the apprentices, maybe?" says Father.

But it isn't. When Mag and I take our flour over that evening, Emma Baker is there, piling the wood into the oven with the apprentice whose mother was sick.

"What are you doing, being a baker?" Mag says, her eyes big and round.

"Someone has to," says Emma. She looks far too cheerful for someone whose husband has just died. Her round face is red and the sleeves of her gown are rolled up. "Don't just stand there gawping, Watt! If that fire goes out, I'll wallop you so hard you won't be able to stand for a week!"

"Are you going to carry on being a baker when the pestilence stops?" I say.

"Well, I don't see who else is going to," says Emma. "Watt! Didn't you hear me?"

"Emma never did care much for John," says Alice, when I tell her all this. "It was her father who wanted them to marry – he thought it was a fine living for his daughter, though I wouldn't want that great oven on my croft, myself. And who's going to run their house, then, if Emma's playing at baking?"

"Maude's big enough," says Father. Alice sniffs.

"Well!" she says. She turns to me. "Don't you get any ideas, young miss. Don't go thinking you'll run this farm if anything happens to your father!"

"I'd do it better than Robin would, anyway," I say.

19. Harvest

Time passes. The days grow lighter and longer. Soon it'll be harvest, and I don't know how we're going to manage to bring in all the barley this year. Harvesting takes every pair of hands going – men at the reaping, women and girls at the binding, old folk and little squirts like Mag at the gleaning, stumbling behind the binders picking up the fallen grains.

Every summer, our barn is full of the harvesters, sleeping in the hay and toasting bread and cheese over the old iron hearth. Harvest time is hard, but it's also wonderful. The harvesters bring pipes and flutes and drums. They light fires on the green and dance and play and tell tales late into the night. Alice always sends me to bed early, while the dancers are still jumping and whirling by the fire, but this year I'd hoped I might be old enough to stay dancing with Robin or Will, into the long evening.

This year is going to be different. Who's going to look for work in a village with the pestilence? A few people have come – beggars, and poor men and women who have already lost everything they have to lose. But there are richer trades than harvesting now. These are our gravediggers and pall-bearers and nurses of the sick, our walkers behind the coffins and ringers for the dead.

I don't know exactly how many people have died, but it's over three score. I think. Maybe more. The church bell rings every day now, sometimes two or three or four times. I often see Simon hurrying past our house, his little bag with his oil and candles dangling from his arm. He's promised us that as soon as the disaster is over, we'll have the funeral masses. At the moment, he's just getting everyone into the ground.

There are more and more empty houses in the village. Twice now, I've seen sick people wandering through the village half-naked, their wits gone. Sometimes, they don't discover that someone is dead until their neighbours scent it out from the stench of the rotting corpse. Muriel-at-Brook was dead for a week before they found her. Her little daughter was still sleeping in the same bed, half-starved and stinking and covered in blood and shit. Her aunt took her, but not all children have found a home. Edward Miller had two chickens stolen by a couple of filthy ragamuffin boys from York. Sarah Fisher had leeks pulled up from her garden by a family who'd fled the pestilence from the south, and now had nowhere to go. These folk don't stay for the harvest. They won't stop in a pestilence village, but they need to eat, same as the rest of us.

Father doesn't seem to notice the bells ringing, or the empty spaces in the church. He's eaten up with worry over his fields. You'd think, watching him, that he cares more about his rows of barley than he does for Robin's mother and Radulf and Muriel and little Joanie Fisher and Geoffrey at the abbey, about whom we've still had no news.

There's far too much barley to bring in on our own. Father's been trying to get other folk to work on our strips. He offered Stephen Dyer 2d a day to work our strips of field instead of his father's. Stephen was tempted – you could see it in the way he bit his lip and glanced from side to side, but his sister Matilda heard and started shrilling at Father, calling him cruel and heartless, to be making money out of others' troubles.

"You're as bad as those gravediggers, you are!" she said, spitting into the dust.

The new gravediggers charge more and more for their services. Since Adam the sexton died, they've asked as much as a whole pig for burying a body – that's what Sir John used to want for saying the mass! Even the beggars who follow the dead-cart only ask for pennies. And then the gravediggers swagger around the village, living off salt-bacon and throwing their farthings away on ale and white bread. There's an uglier rumour too – that they climb down into the graves and steal rings from the fingers and beads from the necks of the dead. I don't know if this is true or not.

"I don't know why you're so worried," Alice grumbles at Father. "It's not like anyone is going to starve this year." And she's right. This year there'll be more than plenty, even if we leave half the barley to rot in the fields.

"Why waste your strength bringing in food that no one will eat?" says Alice, jiggling Edward up and down on her lap. "They're big sillies, aren't they, my love?"

Alice doesn't understand. Neither does Robin.

"*More* work," he groans, stretching his long arms over his head. "We'll be the richest dead people in England!"

Robin isn't used to working as hard as Father makes him. Margaret's land was all rented out, and though Robin worked in their herb garden and did his labouring on Sir Edmund's land and helped with the haymaking and the harvest, most of Margaret's money came from her weaving and her ale. Father takes Robin out into the fields every morning with Richard, to chase away the birds and weed the rows and do the work of the labourers we aren't able to buy. When he comes home he collapses by the hearth with his hood over his face and his long limbs splayed out before him. Father thinks the work is good for him, and maybe he's right. He certainly looks healthier than he did when he first came here. He's got muscles where before he only had bone. Father never takes Robin's complaints seriously.

"Coming to hew some wood with me?" he says, and Robin groans. "You'll need to work much harder than this when you have your own farm, you know."

"The joy!" says Robin. "The excitement!"

Father tries to look stern, but his mouth twitches.

"Leave the poor boy be," says Alice, as Robin and Father both know she will. "Have a mug of ale, lad, and don't listen to him."

It is very strange living in the same house as Robin, and sharing a bed. I've never felt shy about dressing and undressing for bed before, but now, suddenly, I'm awkward about him seeing me in my slip, and even more awkward about seeing him in his breeches. If Robin is shy too, he doesn't say anything, but I've noticed that he pulls the blanket up almost to his chin when he gets into bed, even though the nights are growing shorter and hotter and closer.

I'm shy around him in other ways too, ways I never was before. I'm very aware of when he's in the room, or when he speaks. I catch myself watching him when I hope he's not looking. I notice things about him – when he's weary, or angry, or sad. He hasn't got used to living with Ned and Maggie yet, the way they tug at you like a pair of puppies; Maggie begging for attention: "Look what I've got, Isabel!" "Look what I can do, Robin!" Ned pushing and pushing until in the end you yell at him, or wallop him, and he retreats into wounded righteousness. Robin doesn't understand about little brothers and sisters. He takes it all too seriously, and minds too much when it all goes wrong.

He likes Father and Alice, I think. Alice, at least. And Father is kind enough to him, though most of his heart is busy worrying over the fields and the sickness. Alice is just worried, about us all.

Richard and I are the only ones who understand Father and his worries.

"All that barley rotting in the fields," Richard says, and I nod.

"What a mess," says Richard, and he shakes his head. "What a god-forsaken mess."

20. Death and the Devil

Mid-July, we have two weeks of real summer weather – hot, dry days full of sweat and flies and thirst. All through the village, you can hear people thinking the same thing. Hot weather is when sickness comes. Even a plague sent from God will surely be influenced by the summer, won't it? The days that follow are so dreadful, I think I must be dreaming. Or perhaps the happy memories – Midsummer Day, the day Will kissed me, the mummers at Easter last year, and Christmas, and the day Edward was born and decided to stay – perhaps they're the dream and this is the only thing that's real. I can't unmuddle it all in my mind. I feel dazed, like I did the time Richard dropped a sack of oats on my head once by mistake, and everything was dazed and blurry, and nothing made sense.

At first, when bad news came – when Joanie Fisher or Margaret died – it was horrible, so horrible and unexpected that we struggled to believe it. But now everything is dull. Every day brings news of more dead, and every day all I feel is resignation. I turn my face away from the people at church, or at the well, so I don't have to hear the bad news. I feel like I've been turned into one of Maggie's clay people, and the real Isabel is sitting on the shelf above Alice's loom, biding her time, waiting for the pestilence to pass.

The next Monday, the harvest starts. It's the long slog now, five days' work a week for Sir Edmund, then your own land to work in the evenings after your time on Sir Edmund's fields is done. If there's sickness in your family, one person can stay to tend the sick, but the others have to work. Some don't come. They hide when Gilbert Reeve comes to their houses, and pretend to have left or to think themselves forgotten.

"Better a day in the stocks than a bed under the earth," Amabel's uncle told Father.

"Don't look them in the eye!" I whisper to Robin, but he doesn't smile. Every day, more people are dying. On the Saturday after the harvest starts, nine people die all in one day. At mass on Sunday, tears run down Simon's face as he tries to speak to us. And he's not the only one.

"Today is a hard day," he says. "Harder than any day we ever thought we'd have to face. But it's not over yet."

All around us, people are crying. I know what they want. They want to understand this. Sir John told us that the pestilence punished the wicked – the French and the heathens and the wicked folk in London. But what reason could God have for punishing little Joanie Fisher, or Edward Miller's baby boy? Why does He strike down the monks and leave the grasping gravediggers, who go into the houses of the dead and take what they please? The only reason I can think of is that He's wiping everything out and starting again, that the end of the world is coming, if not today, then soon; next month, perhaps. Nothing else makes any sense at all.

Nine people dying in one day is horrible. But two days later, ten people die. And three days after that, twenty-one.

If we didn't have the monks from the abbey, I don't know what we would have done. How would Simon have given all the sacraments alone? Sometimes I see him about the village, swaying with sleeplessness on his old brown mare. Two of his chaplains have died already, and the monk who came down from the abbey to live is sick too. People have stopped complaining about how young Simon is and how he's started skipping over the difficult bits of the mass. He may not know the services, but he knows how to be a priest. He comes to any house that asks for him, even in the middle of the night, even to families that live right at the other side of the village. He sits by the dying and reads them the sacraments, asks them to confess their sins, even if they are so far gone that it is clear that they will never be able to speak again.

We're running short of oil and candles. I know the abbey sent to Felton for more, but none could be found. Simon has a bottle of oil that he wears on a chain around his neck. He anoints the sick with a tiny speck on their forehead, and whispers the sacraments to them as they lie dying.

He gave the sacraments to a beggar who wandered half-mad and half-naked through the village. Everyone else cowered away and wouldn't speak to him, but Simon set him on his horse and took him to the infirmary at the abbey. He sat by his bed and gave him the rites. I saw him afterwards, coming home with blood down the front of his robes and his hair stiff with sweat.

The bell in the church tower goes from ringing a few times every day to ringing almost continuously; one long, sorry peal of grief for the dead. It becomes a background to our lives – another person dead. People die so quickly you lose track.

"I shared a bottle of ale with Will Thatcher and Amabel Dyer once," I tell Robin, one day. "It seems so long ago now."

"I know," says Robin. "Poor Amabel. I'm sorry, Isabel."

"Amabel's dead?"

She'd died two days ago, and been buried in a trench in her croft with her father and sister. I hadn't even known. And when Robin tells me, I don't feel anything. One more dead means nothing.

This time last year, the whole village would have mourned Amabel Dyer. But now nobody except her family even notices.

The day after twenty-one people die, the bell stops ringing. The space it leaves is incredible. My ears ring with the silence. But the silence is worse than the bell, somehow. Ingleforn has never been silent, but now – suddenly – you notice all the other noises that are gone. The children, who aren't allowed to play out of their gardens any more for fear of straying into the bad air. The babble of voices around the well and the river – vanished. Many people don't have time for washing, what with caring for the sick and doing the farm work of all those who have died. We still do, because of Edward, and because Maggie is still small enough to spill ale down her front and mud up her skirts at least twice a day. But washing now is a rushed and furtive business. Alice starts washing in the evenings, after dinner, because then the banks of the river are empty.

And she stops taking Edward with her.

Other noises are missing too. The forge is quiet since

Robert Smith died. The stocks are empty too. And the archery butts behind the church stand forgotten, fading in the long sunlit evenings. This is illegal – it's the law that every man and boy has to practise his shooting every day – but nobody is punished. Why bother fining someone or putting him in the stocks when he might be dead tomorrow?

"There'll be a pretty mess to sort out here after this is over," Father says, standing in the doorway looking out at the village, the gardens growing over with weeds.

"If there's anything left when this is over," says Alice. And I realize that she doesn't mean *if the world ends* but simply, *if the village is still here*. What happens if so many people die that there aren't enough of us left to keep up the village?

"I'll still be here," says Richard grimly.

"So will I be," I say. And I will. I hope.

One part of the village that's noisier than ever is the taverns. We don't have an inn in Ingleforn – the alewives simply put a sign up outside their door when they've brewed a new keg of ale and everyone goes there. Robin's mother's was always the main drinking house, but since she died the other alewives' houses have been full every night, even with the risk of catching the sickness. In the evenings, now that the bells have stopped ringing, you can hear the singing and cheering from Margery Goodenough's back door until long after dark. Alice sniffs.

"What have they got to be celebrating, I'd like to know?"

But I know. They're celebrating because they're alive, and because tomorrow they might not be. They're celebrating because if you don't, you'll go insane.

"Oh yes?" says Alice. "And your father and I, we're lunatics now, are we?"

"You were always mad, Alice," I tell her. "Nothing's changed there."

Alice still prays every night for the Lord to save us, but I don't know if she still believes the words she says. I still pray every day too, but only because I'm frightened of what might happen if I don't. I don't believe God can be punishing the wicked any more. Not if the people He thinks are evil are the good monks and Robin's mother and babies like Joanie Fisher. I refuse to believe it – even if it sends me to hell. But then what does He think He's doing?

More than half the monks are dead, Simon says. And many more are sick.

"The Lord is punishing those monks, sister," Agnes Harelip says, glancing at Father. She knows all about Geoffrey. "They say in the village they were sleeping with devils and writing Satan's words in those big books of theirs."

"Those who think that don't have to have the monks visit their sick, do they?" Alice says. "Or bury their dead? If I were you, I'd keep your nose where it belongs – in your own house and not in others' business."

Agnes's face twists, the prissy way it does when anyone disagrees with her, which is pretty much any time she comes to visit Alice.

"God won't spare any of those devil-worshippers," she hisses. "You'll see! You'll see!"

21. *My Brother Geoffrey*

My brother Geoffrey lives in that abbey. It's only three miles' walk away, but it's a long time since any of us have been there to see him. I wanted to go when the pestilence came, but Father said no.

"Wait until this is over, Isabel. There's a lot of sickness at the abbey now."

When people first started getting sick, there used to be a lot more monks around in the village, and I used to stop and ask them about Geoffrey – if he was still at the abbey, if he was all right. I always used to send him my love, tell him we were thinking about him. I haven't spoken to anyone from St Mary's in nearly two weeks, though. As the pestilence has tightened its hold on our village, the monks have seemed to slip away. I know there have been a lot of deaths at the abbey. Maybe that's why.

People don't talk about Geoffrey any more. Mag can't really remember him, and even Ned is forgetting, and he's not Alice's son, of course, so why should she care?

Father's the one with the least excuse. He didn't want

Geoffrey to go. When Sir John came and asked if Geoffrey could enter the abbey, Father said no straight off. He said he needed Geoffrey to work in our fields, and what sort of father did Sir John think he was anyway, to send his son away like that?

Lords and ladies send their children away all the time, when they're younger than Ned. Father said it was a barbaric practice, and Geoffrey's place was here, with his family.

But Geoffrey wanted and wanted to go. He was always different, Geoffrey. He was one of the best choristers in the church choir – he learnt the hymns about twice as fast as the other little boys, and he could say all the Latin in the mass, better than Simon can. Geoffrey loved words. He was always running after Sir John, asking him what this word meant, and this one, until they could say things back and forth in Latin like it was a real language or something.

Geoffrey knows ever so much Latin now, of course, and French, and letters and numbers and herbs and planets and whatever else they teach them up at that abbey.

That's why Sir John wanted to send him away. He said Geoffrey ought to be trained as a priest, that he was too clever to work Sir Edmund's fields for the rest of his life. Ned and I giggled when he said that. Geoffrey was eleven at the time, skinny and yellow-haired, with bright blue eyes and hands which were always moving and ideas bubbling up inside of him. We couldn't imagine him as a priest.

But he wanted to go.

"Just think!" he told me, when Father was stamping around the fields with a face like ice, and Sir John was praying special prayers to God for Geoffrey and Alice was making sideways comments like, "Are you sure you want to be a priest, Geoffrey?

Wouldn't you like to have a family one day?" As if Geoffrey ever cared about babies!

"Just think," Geoffrey said. "They have a whole library full of books. Think of all the words there are in Sir John's Bible and then think how many there are in a *whole library*!"

I grunted. Nobody ever learnt anything useful from a book, except if you were an astrologer maybe you learnt astrology, or if you were an infirmarer you learnt herb-lore. But Geoffrey wasn't planning on being an astrologer or an infirmarer he just used to suck up knowledge like a little pig sucking milk. Latin never taught anyone anything useful, as far as I could see. Not useful like how to milk a cow, or plough a field, or weave a blanket, or sail a ship to Aragon. Why learn all those letters and languages just so you could read the name of a plant, which you could find out much simpler just by asking?

Geoffrey was obsessed by Latin, though. He used to wander round the house muttering it to himself. I'm sure it was his way of riling Father. There was a whole long, weary month and a half where he would use all the Latin words he knew for everything, calling Father *Pater* and Alice *Mater* instead of Father and Mother, and asking for *panem* instead of bread. Father used to whack him, and Alice used to worry and fidget, but he wouldn't stop. He's stubborn, is Geoffrey.

In the end, Sir John said he would pay the money to Sir Edmund for Geoffrey leaving the village, and Father stamped and shouted and said he could afford to pay his own fines, no matter what some people thought, and finally, finally, Geoffrey was allowed to go.

I hate it when people leave. People are always leaving me – Richard marrying Joan, and Geoffrey going to the abbey, and that horrible half year after Mother died. When Geoffrey went, Father got sadder and angrier, and things got a lot less interesting. I used to find myself muttering Latin when I was pulling up leeks or milking the cow, just because it reminded me of Geoffrey. I used to run away to visit him all the time. When he first left us, we used to go up to the abbey every year for the Feast of the Nativity of Mary with all of the other monks' families, and to take part in the Vigil. Father and I went last year, but Richard said he had too much work to do, and Alice was big with Edward and couldn't get away.

I haven't been for months now.

All these long, warm days of summer I can't stop worrying about him. Last night, I couldn't sleep for hours, thinking about him. I wondered what it felt like, stuck there surrounded by the dead and the dying. I wondered if he wished he'd stayed here with us. I wondered if he wanted to come home.

Tonight, it's so hot, I wouldn't be able to sleep even if nothing was amiss in the world. Robin is awake too, shifting and rolling beside me. Ned and Mag sleep through his twistings and squirmings, but he always wakes me. Once or twice I think I've heard him crying. Robin never cries during the day. I wonder if he dreams about his mother, and what he thinks when he wakes and finds that she's gone.

This time, when I roll over, the day is feeling her way in through the chinks in the walls. Robin is lying on his side, watching me.

"Isabel," he whispers.

I reach out my hand, and he squeezes it, very gently.

"Do you think Geoffrey is still alive?" I say.

"Are you still worrying about that?" Robin whispers. "Don't worry. They'd have told us if he wasn't."

"They might not have known who we were ... the abbot died, did you know? They have so much work to do. . ."

Robin squeezes my fingers again. "Shall we go and see?"

And I feel something give up inside me. There's nothing I want more than to see Geoffrey, to hold him, to breathe in his inky, herby scent. To know that he's still here walking amongst the living, that the pestilence hasn't taken him from me yet.

"All right," I whisper back.

22. A High-Day, A Holiday

We take our clothes down the ladder and dress in the dark, *shh*ing each other and trying not to giggle. Nobody stirs. As soon as we're out of the house – dressed, but not washed, as we can't light the fire without waking the others – we're filled with a festival feeling.

"No work!" says Robin. He tips his head back and breathes in deep, happy breaths. He looks more like himself than I've seen him since he came to live with us. "Your father will probably whip me, but I don't care – I don't have to be in your fields today!"

"Do you really hate it that much?"

Robin steadies himself and thinks about it.

"I hate the every-day-the-same-ness of it," he says, slowly. "The way you know in the morning exactly what you have to do that day, and then you do it, and you come home so tired you can't stand up, but you know you're going to have to get up the next day and do exactly the same thing again. And again. For the rest of your life."

"But it's not the same!" I'm indignant. "You don't know –

you'll see. There's planting – and weeding – and haymaking – and harvest – and spreading the muck – and—"

"And all of it standing arse-upwards in a field," says Robin. "It's different for you, Isabel. You care what happens to seeds and roots. I don't, and I don't think I ever will. No, don't argue! Look! We're the only two souls in the whole world."

I know what Robin means. We're on the path between the two village fields, Three Oaks and Hilltop – still in our village, but away from the cluster of houses. It's very quiet. The sky above us is still that pale, almost-wakeful pre-dawn grey. We really could be the last two people left alive.

"Come on—" says Robin. He grabs my hand and we run across the dry earth, barley-heads slapping at our legs, till at last we stop, doubled over with breathlessness and laughter.

"What would you be?" I gasp. "If you didn't farm?" I think of all the jobs there are – miller, baker, carter, thatcher, tanner, smithy, pigman, reeve. Most of them you need apprenticing for, and the ones you don't, you either need a licence from Sir Edmund or they earn barely enough to buy a poor handful of rye. That's why Robin's mother had so many jobs – she was an alewife and a weaver and a landlady and she let travellers sleep in the solar, and the soldiers that Sir Edmund billeted on her – not that she had much choice about that.

Robin's brown face is flushed with running. His ears stick out under his dark thatch.

"I'd like to be a sailor," he says.

"A sailor!"

"Or a merchant. Or a soldier, maybe. I'd like to travel. I'd like to go to France and see where the Pope lives, and where the wine comes from, and Canterbury to see Thomas Beckett's bones, or Jerusalem on pilgrimage, like Matilda Tanner did. My mother never went further than twenty miles from Ingleforn, can you believe it? I don't want to spend all my life planting beans, Isabel. I can't."

"But what about me?" I can't be any of those things, not without leaving my land, and I don't want to be any of them either. And Robin and I belong to each other. We've always meant to be together – Robin's land and a little house and my father there to help if we need him. What am I supposed to do if Robin is fighting or sailing or visiting the spot where Noah had his ark or drinking in the tavern where Jesus turned water into wine?

"I know," says Robin. "But that's what I want. I'd come back for you," he says. But I'm not sure it's enough.

The abbey sits in the sheltered place between two hills. Almost until you're at the end of the road, you can't see it and you can't see it, then suddenly you turn the corner and there it is, low and solid and comfortable as always, nestled in the warmest place in the valley, the coloured glass from the monk's little chapel sparkling in the early morning sunshine. The abbey makes me feel safer than almost anywhere else. I don't know what it is; the monks, or Geoffrey, or the way no one is ever hungry or desperate here, or just the knowing that it's rested in this comfortable space with its forty-two monks for nearly three hundred years, and everything has always been well. I'd like to work on an abbey farm, I think. Just so long as no one made me speak French.

I know the monk who answers the door slightly. He frowns at me and says, in a thick Norman accent, "Yes?" Then, "Isabel? You are all right?"

"We're fine," I say. I reach over for Robin's hand, and he squeezes it in his long fingers. "Is Geoffrey here?"

"He is sleeping, I think," says the monk, and some of the tightness that is clenched up inside of me melts, and I'm not sure whether I want to laugh or cry. I grip on to Robin's hand, and he gives me an odd, distant smile. My brother is alive. My body is bewildered between happiness and that clenching fear that won't let go of me. My brother is alive, but how can I stop worrying, even for a moment? My brothers, my sister, my parents, myself. How can I ever relax?

"He works in the infirmary all night," says the monk. All of the monks here speak some English, but most of them grew up in Norman houses where everyone speaks French, like the king and queen.

"I go and find him for you," says the monk.

We wait. The sun is warm against our backs. It's going to be a hot day.

And then Geoffrey is there, standing in the doorway rubbing one foot against the back of his leg. He's grown even since I saw him last, but he's just as skinny and earnest-looking, and his hair is the same, thick and yellow, with the bald, shaven circle at the top to let God in.

"Isabel—"

And suddenly I'm in his arms and I'm crying, and he's holding me and not saying anything, just holding me, and I'm filled with that sense of safeness that I only get around Geoffrey, a feeling of family which is completely different from the warm, busy, noisy familiness of our home. At home, family is about *doing* things. With Geoffrey, family is about me and him.

"Let's go somewhere," says Geoffrey, and I say, "Aren't you supposed to be working – or praying—?"

And Geoffrey says, "Aren't you supposed to be working too?"

And Robin says, "Quick, before she remembers the harvest."

And he and Geoffrey grab my hands and pull me along, and we're off, running down the road that leads to the abbey, and away.

It's heady, the freedom – the freedom, and seeing Geoffrey again. Robin is practically dancing.

"It's a holiday – a saint's day – a feast day—"

"A feast!" I laugh. "We don't even have anything to eat!"

"I don't care," says Robin. "Where shall we go?"

"Let's go to the river," says Geoffrey.

It's cool and quiet by the river. Everyone from the village is out in the fields, or home with the sick. We don't go to the washing-place by the bridge, but further down, just inside the village boundaries. It's getting hot already. The sky above is blue and cloudless, and the air heavy with the heat. The earth is dusty and cracked, even here by the river, and the grass is turning yellow. Robin sees the water and gives a whoop.

"A swim!" he calls. "Come on, Isabel!" And he starts tugging at his shoe. "You too, Geoffrey, or aren't priests allowed any fun?"

The water is cold at first, so cold it makes me gasp, but once you start swimming, it's warm enough. Robin and Geoffrey look smaller naked, their hair plastered to their foreheads, their faces streaming with water. I keep my shift on, but I still see Robin looking at me. We splash each other and the boys swim underwater, grabbing at my legs and pulling me under so my mouth is filled with water and I shriek. In the end, Geoffrey and I scramble out, wet and bedraggled, and sit in the dead grass, little stones and dust sticking to our wet feet and the bottom of my shift.

I tell Geoffrey the news – which these days is mostly a list of the dead. John Baker. Margaret. Little Joanie Fisher. He listens, but I can't tell who he remembers and who he doesn't. Margaret he says he knows. Joanie Fisher he's never heard of. John Baker...

"Was he the big man with the red face? Who used to wallop us for stealing from the bread oven?"

"His face is red all right," I say. "But he's not that big."

Geoffrey smiles.

"He was big to me."

I ask him about all the people from York, and about working in the infirmary. He's silent, picking at the stones.

"All the infirmary monks died," he says, in the end. "You know that, don't you?"

"I didn't," I say. "I'm sorry."

He nods his yellow head.

"That's why I'm there now..." His voice trails off. He pokes at the dusty earth with his twig. "Did you know," he says, "in the library, at the abbey? They have an astrolabe that tells you the position of all the stars and all the planets?"

I don't even know what an astrolabe is, but I don't say so.

"Mercury, Venus, Mars, Jupiter," says Geoffrey. "The earth, the moon, the sun. If you could tell their exact positions – if you could know how they influence each other, what they tell each other in the sky—"

"Yes?" I say. "What?"

Geoffrey turns his head.

"You'd know everything," he says. "All the future . . . all the past. All the grains in God's hourglass. That's astrology. The science of heaven."

The river runs below us, blue and clear, rushing and chuckling and swirling around the stones. Robin floats on his back with his brown face out of the water and his chin pointed up at the clouds. The birds trill in the trees and the sunlight sets the whole water dancing.

"I read something that made me think of you," Geoffrey says suddenly.

"Mm." Geoffrey is always telling me things out of books, and usually they either don't make sense or they don't mean anything.

"Yes," he says. "Listen—

He to whom God has given knowledge,
And the gift of speaking eloquently,
Must not keep silent nor conceal the gift,
But he must willingly display it."

He looks at me expectantly. I wriggle my shoulders.

"*He,*" I say. "It's always *he*. What about *she*? What if *she* wants to speak el – el—"

"Eloquently."

"Eloquently. I bet he didn't think of that, did he?"

"But he did. I mean, she did."

"She?"

Geoffrey nods. "That's why I thought of you. That poem was written by a woman. Marie de France. She was an abbess. She wrote poetry – about King Arthur, and Tristan and Iseult, and – oh, Isabel, all sorts of beautiful things. But don't you see what it means?"

I stare at him stupidly. All I can think is that a woman

124

wrote poetry. A nun – so not exactly a woman like me – but still. A woman.

"It means," says Geoffrey, "anything. It means anything. If you have a skill – or a talent – then that's a gift from God and you have a duty – an *obligation* to use it. So, if you want to be a farmer – and that's what you want, isn't it? To farm your own land, rather than let poor old Robin do it? – Well, if that's what you want and God has given you that skill, then you *have* to do it. Otherwise it's like throwing away his gift – like the men burying the talents, do you remember?"

Vaguely I remember the story from one of Sir John's rare sermons. If God gives you one talent you're supposed to turn it into twenty, you're not supposed to bury it in the ground and leave it there. Except if your talent is for growing seeds; you're probably allowed to bury them in the ground. I remember what I'd forgotten about Geoffrey – his ability to give shape to the problem or the desire that you hadn't even realized you had. Being a farmer. Growing things like Father does. I hadn't known it until Geoffrey told me, but that *is* what I want. More than almost anything.

"Give it to me again," I say, and Geoffrey says the piece of poetry to me, and I recite it back to him until I have it by heart. "I'll look at it when I've got the space," I say carefully, and Geoffrey smiles.

"Same old Isabel."

Then Robin comes running up out of the river, kicking water before him and on to our feet. We squeal.

"Brotherly love," he says. "How sweet. I'm hungry."

"We don't have any food."

"Don't we?" And he scrambles over to his pile of clothes

and pulls out a loaf and some cheese and Alice's salt ham. Geoffrey sits up, the solemn mood broken.

"You thief!" he laughs. "I should sentence you to five Ave Marias and two Pater Nosters."

"You'd better not eat it then," says Robin, and Geoffrey shrugs.

"The sin's been committed already; I can't let good meat go to waste."

The food is warm but good. We eat half-dressed, sticky with sweat and dust. When we finish, Geoffrey stands up, brushing the crumbs from his robe.

"Come on," he says. "We'd better be home. Our thief forgot to bring us some ale."

I haven't drunk all day, and I'm thirsty, so thirsty that I could drink the river water, muddy and full of disease as it is. We kick our way slowly back to the abbey and drink a flagon of good abbey ale in a row against the kitchen wall. The monks don't seem to mind that Geoffrey's been away nearly all the day. How strange to live such a come-and-go-easy life as this.

As we drain the last of the flagon, Geoffrey stands.

"Well," he says. He looks tired. I remember he was working all night.

I look across at Robin. Neither of us wants to go.

"Can't you come home with us?" I say, but even as the words are out of my mouth, I know he can't. You can't eat someone's beef and venison and read their books for four years, then run away as soon as things get hard.

"I want to stay," says Geoffrey, but he doesn't meet my eyes.

He embraces me, and nods at Robin. "Be careful," he says, and we nod.

"Don't look them in the eye," says Robin. He stretches out his hand and grips my fingers in his. Geoffrey laughs.

"Well," he says. "Good luck."

Robin and I walk slowly back down the path, scuffing up dust. The sky is a clear, pale blue above us and the gnats are out, buzzing around the little beck at the edge of Hilltop. The heat and the weariness of the afternoon hang around my shoulders and my sunburnt cheeks.

"We're all right, aren't we, Isabel?" Robin says. "You and me? I know it's strange, with everything, but. . ."

"Of course," I say, but my thoughts are far away.

"It was a good holiday, wasn't it? Even if your father beats us for it?"

"It was a good holiday," I say. I take his hand and squeeze it, and he gives me a sweet, grateful, weary smile.

I never see Geoffrey again.

23. *Today*

Today, Robert the smith's brown cow caught the sickness and died. They found it dead in the yard, and Robert Smith's widow couldn't move it without help, so it lay there, stinking out the walk all night and all day, until Beatrice Smith gave one of their geese to two of the foreign gravediggers, in return for dragging it away and burying it in a ditch.

Today, they found the body of Old Alis, who was old, old, old, bent like a scythe and wrinkled like an old apple left at the bottom of the barrel. She lived in a little house over by the river, and she'd died maybe a week ago, but nobody had found her.

Our Alice, when she heard about Old Alis, was shaking – actually shaking – with the anger and the shock of it.

"To think that nobody helped her! In a village like ours, nobody knew!"

But we didn't help her either. We didn't know.

Today, when we come home weary and aching from the fields, hands cut and sore from the binding, ready for food and ale and for sleeping until dawn, Alice is in the garden, holding

Edward. She brought him home early because he was hot and fretful, and he's still crying now, his mouth open in a red wail, his face wet and furious with tears.

"What is it?" Father asks, and I can hear the fear spurring at his words. Alice's blue eyes are cloudy and distracted.

"I don't know – maybe we should put some rosemary on the fire? Rosemary and lavender. Something sweet. I don't – we need—"

I've only seen her like this once before. The first time she was pregnant and her pains came too soon and the baby only lived a day, a small, shrivelled little sister who was never baptized and so was buried outside the churchyard walls and never went to heaven. Alice wept at the mass we held for her soul, and then afterwards she seemed to shake herself and lock it all up somewhere. I never saw her cry for that little girl again.

"Alice—" says Robin, and Alice's blue eyes fill up with tears. Robin goes up to her and takes Edward from her arms into his. His baby face is hot – his face is red – and his eyes are screwed up with crying.

"He won't stop screaming," says Alice, and the tears spill out of her eyes. Behind us in the village, the bell starts up ringing again.

"Who—?" says Alice, turning to meet it, and Robin says, "It's vespers," and suddenly I want to cry too.

In the night, I'm woken by Edward screaming, a thin, high wail that won't be comforted. In this hot weather the blankets are up to let out the heat and from my bed I can see Alice walking him up and down, her face red, tears wet on her cheeks. Father comes and tries to take Edward from her, but she pushes him away, her movements nervous and restless, sharp with fear.

When I wake the next morning he's still crying, high and urgent, like a pig being killed. Father's at the door, jiggling him up and down. Father never comforts Edward. He never changes his napkin, or cleans him, or washes or dresses him, or does any of the things Alice does. He might hold him for a moment, if Alice is busy, and he'll rock the cradle in an absent sort of way as he goes past, but that's it. Yet here he is now, in the doorway, jiggling him and saying, "Shh ... shh..." as Edward howls.

"Father?" I say, from my bed, and he looks up and says, "Isabel, can you come down here, please, and take the baby?"

Edward's face is open in a huge, wide-mouthed baby squall. His cheeks are a furious harvest-poppy red, the drops of tears clearly visible against the skin. I hug my arms around his fat body.

"He's hot," I say, but Father's disappeared. "Robin? Feel – he's got a fever."

Mag – in bare feet, shift and green nightcap – pushes against my arm, saying, "Let me take him. He's *my* brother. I want to feel!" Edward is still squalling. Ned is lying in bed with his hands over his ears.

"Isabel! Make Edward stop *screaming*!"

Babies get fevers, I think, *don't they, all the time?* Mag tugs on the sleeve of my shift. I pull my arm away and she yelps. What I want is space, quiet, an empty moment to take a breath and work out how I'm supposed to feel.

"He's wet," I say. "That's why he's crying. Mag, let me alone! I need to change him."

I start unwrapping Edward's swaddling. He's still howling.

Father has disappeared into his and Alice's sleeping space. The cow is making restless noises behind the wattle wall. She needs milking. Everyone needs feeding. Someone needs to fetch water and light the fire and set the day in motion. The world doesn't stop turning just because Edward is ill.

Edward's arms and pink baby stomach are covered with blotches under the skin, like bruising but a reddish purple, blood-coloured. He's still howling, and now I can see why. There, in his groin, is the ugly swollen buboe. It's about the size of a pigeon's egg, and already it's beginning to turn black.

"Robin. . ." I say. "Robin. . ." Then, "Father!"

The end of the world.

24. My Brother Edward

These are the things I know about the pestilence.

It swarms around those who catch it, like a cloud of flies. If you find yourself caught in the cloud – or look in the eyes of somebody who is sick – or offend God – or are loved by someone who offends God – or walk in a particular place when the wind is in the wrong direction – you die too.

You can travel far from the city where your family died, thinking yourself safe, only to reach a place of sanctuary and fall down dead, bringing the sickness down around you.

There's no cure.

Once you have it, you die.

These are the things I know about Edward.

He's small and fat and solemn.

He can almost crawl.

When you take him out of his swaddling, he never stops moving. He's always waving his arms and nodding his head and arching his back and making happy baby noises.

Alice wanted him and wanted him and wanted him, and

almost the whole of his life, he's been living under the threat of this terrible thing, blowing towards us on the winds from the south.

And now he's going to die.

It's a terrible thing, watching a loved child die. Edward screams and screams and Alice cries, holding him and rocking him as though she doesn't care about the pestilence. She buys a magic powder from a travelling magician, which he says is made of myrrh and bole armoniac, tragacanth, spikenard and red sandlewood. He still screams.

The buboe grows until it's hard and black, too hard to burst. If you touch it, Edward screams, but how can you avoid it? Red marks grow under his skin, purpling and mottling until his skin is almost black.

Father sends us out to bring in the harvest. The field is half empty. The other villagers avoid us.

On the third day, when I come home from the field, Alice is sitting by the hearth, watching Edward cry. I go over to his crib and pick him up and he wriggles in his swaddling bands, arching his back and screaming. I rock him and murmur to him, trying to soothe him.

"Can't you take him?" I say to Alice, but for once she's quiet and just shakes her head.

"Are you all right?" I say, and she nods.

I rock my brother until his cries stop, and then we sit by the hearth and watch him sleeping. His skin is more red-and-black than clear, but his hands are quiet.

He dies that night.

25. *By Candlelight*

Alice falls ill next. My Alice.

Father sends us out to work in the fields.

"Can't I stay?" I say, frightened. "Can't I stay and help look after Alice?"

"No!" says Father, too quickly. Then, "Isabel, please. Just go. Let me work out what we're going to do."

We're quiet as we walk down the track towards Three Oaks. I look around at the other people walking to work with us. So many people missing! It shocks me, whenever I look around. But surely all these people can't be dead? Some of them are hiding – or running away – or staying at home to look after the sick? Please God, that's why there are so few people coming to work today, surely?

In the fields, people look at us and whisper, but no one comes near or asks where Father and Alice are. When we come home, the sheet and the blankets from our bed are in the barn. There are pots and cups in a pile, and the leg of smoked ham from the house, and two round cheeses. A bag of flour. A bucket. The ale-barrel. An axe. The old iron hearth that the hired labourers use when they sleep here has been pulled out into the middle of the barn, and there's a pile of new wood stacked up behind the door.

"What's going on?" I say.

"This is where you're going to sleep from now on," says Father. "Just while Alice is ill."

"What about you?" I say, frightened.

"I'll be all right," says Father, but he doesn't meet my eyes.

"I don't want to sleep here," says Ned. He sounds much younger than he usually does, little red-haired Ned who tries so hard to show that he's bigger than Maggie. He pushes out his lower lip and glares at Father. "I want to see Alice! Why can't we see Alice?"

"You saw Alice this morning," says Father. "But now she's ill and you need to let her rest." He rubs at his forehead. He looks tired, and blurred around the edges somehow.

"Are you sick too, Father?" I say, before I can stop myself.

Maggie cries, "Father!"

Father draws in his breath and steps back.

"Please!" he says. "Please! Just – just do as I say, can't you? Just for a few nights."

"No—" says Ned, and he kicks at the floor, so the straw and dust flies up into our faces. Father sighs, and I cuff him over the back of his head, which makes him shriek.

"Isabel," says Father. "Ned, behave! Isabel, please." He takes my hands and looks at me, as though he's trying to say something bigger than his words, but my heart is cloudy with fear, and I can't work out what the shapes behind his words are – or perhaps I don't want to look too closely for fear of what I'll see. "Isabel, you're in charge, all right? You and Robin.

You'll have to have the animals in here with you for a couple of days. You can manage that, can't you?"

I shake my head, dumb and fearful. I can't do anything. I can't look after anyone. I want Father to stay and look after us. I want Robin to be the leader – he's older than me, after all. I want Richard to come and take charge.

"Can't we go to Richard?"

"No." Father drops my hands. We haven't seen Richard since we buried Edward. He and Father stood apart by the grave, speaking together for a long time in low, urgent voices. I don't know what about. I didn't say anything. I was too angry. Richard never liked Edward. He always thought Alice would give him all of our land. He never wanted Edward around, and now Edward was dead, he didn't deserve to come to his funeral and bring his pretend grief to stand by our real sorrow.

"Don't bring this on Richard," says Father. "He's got enough to worry about, with the baby coming. Just . . . look, you'll just have to manage on your own for a couple of days. You can do that, can't you, Isabel?"

"We can do it," says Robin. He comes behind me and puts his hand on my arm. I feel myself shaking against him. "Isabel. Don't. We'll manage, sir."

Father nods a couple of times. Then he embraces me, tight. I breathe in his musty, earthy, leathery smell, trying to keep this essence of Father safe inside me. "You're a good girl," he says. "I wish you had a better world to live in."

I'm shaking inside my skin. I'm rigid with anger and fear – no, terror, I'm terrified – and shock, I'm shocked. I don't know what to do.

Father lifts Maggie up. She wraps her arms tight around his neck. "You'll be good for Isabel, yes?" he says. Maggie nods.

She doesn't really understand what's going on, but you can see that she knows Father is upset and that whatever is happening is serious.

"I want Alice," she says, but when Father lowers her to the floor, she doesn't argue.

Ned jerks back when Father tries to touch him.

"No!" he shouts. "I want Alice!" and he runs out into the yard.

Father sighs and tugs his fingers through his hair again.

"It's all right, sir," says Robin. He's still got his arm across my shoulders. "He's all right."

"No, he isn't," says Father. He sighs again. "Well then," he says. He nods a few times, and then he goes into the house, shutting the door behind him.

With the harvest only half gathered-in and no labourers this year, there's room in the barn for all the animals. Father has corralled them behind the wattle wall from the house, but we have to spend some time making sure the wall is fast, and moving the sheaves of grain into a pile in the corner, so that there's room for us to sleep. The oxen are restless, stamping and snorting, and the chickens keep trying to run back into the house where they know they ought to be.

"I'm sorry," I tell them. "I don't want to be here either."

The barn is cold, even with the warmth of the cow and the oxen and Gilbert Pig. We wedge the candles into hot wax on the beams and push aside the straw to make space for a fire. There's plenty of wood piled up against the wall but it's damp, and it takes a lot of puffing and blowing before it catches. Ned wants to go back inside for more, but I won't let him and there's nearly a fight.

"Make up the beds instead," I tell him.

There's plenty of straw and there are plenty of blankets, but Maggie's too little to do it properly and Ned won't. He just kicks at the straw until it's piled into a heap, then wanders off.

"I'll do it!" says Mags. "I can do it!"

She pats and pulls at the straw, trying to make a mattress, but her bed wouldn't support a cat, let alone any of us.

"Ned," I yell. "Ned!"

He doesn't come.

I go and stand in the barn door. He hasn't gone far. He's stamping about the yard, throwing stones against the side of the house. I go and grab his arm.

"What are you *doing*?"

"Nothing." He pulls his arm away. "Let me *alone*."

"You were trying to get Alice, weren't you?" I say. And, when he doesn't answer: "You *can't*. We promised. Remember?"

Ned doesn't answer. He pulls his sulky face and kicks at the dirt.

"You *have* to do what I tell you," I say. "Me and Robin."

"I do not!" says Ned. "You can't make me!" I want to kick him.

"Fine."

I stamp back inside and slam the barn door shut. It's dark, like the inside of a cave, with only the dull firelight from the hearth and the long, narrow beams of sunlight from the high windows.

"Where's Ned?" says Robin.

"He's in the yard." The fire is sending off great clouds of smoke, but it's burning properly at last. Robin has cut the cheese into pieces and torn yesterday's bread into chunks.

"I thought we could toast the cheese on the fire," he says,

and I give him a grateful smile, because I don't have the wits to think about making anything more complicated right now.

Ned comes in halfway through the meal, his face tight and sulky. He doesn't look at us, but I hand him a lump of bread and he takes it silently and holds it in his lap. After a while, he takes up a stick and a slice of cheese.

Nobody says much, except for Mags, who won't stop talking. "We're staying here all night, aren't we?"

"Yes, Mags," says Ned, in this fake-weary voice. "We're staying here all night. And the next night. And forever until Isabel says we can go inside again."

"Until it's safe to go inside."

"Until everyone's dead."

Maggie looks up, startled. "Are Father and Alice going to die?"

"No, of course not," I say. Alice might, but not Father, please not Father. I feel Ned's eyes watching me. "I don't know. Maybe not."

Maggie settles back, reluctantly. I pass round the ale jug and we all drink. Will everyone really die of this thing? Will it kill us all, then all the dogs and cats and oxen and sheep? When all that's human is gone, will it be happy? Or will it move on to the scurrying things of the moorland, the rats and foxes and little prickly hedgehogs that Maggie likes so much? Can flies get it? Can fleas? When it's finished, will there be anything left?

Maybe somewhere there's a virtuous man or woman, like Noah and his wife, who will look out one day on to a clear, empty morning, and find a world with nothing left alive. Will they be sorry? Or will they smile and step out of their hiding place and walk into the empty farmland and build the world anew? What will the new world be like? Will it be better, with all our squabbling and bickering and wickedness gone?

Outside the barn, it's growing dark. Ned dumps some more wood on the fire, and it hisses and steams. I look across it at Robin. He's hunched up next to the fire, his arms wrapped around his legs, head resting sideways on his knees. Is he thinking about his mother?

If Robin and I both survive this, we're betrothed to be married. I wonder what he thinks about that. Does he want to marry me? Do I want to marry him? I've been starting to think that I might, since he came to live here, but tonight my heart is too full and weary to be able to work out what I think about anything. All I know is that I'm glad he's here.

Ned is poking at the fire with a bit of stick. His face in the firelight is sulky.

"I don't see why we have to do what Isabel says. She's not our mother."

"I will be if Alice dies."

"And Robin will be our daddy!" says Maggie. She grabs Robin's leg and squeezes it. Robin makes a half-hearted attempt at a smile.

"Don't treat your father like that!" I say. Maggie giggles. Ned scowls.

"He's not my father. You aren't even married."

"That's right," says Robin. He lifts his head from his knees and watches me across the flames with an odd expression on his face. "Isabel, will you marry me?" he says.

I look back at him. He's got straw in his hair and dirt on his fingers. There's an ale stain on his cote. His face is all shadow and candlelight and secrets.

I know him deeper than I know anyone else in the world.

"All right," I say.

"Good." Robin turns to Mag. "There," he says. "Now we're married."

"You are not!" Mag tugs at his cote. "You need a priest to be married."

"No, you don't!" says Ned. "John Felton and Amabel Farmer got married just by telling each other they were going to. And then Amabel changed her mind and got married to John Tanner instead and she was going to have his baby and John Felton took them to the manor court and said she was married to him already and the lord said she was and her baby was a bastard, only John Felton said she could marry the other John because he didn't want to have to raise some other man's baby and then they had a fight and—"

"Who are these people?" says Robin, which is what I've been wondering, and Ned says, "They live in Will Thatcher's uncle's village – Will told me about them."

"Ned's right, though," I say, quickly. "We are married now. That's the law."

"Let's have a marriage!" Mags sits up. "Ned can be the priest and I'll be Isabel's mother and cry because I'm giving my daughter awa-a-a-ay!" She pretends to sob into her skirt like Joan's mother did when Joan married Richard. I glance at Robin and he shrugs.

"All right," I say.

Mags takes charge.

"You stand here," she says to Robin, pulling him up. "And you here, Isabel. And Ned, you stand there and hold the candle—"

"I'll hold the candle," says Robin. He takes it from Ned and holds it wrapped in his long fingers, so that the yellow light shines up onto his face. I reach out a hand to touch his cheek, and he stands there watching me all big-eyed and smiling. But when he raises his head again, his eyes are dark and all the laughter is gone and something like a shiver goes down my back, and I'm almost afraid.

"You first," says Maggie, tugging on my arm. "Isabel. Say the words."

I've been to lots of marriages – Richard and Joan's, and Father and Alice's, and Matilda-at-the-Wood's last year and others I've forgotten. I look at Robin and I say the words.

"I take you, Robin, to my wedded husband, to have and to hold, from this day forward, for better, for worse, for richer, for poorer, in sickness and in health, in bed and at board, till death us depart, if holy church it will ordain. And thereto I plight you my troth."

The words start out in silliness, but somehow, halfway through, they become real. Robin is holding the candle cupped in his two hands like it's a flower. I can see by his eyes, and his voice when he starts speaking, that he means this too.

"I take you, Isabel, to my wedded wife, to have and to hold, from this day forward, for better, for worse, for richer, for poorer, in sickness and in health, till death us depart, if holy church it will ordain. And thereto I plight you my troth."

We stand there in the barn, staring at each other. Neither of us speaks. I want to kiss him, but I'm not sure I dare, not with Ned and Maggie watching us. Ned will squeal and laugh and what if Robin doesn't let me? Though I think he will. We're man and wife now – aren't we? Can you be married – properly married – at fourteen? Kings and queens and lords and ladies get married as little children, don't they? The old queen, Queen Isabella – King Edward's mother – Geoffrey told me she was married at seven. I duck my head and look at Robin through my falling hair, shyer now that he's my husband than I've ever been shy of him before.

All evening, I sit by Robin with my hand in his hand, safe in his lap. When we come to bed, I won't be parted from him, even for a moment. I feel like the child at the fair who won't leave her mother for any temptation, not to play on the sideshows, not to join in the dance. When Robin blows out the candle, I worry myself up against him and lay my head on his breast. He puts his arms around me, and I feel like a little bird who's found her nest, a little bird who's never going to leave it, who's going to stay here for ever.

Now that the candles are out, the only light is the red glow of the fire embers. One by one, they'll dim and wink out, until there'll just be warm ash, then cold ash and then nothing. On the other side of the fire, the animals snuffle and sigh.

"There's rats in this barn," Maggie whispers.

"You're not scared, are you?" I say, and she shakes her head.

"Only if they bite," she says, and nods to herself.

She falls into sleep almost immediately. Ned takes longer, but soon I feel his body relax against mine and his breathing slow. I lift my head to look at Robin and see that his eyes are open, black and shiny in the darkness.

"You're my family now," I say.

"Yeh," he says. He sighs and closes his eyes, his hand still draped across my chest. He's falling asleep. I rub my head against his shoulder bone.

"Do you think Geoffrey's still alive?"

"Yeh," he mumbles, though how should he know?

"What's going to happen to us, Robin?" I whisper. He

doesn't answer, but he grips my shoulder tighter against the darkness. And so the first night of my married life we sleep like that, huddled together in the straw, with the barn door bolted against the night.

26. Isabel Alone

The next morning, I wake early. The sun is coming up through the crack in the barn door, and the cow is making restless noises in the gloom, waiting to be milked. I feel almost happy. I know that's a dreadful thing to say, but I do. I roll over and I see Ned, awake much earlier than usual, sitting up in his blankets with bits of straw all stuck into his red hair.

"What?" I say at him, still waking up.

"We don't have to work today, do we?" says Ned. "Not if we don't want to."

"Of course we do." I hate being idle. "The cow still needs milking, doesn't she? And the chickens need feeding. And—"

"I don't think we ought to work!" says Ned, in his high little voice. "I don't want to bring the harvest in if Father's not!"

"Who says we're bringing in the harvest?" says Robin, sitting up with his thick hair falling like a tumbledown haystack over his ears. "Isabel? Don't listen to Isabel – I'm father here."

"What would we do instead?" I say. I don't have the heart for the harvest, it's true, not with Alice sick and Edward . . . I

145

feel all tangled up and out of sorts. But I can't bear the thought of sitting here all day doing nothing.

"Let's go fishing," says Robin. "We'll catch Walt and Alice a fish for supper."

Fishing turns out to be a good idea. The best spot is upriver from Ingleforn, but it's empty, of course – everyone is dead or out in the fields. Maggie and Ned splash about in the shallows, then settle down trying to build a dam across the river – which doesn't work, because the river is much too wide here. You want the beck by the abbey for dams.

Robin's a good fisherman. He's patient, and he doesn't mind standing in the shallows for hours. I watch him, his clever face dappled and danced by the light which plays through the leaves. Shouldn't we tell Geoffrey about Alice? Wouldn't he want to know? Or am I just being cowardly, wanting him here?

The door is still shut when we get back home, but there's smoke coming through the thatch, so Father must be there. I leave Ned and Robin to gut the fish, and search amongst the pile of things by the door for some flour. Maggie crouches in the straw twisting her skirt around her fingers, watching me.

"Can't we go and see Alice?"

"Alice is sick," I say, for about the hundredth time.

"I want to see Alice!"

"Well, you can't!" I tell her. I should know better, with all my years of big-sistering. She starts to cry, not usual Mag sobs, but dirty, hiccuppy, almost silent tears.

"I want Alice!" she says, and I lift her on to my knee and put my arms around her. The hem of her dress is choked with mud from the river, and her long, yellow hair has a scraggly look to it already. I hold her like a good sister and say, "Shh, Mag. It's all right – I'm here," but she spoils it by elbowing me in the stomach and shouting, "I don't want you! I want Alice!"

"Here—" says Robin, coming to my rescue. "Here, Mag, leave Isabel now, she needs to go to the baker and bake us some bread. How about you play cat's cradle with me? Eh?" Mag scowls at him, but he picks her up by her armpits and carries her over to the bed, so at least I can find the flour and take it to Emma Baker's.

What will I do if Father and Alice die? How can I bring these children up on my own?

The houses in the village are quiet. The stocks are empty. There's a man – Will Thatcher! – firing arrows into the archery butts, but he doesn't see me and I don't call out. A few children are playing on the green, and they stop and stare as I pass. I wonder, could I leave Mag with them sometime, or would their parents be too frightened?

Emma Baker is working in the oven with the one apprentice left, a red-faced boy called Philip, who's pumping on the bellows with his sleeves rolled up and the sweat glistening on his cheeks. She looks up as I come with the bread and says, "Isabel! How's Alice?"

"She's ill," I say, and I wait for her to tell me that I'm not welcome here. I wouldn't blame her – she's got three children of her own to think about.

But all she does is suck her teeth and say, "That's bad, Isabel, tell your father I'm sorry," and she takes the flour. "Come with me," she says, nodding to the red-faced Philip, who gasps and wipes the sweat from his forehead. I follow her into the house, where she takes a plate from the table and gives me three smoked trout, still warm from the oven.

"There," she says.

I want to cry, suddenly. I can take people being horrible to me – but people being nice always unmans me. I blink at her and mumble something, and she pats me on the shoulder and starts shouting at her daughter Maude for letting the cauldron boil over.

I don't see Father, but I leave the bread and fish on the doorsill and call, "Father! There's food!"

Then I pull the others away round to the yard, and we eat our loaves and fishes sitting on the cow's drinking trough all in a row. When I go back round to the front of the house, the food is gone.

On the second day, I'm milking the cow when Gilbert Reeve comes swaggering up to our gate with his fat belly hanging out of his cote and asks me why we weren't in Hilltop an hour ago, and what happened to us yesterday, and don't I know they need our oxen for the haycarts? I tell him Alice is sick and Father is looking after her, and he says that's all very well, but we're not sick, are we? And how is Robert Thatcher's team supposed to pull a cart with only three oxen?

I can see we aren't going to win this argument, so Robin and I gather up the little ones and we spend the day bringing in the barley, Robin and I as binders and Ned and Mags as gleaners. The others are distant but polite – my brother Richard is there and he nods at us, but Father must have told him not to come near, because he doesn't say anything to me. Some of the other women stay clear of us too, which puzzles Maggie, but I don't care. If they don't want to talk to me, I don't want to talk to them either. Not after Alice has been so good to the village, taking in Robin and letting me visit Margaret, and inviting Robert Smith's daughters over for food. Agnes Harelip sniffs and turns away when we come into the field after Gilbert, but Robert Smith's widow, Beatrice, comes and sits by us when we're eating and asks after Alice, and gives Maggie a bit of bread with raisins and honey in it.

"Alice is a good woman," she says. "Tell your father, if there's anything we can do."

Should I go to the monks and ask for help? Should I tell Geoffrey?

Robin hates being here, I can tell. His body is stiff as a plank of wood, and his jaw is clenched. The last few weeks, he's been working with a man called Hugh – binding the sheaves as Hugh scythes them. Today, though, Hugh is working with Alison Spinner, and he moves ever so slightly aside when Robin makes as though to go up to him. It's a small thing, but Robin flushes, and goes to bind for Beatrice instead.

I touch his arm when we're eating.

"Robin—"

"Why are we even here?" he says. "They don't want us here. *I* don't want us here. How would you feel if Alison gets sick – or Beatrice – or one of the little ones—" He nods at Maggie and Ned and the other children who are chasing each other through the stubble. "If they died?" he says, his voice high like Ned's. "And it was your fault? How would you feel?"

I touch his arm. Was Edward's sickness Robin's fault? Did he bring the miasma into our house? I thought the miasma was supposed to smell bad, and Robin doesn't. But could it have been Robin's fault anyway?

27. Breathing Through Smoke

The next day, when I go for our bread, Emma Baker's flustered and distracted, wiping her floury hands on the front of her gown.

"Isabel," she says, "oh, Isabel, have you heard?"

From the tone of her voice, I wonder if King Edward has died, or the Scots invaded, or something equally dreadful.

"Our poor little village," she says. "There won't be anything left of us when this is done."

"What is it?" I say. Beside me, Maggie tugs on my gown with sticky fingers. I didn't want to bring her, but she wouldn't be left. I've got so much to do this evening – I'm off to the well for water after this, and then there's the cow to bring back from the pasture, and the pig to fetch from the swineherd, and the chickens to put to bed, and the garden needs watering, and I haven't even started thinking about the evening meal.

"The poor priest," she says. "That poor boy. Two priests in less than a month!"

Except that Sir John didn't die, and Simon. . .

"Is he dead?" I say, and my voice goes up a notch. I don't

want him to be dead, I realize, this gawky fair-haired boy-priest, who reminds me so much of my brother Geoffrey, who I hope – please, God, I hope – will grow up one day to be a priest like Simon is.

"Taken with the sickness, I heard," says Emma Baker. "Last night. He was coughing blood, Agnes Harelip said. He won't have long."

"Isn't anyone nursing him?" I say. "Is he there on his own?"

Emma Baker sniffs.

"Who'd go into a house with the sickness?" And I'm angry – with her, and with the villagers, for leaving this boy alone to die, until I remember the baby no one ever talked about, and the old couple from Great Riding Amabel told me about, who were six days dead and half-eaten by pigs by the time someone found them, and my brother Geoffrey, and how I don't even know if he's alive or dead.

All evening I'm angry. I snap at Mags and shout at Ned and send him running off to the green to play with the Tanner boys. Robin raises his eyebrows at me and I want to slap him. Everyone's been grumpy all day today, and I hate it. I hate it. I hate everything about this. I slop Father's dinner on our doorstep with undeserved force. I'm angry with him and Alice too – for getting sick, for leaving me, for leaving Geoffrey, for forcing me to make decisions I'd rather not make.

"Do you know that boy-priest is sick?" I tell Robin, angrily. "And no one's going to help him? Not one person? After all he's done for everyone in this village – he's lying there in his own shit and no one has even gone to give him a mug of ale!"

"Isabel," says Robin, and his voice is frightened. "You promised your father. Don't you even think about going into a pestilence house! How would you feel if you brought that sickness back to Mag and Ned?"

"I know!" I say, irritated. "I wasn't going to! I just think. . ."

"Don't!" says Robin fiercely. "Don't you even think it! Don't die on me, Isabel. I won't let you!"

"Robin. . ." I say. *It's not your fault*, is what I want to say. But who knows? It might be.

But when we go to bed, I can't sleep. I keep thinking about Geoffrey. The Geoffrey I keep thinking about is alone in that big abbey. He's sick, and all the monks are dead, and nobody is coming to help him. He calls out for me, and for Mother, but no one answers. I lie on my back and stare into the darkness, and tell myself that Geoffrey has all the monks, and surely we'd have heard if they were all dead?

But now my mind is wandering, to that baby that nobody took out of that house, to Father, staying by Alice when he could have run away, to Alice letting Robin come to us. And I think about how young Simon the priest is, how he probably has a mother and a father and maybe a sister like me somewhere, and how he went into Margaret's house even though he knew she had the sickness, even though he didn't even know who she was.

At last I get up, slowly and carefully, so as not to wake Robin. I put on my gown and my shoes, and kneel down by the embers of the fire to light the lantern. Maggie stirs as I blow on the ashes, and calls out, but I hush her.

"I'm just going to the privy, Mags. Go back to sleep." She murmurs and rolls over, back into Ned, half asleep already.

The moon is full, and the sky clear. It's a shiny, silvery, moonlit night and the sky is glorious with stars. I didn't need a candle. The village is very quiet as I walk through it.

There's a light in the window of the Tanners' cottage by the millpond, and I wonder what's happening inside. Someone dying, probably.

Simon's little house is dark, and my single, flickering lantern doesn't drive away the shadows that cluster at the edges of the walls. The shutters are closed and the fire has burnt out long ago. There's that smell again, the pestilence miasma, that choked our house when Edward was sick – a foul, sickly scent somewhere between rotting apples and blood.

"Simon?" I say, as I push open the door, and something stirs at the back of the house.

Sir John's box is open on the table, but the oil and the candles and the little rosewood cross are gone. Someone came in while he was lying there and stole them. Someone who thought having oil at a funeral was more important than the Ten Commandments.

"Simon?" I say again, and my voice hardly shakes at all. "It's me. Isabel. Isabel from the green."

Simon is lying cross-ways on his bed. The smell is stronger here – even with my hood pressed against my nose I can still smell it. The bed sheets are filthy with blood and vomit and probably worse. Simon's narrow face is yellowish-white in the candlelight, and his hair is matted with sweat. There's dried blood on his chin and neck, black and horrible. The candle flame flickers as my hand shakes. I think of Geoffrey, my brother Geoffrey, and the way his chin stuck out as he said, "I want to stay," and wouldn't meet my eyes. I think of all the strangers in the abbey infirmary, and Geoffrey cleaning up the blood and piss and carrying the corpses out to the plague pits. Compared to what Geoffrey is doing, I think, this is nothing. If I were a monk, I'd have to do much worse.

Simon's eyes open. They're dark, darker than Geoffrey's, and they move restlessly in the bones of his face until they see me there. They focus and his lips move, his tongue running against his cracked lips.

"Drink—"

Sir John's ale barrel stands by the table in the corner. I don't know how fresh the ale is, but I don't suppose Simon will mind. I fill a goblet and lift him so he's sitting high enough to drink. He's not much heavier than Ned, and so thin that I can feel the bones of his shoulders digging into my arm. His Adam's apple bobs convulsively as he swallows.

I feed him about half the goblet; then he starts to cough. I pull my arm back, but not quickly enough to stop the blood spattering on to my sleeve and into the ale. His whole body shudders in my arm and I hold him as best I can, terrified that I'm going to drop him. How many years in hell do you get for dropping a priest? The coughing is almost more frightening than the blood, which isn't much, and stops eventually. His eyes close again, and I lay him back on the bed.

I go and fill a bucket from the water butt and bring it back to the bed. With a bit of cloth, I clean Simon's face and hands, rubbing at the dried blood and vomit until it comes away. I ought to change the sheets too, but my mind baulks at the thought. He lies back on his pillow, watching me, not moving. Is he still inside there somewhere? Does he know who I am?

"Simon," I say, and my voice hardly wobbles. "You need to make your confession before God." Simon watches me, but he doesn't say anything. Sir John only ever heard my confession once, at Easter, and I've forgotten the words he used. "Do you have anything you want to confess?"

The candlelight shines in Simon's eyes. He jerks his hand on the bed sheet and I grip his fingers. There's blood and dirt under his fingernails, where the cloth didn't reach.

I wrap my hand around his long, white fingers and squeeze them. They're very cold. The skin is dry and papery.

"I'm afraid—" he says.

"Of what?"

I wait, but his eyes are wandering again, over the bedclothes, over the rough surface of the walls. I swallow again.

"I forgive you," I say. "God forgives you." I dip my finger in the goblet of ale and draw the cross on his forehead. His eyes close.

I lay his hand back down on the blanket and sit there quietly on the edge of the bed. I don't want to leave him. I fill the goblet up with ale and put it back beside his bed. I make up a fire in the cold hearth, grateful for the flame from the candle because my hands are shaking too much to use the tinder. I can't leave the candle burning, but I kick the straw away from the fire and it'll probably be all right. I scatter some feed for the chickens, who'll be hungry in the morning, and then I go back and look at Simon.

He's lying with his head lolling on the pillow. His breath is low and rattling in his throat, like he's trying to breathe through smoke. The stench is strongest over his body. He's going to die soon.

"*In nomine Patris et Filii et Spiritus Sancti*," I murmur over his head, the way Geoffrey taught me. I hold his hand and I pray silently inside my head, for Alice, and Father, and Edward, and Geoffrey, and the baby in the empty house, and the couple in Great Riding who were eaten by pigs, and the nun in France who drowned herself, and all the good men and women who died with no one to wait beside them. Then I sit there on the bed and watch him breathing in and breathing in, and breathing in and breathing in, until he dies.

28. *Inside the House*

It's late when I wake. Usually, I'm the first one up, but today the light is streaming through the cracks in the doors and the cow at the other side of the barn is making urgent noises, wanting to be milked.

Magsy and Ned are already up and playing campball in the yard. I can hear them calling.

"To me! To me!"

I pull on my clothes and go outside. Something's going to change today. It has to.

Robin's sitting on the edge of the animals' drinking trough, eating a bit of cheese. He holds out his hand to me and I go up and sit beside him.

"The food's still there," he says, in a low voice. "From last night."

Every evening, I leave ale and food outside the door of the house. Every morning the food is gone and the flagon is there, empty.

Today, it hasn't been moved.

The house is quiet. There's no smoke coming through the thatch. The shutters are closed.

I feel very tired. I lean my head against Robin's shoulder, and he puts his arm around me. Maggie and Ned are playing with their ball against the wall of the house, but I can't seem to pull my thoughts together enough to worry about them, to tell them to keep away. I ought to go in. I know I ought. But I'm frightened. Not of dying. I'm frightened of what the bodies might look like. I'm frightened of the blood and the pus and the stench, and I'm frightened because these things have no place in our neat little house, in my warm and orderly home.

"What are you going to do?" says Robin.

I bite my lip. Father made me promise not to go into the house, but all today I've been wondering if that was a fair thing to ask me to promise, and if I can live with myself if – when – they die alone and unsanctified.

Watching me, Robin says, as though reading my mind, "Walt never said you couldn't go to the monks."

That isn't true. Father said again and again – since the pestilence came here – that I wasn't to go to the abbey, that I wasn't to go and see Geoffrey, that he didn't care if I'd suddenly decided I wanted to run away and be a nun, I had to wait until the sickness had passed. It's just that now – since Alice fell sick – all his prohibitions have been about the house. But he wouldn't have wanted Alice to die without a priest. I'm sure he wouldn't. And when – if – Alice dies, he wouldn't want her body left to rot in the house, would he?

I don't take the others, because I know the abbey is dangerous. I go through the village alone, with nothing but a handful of lavender from the garden pressed against my nose. It's a heavy, wet day, with a faint mist curling around the edges of the trees.

The village is eerily empty. A few chickens scratch about in the road, and a pig is nosing at the fence by Richard's garden, but that's it. It's like everyone has run away or died and we're the only people left alive, though I know of course that that can't be true.

But there must be monks left. Mustn't there?

The stench of the pestilence is stronger at the abbey as well. I take deep breaths of lavender as I bang on the door with my fist, until I think no one will come, that everyone is already dead. At last, a brother I don't recognize answers the door. His hair is wild and his eyes weary.

"Well?" he says. "What?" He speaks real English, as though he's spoken it every day of his life, rather than learnt it from a book like most of the monks.

"Please," I say. "My parents—"

The monk sighs. "Half of the brothers are sick," he says. "And the other half are dead. And now every bastard in the village wants a miracle. All right. Wait there. I'll get my things." He tugs his hand through his hair.

"Do you have a miracle?" I say. The words tumble out of me like grain from a barrel. "We have St Bede, and rosemary—"

"Rosemary and St Bede!" The monk gives a bark of a laugh. Then he sees my face and seems to collapse. "I'm sorry," he says. "I've not slept all last night, and I'm not going to sleep tonight either. You can't cure this. You do know that, don't you? Once you've caught it..."

He sighs. "Come on," he says. "I'll give them the rites, at least. I can do that much."

We don't talk much on the long ride back. The monk has a scrawny brown horse, which looks as ragged as he does – it's got some sort of mould around its eyes, and there are patches of discolouration across its back and head which give it a worried, half-finished look. The monk rides with a concentration which suggests that he hasn't had much practice. Maybe he's a villein's son, like Geoffrey.

I'm glad he doesn't say anything to me. I don't feel much like talking.

Robin is milking the cow when we come back to the yard. He nods to me, but doesn't come over. I can't see the little ones. I don't know where they are.

"Hello! Open up! Open up!"

The monk raps proprietorially on our door with the back of his hand. I stand a few paces back. He isn't like any monk I've ever met before. His thin face is unshaven and his eyes raw with sleeplessness. The shaved pate of his head has a raw, scabby look to it.

"I don't know if—" I say. The monk looks at me.

"Well?" he says.

"We've been sleeping in the barn," I whisper. "I leave them food, but—"

He gives me a hard look then.

"God almighty," he says. Then, "How many of you are there?"

"Three," I say. "Four with Robin. Six with my brothers who aren't home. There were seven, but. . ."

He runs his fingers through his hair so it sticks up again. Then he says gently, "Do you want to come in with me?"

I shake my head, blind, tears starting in my eyes for the first time all day at his kindness. Kindness always makes me cry.

"All right," he says, and he goes into the house.

I wait outside. He's gone for what seems like hours. I hear

scraping on the floor, as though he's moving the bed. Perhaps they're all right after all.

He comes back to me at the door.

"Don't be frightened," he says. "Come and see."

Coming in from outside, the house is dark and stuffy. It smells of lavender drying, and rosemary and juniper, and straw and smoke and pig and cow, but also the sickly, rotten scent of death. The fire is dead, and the candles are out.

The smell is worse in Father and Alice's little bed-space. The monk has arranged them flat on their backs together in the bed, but he couldn't hide the mess – the blood and pus and worse on the blankets. Their skin is marked with bruises, blossoming under the skin, bruises and blood.

They are both quite dead.

I feel like I'm falling. I feel like I'm standing on the top of Riding Edge, just about to tip over the face of the cliff, and there's nothing I can do about it. My mind is dull. All I can think about is Ned and Maggie and Robin, and how it's my job to look after them now, and how am I supposed to do it on my own?

"Their confession," I whisper. "I never heard it. They died unshriven."

"Here," says the monk. He makes the sign of the cross over the bed.

"But if no one heard their confession – aren't they going to hell?"

"Perhaps they heard each other's confessions," says the monk. He puts his arm around my shoulders and leads me gently away from the bed. "Yes. I'm sure that's what must have happened. They knew what the bishop said, didn't they?"

Outside, the sudden brightness makes me blink. Robin has taken the cow to pasture, and Mag and Ned are nowhere in sight. My head is stuffy, as though I haven't properly woken up. I can't think what to do next. Should I tell the others? Find Geoffrey? Run away? What can I do with these ruined people? I'm supposed to bury them, I know, but the thought fills me with terror. I want to run back to the barn and lock the door and never leave it again.

"Your brothers." The monk is talking to me. "Little girl. Listen to me. Where are your brothers?"

"Geoffrey's at the abbey," I say. "Richard's in his house – it's not far. He's got a wife who's going to have a baby. Do you know Geoffrey? Is he all right? Can we go back and tell him?"

The abbey rushes into my head, the abbey infirmary where Geoffrey was working, that cool, safe place rich with the smell of dust and sunlight, green leaves and apple blossom, paper and old stone. Maybe we could go there, and the monks could look after us. They wouldn't ask Mag and Ned to work in the infirmary, surely? Maybe there's somewhere safe they could hide us. But even as I'm thinking it, I know I'm dreaming. Nowhere's safe any more.

"Geoffrey," says the monk, as though he's tasting the name. Then, "No, don't go to him. Better not bring your family to the abbey now. Take the others to Richard – he'll look after them."

"But I can't!" I cry. "Father told us we weren't to. Why can't I see Geoffrey? What's wrong with him?"

"Little girl," says the monk. He says it calmly, but very firm. "Listen to what I'm telling you. The abbey can't help you now. You need to go and find your other brother."

Does that mean Geoffrey is dead, and he doesn't want to

tell me? I bite my lip, hoping to make the blood come, but I don't ask any more.

"All right," the monk says. "Good girl. Come on." He leads me away from the house and towards the gate. He hauls himself back on to his horse, rubbing at his bloodshot eyes, yawning hugely. Then he leans over and touches my forehead. "*In nomine Patris et Filii et Spiritus Sancti*," he murmurs, like I did to Simon, and I stand there at the gate to our house, watching as he rides away and the empty land that is the rest of my life rises up to meet me.

Richard.

Richard will help. I know I promised Father not to go to him, but I can't do this on my own. How can Robin and I dig the graves? How can Robin and I bring in the harvest alone? How can I keep Mags and Ned fed? How can I go back to that house, once so warm and safe, with the stench and the blood and the dead people already starting to rot inside it?

When I rap at the door, Joan answers, her belly heavy and swollen, and my hope sinks a little. I'd forgotten quite how pregnant she was. At the same time, it's so wonderful to see someone grown-up and related to me – someone whose problem Ned and Mag and those dead bodies are now – that I grasp at her sleeve.

"Joan! Oh, Joan. It's so good to see you."

"Isabel! Isabel, whist." Joan steps awkwardly off the doorsill, shutting the door behind her. "You'll wake Richard."

Wake Richard? The sun is already halfway through its journey into the heavens. Why would Richard be sleeping?

"Can I talk to him?" Tears are pricking at the back of my eyes again.

Joan hesitates. There's something wrong with her face – it's stretched taut with sleeplessness and her eyes won't meet mine. Who of her people have died – her father? Her sister? I don't want to see whatever sadness is there and I look away, to the church and the faded cloth of the archery butts and the three beehives round and content and all unknowing in a row in Sir John's herb garden.

"Isabel. . ." she says, and something in her voice makes me turn back to her. "It. . ."

"What? It's what? I need to speak to Richard, Joan."

"I think it's the pestilence. . ." says Joan, and her face crumples suddenly into tears, and she's crying, this grown woman who I'd hoped would solve all my problems is crying in the doorway.

I hate Joan. I hate her and I hate her stupid tears.

I back away. Joan's shoulders are shaking, but I can't help. All I can give her is more grief, and I can't bear to bring my unhappiness here, to another human's shoulders. I'm a coward, I know, and a fool, but I can't help it. She'll hear soon enough. I stumble back up the track, as Joan closes the door behind me, back to my two dead bodies and what is left of my family.

Last week, I had four brothers, two parents, one sister and Robin.

Now I have one brother, one sister and a husband.

And it isn't over yet.

29. Judgement Day

The future stretches before me, bare and terrible. First I have to talk to the others. Then I have to do something about the dead things in the house. Probably then I have to clean up the house and make it into somewhere we can live again, but my mind revolts at the horror of it. Maybe we could just live in the barn for ever, where it's clean and quiet.

Once we've done those things, then I'll worry about what we're going to do next.

Robin is feeding the chickens – so late in the day! – when I come back to the yard. He sees my face and he comes over and puts his arms around me. I don't have to tell him anything. I just rest my head against his shoulder and breathe in his warm leathery earthy scent.

"Richard wouldn't help us?" he says at last, and I rub at my face with my hands.

"He's sick. And Joan has the baby coming. It's just us now."

I sit Maggie and Ned on the water trough and tell them what's happened. They're quiet, and they look as bewildered as I feel. Maggie seemed to understand about Edward, but Father and Alice together is too big for her to hold.

"But where are they?" she says. "Where's Alice?"

"Alice is in heaven," I say. "But her body's in the house. Do you want to see it?" She shakes her head. She knows what a dead thing looks like, from Edward's cold little corpse. She doesn't need to see another.

"What's going to happen to us?" Ned demands. "Who's going to look after us, if Richard isn't?"

"I don't know," I say wearily. "Me and Robin, I suppose."

"You can't!" says Ned. "You're not grown-up enough!"

"Fine," I say. "Feed yourself then," and he bares his teeth at me. I've only been his mother for an hour, and already I'm a failure.

"Isabel," says Robin, quietly. "How are we going to bury them?"

How indeed? I think of the people I would have gone to for help in another life – Alice's mother, who died of the ague three years ago, Robin's mother, Emma Baker, Edward Miller, the priest. Emma Baker is the only one left alive, and can I ask her to dig a grave for two grown people? But the sexton is dead, and I hate the gravediggers, I hate the thought of giving one of our animals to them in payment. But what choice do we have?

I start shaking my head from side to side, blindly, like a hurt animal. I don't know how we're going to bury them. I don't know how I'm going to look after Mag and Ned. I don't know what we're going to do.

Robin puts his arms around me again. I rest my head on his shoulder. There's so much that needs to be done. I can't do any of it.

"Come on," says Robin. "Let's go down to the churchyard and see who's there."

The churchyard is quiet. It got so full these last weeks, they stopped burying people there. They've opened a pit in Sir John's pasture behind the church. The dug-up earth is heaped up in a pile. The pit itself is low and uneven and stinks of lime. Unconsecrated ground.

Adam the sexton was one of the first in the village to die. Dirty Nick, who's mad, and the gravediggers who follow the funeral carts now open the pestilence pit and throw the bodies in, and then they feast off the beasts of payment, or if there isn't anyone left to pay them they go into the houses of the dead and take what they like.

I can't bear it.

I go into the church and call, "Hello? Hello?" but nobody answers.

Nothing stirs in the cottages by the church. A goat chews at the carrots growing in the sexton's garden. Nobody stops him. The door to Nicholas Harold's son's house stands open, but the inside of the cottage is dark. Nicholas's pig is digging up their herb garden unchecked. I don't want to think about what might be inside the cottage.

"Where is everyone?" whispers Robin.

There are people still alive in the village. There are. There's smoke rising from the oven, and from one or two of the cottages by the forge. One of the beggars is wandering over the green, with the aimless, half-crazy motion of one of the sick. Most people are at the harvest, I know. But Robin is right . . . the village has an emptiness to it that isn't usual even in harvest-time. Perhaps it's because the forge has been silent since Robert the smith died. Perhaps it's because so many animals are dead. Perhaps, perhaps.

I wonder if Noah felt like this, standing on a mountain looking over his flooded world, trying to work out how to remake his life from the beginning.

"There's someone over there—" Robin says, pointing.

In the mist at the edge of the churchyard, there's a low shape, no higher than a child and moving. I draw in my breath. It looks like a devil, a black devil digging up the bodies to take them down to hell. But Robin is moving towards it, and I'm more scared of being left on my own than I am of whatever it is.

"Hello!" Robin calls. "Hello—?" and then, "God, Isabel!"

He turns away, like Maggie when she's frightened, his head ducked down, as though shielding off a blow. I move towards the shape, questioning, and the wind turns so that it's blowing in our direction and I catch a lungful of the pestilence smell, so strong I nearly gag.

"What is it – Robin—?"

It's a pig. One of John Adamson's red-haired pigs, with his snout in the shallow earth. At first I don't understand Robin's horror, then I see that the pig's snout is muddied with blood, and I see what it's been gnawing at, and my stomach rises to my throat and I have to turn away to be sick.

"Isabel," Robin says, and I can hear the tears in his voice. "God, Isabel—"

His voice sounds small and childish and frightened, and I'm suddenly furious with him. It's *my* mother and father who are dead. It's *me* whose world has tumbled topside up. Why am *I* supposed to look after *him*?

"Shoo!" I shout at John Adamson's pig, stamping my feet

and flapping my arms. "Shoo! Go away, you horrible thing!" I run at it, and the pig lumbers away a few feet, but then stops, looking at me with its little piggy eyes. There's another pig at the other edge of the grave – old Sarah Stranger's fat sow, which just looks at me and then carries on with her dinner.

This must be the plague pit. The mud is so shallow here that you can see low, swollen shapes in the earth where the pigs have been rooting – a mottled arm here, a swollen stomach there. My belly rises in me again, and I swallow to keep it down. My eyes move almost of their own accord, catching on scraps of cloth and hair, trying to tell *which* and *who* these people are, and I turn my face away in horror. My hands find Robin, and I clutch at his tunic. He puts his arms around me, and I bury my face in his chest, feeling the tears rise again. How can I do this? How can I put Alice and Father in here?

"There's Dirty Nick," Robin says, and I feel the panic rising in me.

"I'm not asking Dirty Nick!" But what choice do we have? A small – no, a large – part of me just wants to put them in the ox-cart and leave them by the churchyard and hope someone comes and buries them for us. But what if no one does?

Robin is looking over my shoulder, into the churchyard.

"There's someone there," he says.

He's right. There's someone there, where a moment before there was nobody. A man, taller than any of the men I know, standing in the mist by one of the gravestones. He looks like an angel, coming to blow the last trumpet and raise the dead. Or perhaps he *is* one of the dead, rising from the tomb. The Day of Judgement has come at last, and I can lay down all my burdens and put my future in God's hands. I should be frightened, I know, but actually what I feel is relief. It's the same as the feeling you get at the end of a long task, when an adult comes back and takes over the cooking pot or the loom or the plough, and you know that all that effort is lifted out of your hands, that the meal or the cloth or the field may have been worked well or ill, but whatever happens, it's not your business any more.

I don't have to worry any more, is what I think, very clearly. I'm so sure of it that when the man turns, I walk easily and happily towards him, the way a Michaelmas pig walks easy and happy towards the woman who has fed him all throughout the long summer, unaware that this day her hand holds not the slop-bowl, but the knife.

BOOK TWO

YORK

BOOK
TWO

He to whom God has given knowledge,
And the gift of speaking eloquently,
Must not keep silent nor conceal the gift,
But he must willingly display it.

Marie de France
Twelfth century

30. *Thomas*

I t's dark. It's cold. The rain has been falling on and off all day, and though the last fall was a few hours ago now, the sky is still heavy with clouds. The road – the road all those exiles travelled down from York, all that time ago – is swamped with mud and water. My hose and the hem of my gown are splattered and soaked. When I rub my face, water splashes off my hand and down my sleeve. Every time I lift up my foot, my shoe rubs at the broken skin on my heel and my feet squelch. On either side is farmland – beans and oats and barley like Father's strips. It's still harvest, so they should all be full of people, but again and again we pass fields with the yellow barley heavy and abandoned. The harvest is rotting away ungathered. Cows moan in the fields, their udders swollen and unmilked. Sheep with what looks like the murrain lie untended in the grass. In one field, all the cows are dead and the stench is astounding. Foxes and ravens are gorging themselves on the carrion, greedy and fearless and unchecked.

In the doorway of a house, a little boy Maggie's age watches us pass. He's got mud all down his tunic, and his face is red

175

with crying. I wonder where his parents are, if they're still alive, if there's anyone looking after him at all. But there must be someone, mustn't there? There must be.

My feet hurt. My legs hurt. It's all right for Thomas, he's got a horse. It's the most beautiful horse I've ever seen, a black palfrey with a white diamond on its nose. He has Mag up on the seat in front of him. She's half asleep, lolling back into his arms with one finger and the edge of the blanket stuck half out of her mouth. Ned, stumping along beside me, is close to his limit.

"My *feet* hurt. Aren't we *there* yet?"

I want to shake him, but I'm so tired I can't manage more than a, "Be quiet, can't you?"

Not because I care what Thomas thinks. Not because I don't want Ned to mess up this journey as much as possible. Just because if I hear any more complaining, I think I'll turn round and run back home.

Thomas sits on his horse, pretending he can't hear us. I suppose he thinks he's being polite.

Thomas.

I hate him already.

In the saddlebags on either side of the horse is all we've been allowed to bring. There's not much. Most of our things are useful, not precious. We've got St Bede, and the dice, and the little wooden animals Father made for Ned and Mag. Mag has Alice's coloured beads round her neck and the pewter badge that came from Duresme Cathedral. She wanted to bring Father and Alice's bed, but Thomas laughed and said it wouldn't fit on the horse.

"But it's our bed," said Maggie. I knew exactly how she felt. I wanted to ask if we could take Alice's red salt-pot, and her green flagon that came all the way from France, but I didn't want Thomas to think I was a fool.

Thomas is a rich merchant in York.

He probably has whole chambers full of green flagons from France.

I know I ought to be grateful to Thomas. He spent hours helping us dig the narrow grave where Father and Alice are lying now. He and Robin lifted them on to the cart, and off at the other end, so I didn't even have to touch them. I *am* grateful. I am. Now that the bodies are gone, everything is easier, though Thomas said that the grave is too shallow to leave the corpses in safely for long.

"When all this is over," he said, "your priest will have to sort all this chaos out."

"Our priest is dead," I said.

Robin and Thomas and I dug the graves, with Father's spade and another from Simon the priest's house. It took hours. We brought Maggie and Ned down to the churchyard, and I could see Thomas watching them, though he didn't say anything. Robin was looking at Thomas like he was Jesus resurrected and given a broadsword and a chest of gold.

"You know a lot about graves," he said. "Are you a sexton?" which was a ridiculous thing to say. Anyone could see Thomas wasn't a sexton, with his beaver-fur hat and his mantle lined with moleskin.

Thomas shook his head and said, "No, I work in wine. I have two ships that bring wine from France – though the docks are closed now, of course." As soon as he said *ships* and *France*, I could see Robin was gone. His eyes never left Thomas, all the time they were digging. It was like there was a little bell-ringer in his head, ringing it out, *France, France, France*.

France is where the pestilence came from. It's people like Thomas with his wine ships who brought it to England.

Robin didn't care, though. He insisted on taking Thomas back to our barn, insisted on pouring him the last of our ale and cutting him thick slices of our cheese and our ham.

"What are we going to eat when that's gone?" I whispered.

"Isabel!" Robin looked shocked. "He's just dug two graves for us – we can give him some ham!"

I knew we could. I knew I was being ridiculous. We're not short of barley or oats, and the cow and the garden are full of milk and herbs. But I could see what was going to happen. Thomas with his kind eyes looking all round the barn, noticing the straw mattress and the hearth, noticing that we haven't invited him into the house, because I can't think about what that house looks like yet. He was going to be kind and charming, and end up taking charge of everything. And while I was grateful for his help, our other problems were *ours*, not his.

"You're sleeping out here?" he said, casually.

"Just while Father and Alice were sick," I told him.

"I expect we'll go back inside now," said Robin. And I could see the thought trailing off as he said it.

"Nice enough out here," said Thomas. He looked so polite and ... dignified, sitting there on Maggie's hay-bed, that I found myself liking him a little, before I could stop myself.

Mags was still shy of the stranger, burying her head in my skirts and peering out at him from behind fistfuls of cloth. Ned was like Robin – fascinated.

"Do you live in a manor house?"

"Not quite." Thomas stretched out his legs – he had soft leather boots with buckles that glistened even through the mud. "I have a house, and a big shop in York."

"Do you have children?" said Ned. I could hear him wondering what they looked like – if they had leather boots, and horses, and if they sailed on ships to France too. But Thomas's face shut itself up like the big chest in the tithing barn with the seven locks and the seven brass keys.

"Not any more."

"Did they all die—" Ned began, but Robin kicked him.

Thomas steepled his hands and looked at us over the top of them.

"Do you have someone to go to?" he asked. "Other family?"

"There's my grandmother. . ." said Robin, his voice trailing away. Robin's grandmother is small and blind and gnarled like an old tree. Her hands are twisted with rheumatics, and her back is bent forward like the beams in a roof. She lives with Margaret's brother's wife in a poky little house – Margaret's brother died years and years ago. There might be room there for Robin, but there isn't bread or room for us all.

"We don't have anyone," Ned said. "Isabel's going to look after us, aren't you, Isabel?" He looked at me, and I felt sick. I ducked my head, pretending to fuss about Mag's long tangle of yellow hair.

"That's right," I said, trying to sound braver than I felt.

Thomas was quiet. I could feel his eyes watching me, and I looked up, staring straight into his long, sallow face. It looked tired, I realized. There was something about it which reminded me of the monk swaying with sleepnessness on his old farm horse, which reminded me of Simon stumbling over the Latin in the mass with his yellow hair all wild and sleep-tousled. I looked down. I didn't want this well-spoken stranger tangled up with my memories of kindness and bravery. Though I supposed he might have been brave. Burying two victims of the pestilence.

Thomas's fingers were playing with the hilt of his sword. I'd seen Ned eyeing that sword – the sheath was worked with silver and bronze: leaves, with little animals peering out behind them. My mind couldn't focus on Thomas, couldn't give him the attention I knew he deserved. My thoughts were going round and round and round in the same old rabbit-tracks. *Alice is dead. Father is dead. What am I going to do? Alice is dead. Father is dead. What am I going to do? What am I going to do? What am I going to do?*

"There's space in my house," said Thomas. I couldn't really understand what he was saying. Who cared how many rooms he had in his house? "It's a big, lonely house now so many people have died," he said. On the other side of me, Robin sat up, all excited, but I barely noticed. "I'll understand if you want to stay here," he said. "It's up to you of course, Isabel, and you, Robin. But the offer is there if you want it."

31. York

I've never been to York before. I've been to several of the towns around our village – to markets, or fairs. Father went all the way to Scotland when he was a soldier. And Alice went to Duresme, to visit the bones of St Bede. But no one's been to York.

It takes two days' walking to get there, even with Mag up on Thomas's horse. By the end of the first morning Ned is moaning about his feet and his legs and a whole lot of other nonsense. If he can work all day through the harvest, he can't be that tired just from walking.

Ned just doesn't want to go, same as me.

We spend the night in an inn called The Star, which is horrible. The landlord won't let us in at first, in case we carry the pestilence. Thomas has to pay him double. And inside it's dark and smoky, and it stinks – half the servants have run away or are dead, so no one has changed the reeds on the floor or emptied the latrine. Most of the beds in the long bedchamber are empty, but the landlord says we still have to share – Ned and Maggie and me in one, Thomas and Robin in another. I nearly tell Thomas that Robin and I are married and ought to have a bed to ourselves, but in the end I don't. Outside of the barn, the wedding feels like a game we played a long ago time, when we were still children. I'm shy of telling Thomas about it in case he laughs at us. Not that I think he would – he's been very respectful so far.

But I don't trust him.

It's evening of the second day when we get to the city gates. The road is quiet – like nobody lives there. There's still a watchman on the gate, but he just nods when he sees Thomas and waves him in.

"Isn't there a toll?" says Ned. Father always has to pay a toll when we go to Felton – one to enter the town and another to pitch our stall at the market.

"Shhh," I say. I'm exhausted by Ned and Maggie and all their questions, all the way here, on and on, like a saw against my skull. "Don't be so stupid. Thomas must be a freeman of the city."

A freeman of the city. And if he adopts us as his children, we'll be free too.

This is what I've wanted for as long as I can remember. Freedom. Freedom to live my life as I want to, without being pushed hither and thither by Sir Edmund's whims. But I don't feel happy. And I don't feel free. I feel like I've exchanged one master for another, and while Sir Edmund's demands were straightforward and easy to understand, I still don't understand what this master wants from us. From me.

I don't like Thomas. I didn't want to come here. I only came at all because I'm so terrified of our house and the bloody bed where Father and Alice died and that stale, rotten smell that even the Alice's rosemary and lavender can't mask. Which was a stupid reason to come, because York stinks worse than our churchyard, worse than the pit in Sir John's pasture, worse than anything I've smelt before – a sickly mixture of dung and sickness and death.

"Robin, I don't think we should have come," I whisper. "What are we going to do in York?"

"He's going to look after us," Robin whispers back. "He owns ships that sail to France – imagine that, Isabel! Maybe he'll take us to France!"

I'm starting to wonder if Robin is maybe going a little bit mad.

York is unlike any city I've ever been in. Felton on market day is always full of people – selling things, making things, buying things, talking, eating, stealing, dancing, playing. York is empty. What people we see move hurriedly, heads down. Animals forage in the ditches – wild pigs, stray dogs, even a starved-looking horse or two rooting around in the mud. Most of the market stalls are empty or dismantled. And above our heads the church bells are ringing, three or four different bells in three or four different churches across the city, tolling the dead.

Here we go again.

"Isabel," says Ned. "Look!"

A figure half sits, propped against a church wall. It's a woman in a dark green gown. Her head is slumped against her chest. It's hard to tell from this distance if she's asleep, or drunk, or dead, but Thomas doesn't wait to find out. He pulls the head of his horse around, away from the figure.

"Is she dead?" I say. "What's going to happen to her?"

"The dead-carts will take care of her if she is," says Thomas.

"They'll be along at sunset. If she's alive, she's in God's hands now."

He says it so calmly, I'm shocked. For a moment, I'm angry, but then I remember the baby that nobody helped. I remember Father and Alice, who died alone while I was playing weddings in the barn. I never helped them. I never even sent for a priest to hear their confession. I turn away, furious tears stinging at my eyes.

The streets are wet with excrement and other foulness – blood from the butchers' shops, and dye from the dyers'. I clench my nostrils together, but I can't escape the stench. Mag whimpers and buries her nose in my skirt.

The city is cramped. The houses bend their heads close together across the alleyways, almost touching in places. They are two- and sometimes three-storeyed buildings, much more imposing than the little one-storey houses in our village. In many of the houses, the shutters are hinged at the lowest edge, so that they can be let down to make a shop window, big enough that you can see the workshop space below, where men hammer iron, or melt gold, or weave, or bake, or make shoes. Many of the windows are shuttered up, but some are still open. One baker catches at my arm as we pass.

"Buy a penny loaf, mistress!"

I pull back. "I don't—"

"She's with me," says Thomas, and the baker bobs his head and drops his hand.

"Beg your pardon, I'm sure."

Like in Felton, the houses in York are all built higgledy-piggledy around each other. Big houses peer down on the little ones that have been built in the cracks between them. Shophouses are next to merchant halls are next to churches are next to tiny houses even smaller than ours back home. The bells are still ringing, making my head ache, making it hard to think, hard to care.

In one square, there's a figure standing halfway up the wall. I think it's a statue at first, but as we get closer I see it's a man. He's hanging by the neck from a gibbet, and he's obviously been there for some time. Half his face is eaten away by maggots, and as we pass the wind blows the stench in our faces and makes Maggie shriek.

"Who was he?" says Ned, whose face is very white.

"Some criminal," says Thomas. "A murderer, or a thief. A brigand, maybe. Don't they hang thieves in your village?"

They do – they used to, Alice can remember it – but I've never seen one. If Sir Edmund's steward wants to punish us he mostly just fines us or puts us in the stocks. I saw a man once at the market in Felton whose hand had been cut off for stealing, but I've never seen a man hanging there like that in the square.

Maggie is terrified, much more so than I'd expected. She cries and hides her face in her hands, refusing to move or look out. In the end I pick her up and carry her, and she buries her face against my neck to make certain she can't see anything else. She's heavy, and my arms ache, but it's easier than fighting.

"It's only a dead man," I say. "He can't hurt you." I don't understand why she's so upset; she's used to dead things – dead oxen, dead pigs, baby chicks small and unmoving in the straw. She wasn't bothered at all by the huddled woman against the wall. "Where did all these tears come from?" I say. But she just whimpers and won't answer.

When at last Thomas turns into a courtyard, I'm so tired that I don't realize we've arrived.

"Halloo!" Thomas is calling.

His man hurries out of the door to take his horse. He's a servant, but he's wearing high leather boots and a fur mantle, like Sir Edmund's steward back in Ingleforn.

"We didn't expect you," he's saying. "And so late!" He sees us and glances at Thomas, but he doesn't say anything.

"Very good, Ralph," says Thomas. He swings himself down from the horse in a practised motion and Ralph gives him a lantern and leads the horse away, saying nothing.

The door opens into a warehouse – or perhaps a shop. Barrels of wine are stacked up against the wall. There's a table with an inkhorn and parchment and quill pens. There are wineskins in a pile. Thomas's lantern casts long shadows and in the yellow light everything seems darker and bigger than it ought to be.

"Stand up straight," Alice's voice says in my head. "Hold up your head. Show these folk what sort of girl you are." But what sort of girl I am is nothing. I feel like a corn husk with the corn inside gone. I feel like an eggshell, cracked open and empty and useless.

"None of that," says Alice fiercely. "You've got to look after your brother and sister now." But I can't.

"This way," Thomas is calling.

We're through into the hall. The fire is out and it's cold and dark. The lantern light catches on heavy, embroidered hangings and long wooden tables. And then we're going up the stairway, into the chambers above.

"This is the scriptorium," says Thomas. "You boys can sleep here."

There are two low beds against the wall. Ned wraps his arms tighter around his bundle from the saddlebags and looks at me. *I want to sleep in Isabel's bed.* That's what his eyes are saying. Beside Thomas he looks very small and fragile. Tears start behind my eyes again.

"Please—" I say. "Can't the boys come in with us?" But Thomas is shaking his head.

"It wouldn't be proper," he says, and the tears threaten to rise.

"Come and see," he says. "You can sleep in Edith and Lucie's chamber."

He turns away. I mouth at Robin, *Edith and Lucie?* Robin shrugs.

"Edith and Lucie are my daughters," Thomas says, over his shoulder.

Were. Edith and Lucie *were* his daughters.

Edith and Lucie's bedchamber is about half the size of our whole house. Thomas lights the candle by the bed from his lantern. They're both real beeswax candles, and they cast a yellow glow across the chamber, a brighter, cleaner light than the tallow candles we have at home. It's a fine chamber. There's a wooden floor and windows made of a hard, flat substance, pale yellow, paler than wax. Horn. Horn windows. Thomas really must be rich. There's a big wooden bed, bigger than Father and Alice's, with a wooden chest at its foot. There's a loom with a piece of cloth half-woven, and a desk like the one in the scriptorium in the Ingleforn tithing barn.

"Is it another scriptorium?" says Robin.

"No," says Thomas. "Those are Lucie and Edith's."

Mag hangs back, clinging to my hand, but I follow Robin

to the table. There's a cup with quill pens, an inkhorn half full of ink in a hook on the side of the desk and pages of parchment with black letters scratched on to them. Thomas's daughters could write! They could read too, because there are books on the table, two big, thick volumes like they have at the abbey. I touch the top one with my fingertips and close my eyes. This isn't Lucie and Edith's book; it's Geoffrey's and he's trying to get me to listen to something important, some piece of verse or idea that's more urgent than the cheese I'm making or the cloth I'm weaving.

"*The Romance of Lancelot*," says Thomas, and then, casually, "I could teach you to read it if you like."

I pull my fingers away from the binding as though scalded.

"I don't need books to read, thank you."

Thomas gives a little shrug.

"There are clothes in the chest," he says. "I'd like you to wear them please. You're going to be living here as my daughters, after all."

I'm not his daughter. I'm Father's daughter, and Mother's, and Alice's, but I'll never be his, no matter how many fancy clothes he makes me wear. When did he decide that he was my father? Was that why he went riding out, alone, to find children to kidnap? Was this planned all along?

I glare at Thomas, but even as I do so there's a part of me that knows I'm being unfair. Whatever else he is, this man isn't evil. He's trying to be kind to us. Even as I try and hate him, I can see that he's trying to be kind. I might even have liked him, if I'd met him at the market, or the fair.

His sallow face looks tired, and sad.

"Maybe it's time for bed," he says, and suddenly I feel as bereft as Ned. I've been angry with Robin all the way here, but now I can't bear the thought of sleeping apart from him. I want to lie in his arms like we did in the barn, and forget that we ever left home.

"Robin—" I say, but Thomas's hand is on his back.

"Isabel—" says Robin. I can't tell if he cares or not – does he want to stay with me or is having his own bed part of the reason he's so happy to be living here? "I won't be far away!" he says, but Thomas is leading him out of the room, leaving Maggie and I alone.

Maggie is exhausted. She won't let me take her gown off, and she whines when I try to put her to bed.

"I don't want to go to sleep! I want Alice! Go away!"

"Alice is dead," I say and I yank her gown over her head and make her cry. "You know that, Maggie!"

"I want Alice!" Mag whines, and she kicks me hard on the shin.

"Go to sleep," I say, lifting her into our bed. She kicks and cries, but she doesn't get up, she just lies there sobbing in the dark. Eventually, she's quiet, but it's a long time before I climb into the bed and fall asleep beside her.

32. *The House That God Built*

When I wake the next morning I lie in the strange bed, under the fine bedlinen, and stare at the bed's canopy above me. From out of the window, a church bell is ringing. Another funeral? No, because another bell starts up across the city, so they must be ringing in the hour.

Soon we'll all be dead, I think. It can't be long now. How many more people can there be left in the world? Soon God will come down from His heaven, and the dead will wake, and all this will be over.

I climb out of bed and open the shutters. Below me, a shopkeeper is opening up his shop. A carter rattles by in a laden cart. There's the sound of water falling as someone tips a chamber pot out of an open window into the drain below. I can smell the drain even through the horn windows. The whole city stinks of death and human foulness.

Magsy stirs in the bed beside me.

"Alice. . ." she says sleepily.

"Alice isn't here," I say. "Come and look at our new clothes."

Lucie and Edith had a lot of clothes. I sort through them.

One girl was a bit taller than me, the other was somewhere between me and Maggie – her clothes would probably fit Ned, but they're enormous on Mags. They're beautiful, though. All of the dresses are beautiful. There's a soft green gown with flowers and birds embroidered round the collar in yellow silks. I pull it on over my head, but I don't have anyone to lace it up for me, so in the end I have to wear my own clothes from Ingleforn. There are no shoes – perhaps the girls were buried in them? – so I keep my own on. Mag is lost in the smaller gowns, but that's not my problem. If Thomas wants her to look ridiculous, so be it. Mag adores them anyway. She insists on trying on all the younger girl's clothes, before settling on a dark red gown. She's much livelier than she was yesterday – dipping her finger in the inkhorn and smearing ink on her skirts, crawling under our bed to check that there's nothing else hidden there, taking all the pens out of the pot and twirling them around, pretending to write.

"Hey—" I say. "Hey, Maggie – leave that. Let's go and find the boys."

Robin and Ned are up and dressed. There are other men in their room – Thomas's man, whose name is Ralph, and another servant with a thick black beard. Other beds rest against the walls, but these are empty. I wonder if the people who slept in them are dead.

Robin is sitting on the bed talking to Ralph. He's explaining about us.

"We aren't anyone," he's saying. "We just met Thomas and he helped us bury Walt and Alice and—" He stops when he sees us come in.

"Isabel – look!"

Robin has new clothes too – a dark green hose and a brown

tunic, with a soft leather belt and leather shoes that turn up a little at the toe. Thomas's son must have been almost the same age as Robin, because Robin's clothes fit better than Maggie's do. He looks good – handsome, almost, if a little awkward. Ned – like me – is still dressed in his old tunic and hose. There mustn't have been a right-sized son for Ned to step into.

"Look at Mag!" Robin says. "You look like a princess!" Mag smiles at him uncertainly. She's gone shy again.

"Aren't there gowns for you?" Robin asks.

"They all need tying together," I say. *Like a parcel*, I think, but I don't say it out loud. "Besides, I'd look like a fool in them."

"No, you wouldn't," says Robin. He takes my hand. "Come and look what Thomas has!" And he leads me to a mirror built into the wall.

I scowl into it. A white, square-faced girl scowls back. Her hair hangs around her ears, an odd, pale colour somewhere between Ned's copper and Margaret's corn. It hasn't been combed in several days. Robin looks like a merchant's son, and Maggie looks sweet, but this girl looks like a wooden doll. A whole boat of silks from China wouldn't make her look like a lady.

"I look hideous," I say.

"Hardly." I jump. Thomas is standing in the doorway with an odd smile on his lips. Odd and a little bit sad. I wonder which daughter I'm supposed to be – Lucie or Edith.

"I can't put any of those gowns on by myself," I say, defensively. As though I've been caught out doing something wrong. Which I suppose I have. Pretending to be Isabel, instead of pretending to be Lucie or Edith. I wonder what Thomas is going to do. There's no sign of any other women living here, though someone must wash all these men's clothes, and Lucie and Edith must have had a maid to tie them into their gowns. Perhaps she died too.

"I'll think of something," says Thomas, but his eyes are already moving away towards Robin. "I've got work I need to do this morning," he says.

"Do you want me to come?" says Robin, and the blood rises in my cheeks. Thomas can't have Robin. He's ours. But Thomas shakes his head.

"You go and have a look at the city," he says. "I'll show you what we do here tomorrow."

Thomas's house is big. There are three or four chambers upstairs, for sleeping and working in, a big kitchen where the bearded man, whose name is Watt, cooks Thomas's meals with his son Stephen, the warehouse shop we came through yesterday and a hall, with three big tables and a square hearth in the centre of the floor. There's even a parlour, with high-backed wooden chairs and tapestries on the wall, for the family to sit in. Thomas's wife's loom is in here, and some embroidery that I hope belonged to his wife and not his daughters, because I know I'll never, ever be able to sew anything nearly as fancy as that. There's also a privy built on to the side of the house, so Thomas doesn't even have to leave his chamber to go. It stinks.

"That's disgusting," says Ned, screwing up his white little face.

"It's very sensible!" says Robin. "And you'll have to get used to it if we're going to live here, if you don't want to piss in your bed!"

Eugh.

The garden is at the back of the house. It's a long, narrow

strip of land, fenced in on both sides to stop other families' animals trampling his herbs. The chickens are here, and a pigsty with two black boars, and stable for his horse and his man's horse – a sturdy grey palfrey. He's got more herbs than we have at home, including a few that I don't recognize, but nobody's thinned out the carrots and they all look dry and in need of watering. I wonder whose job it is to look after them and if I'll be allowed to help now I'm a rich man's daughter.

None of this feels real. Father and Alice, Edward, Thomas. It feels like a game we're playing, like some joke the devils are playing on us. I keep expecting to wake up and find that it's all been a dream.

Thomas's horse is just as beautiful this morning as it was yesterday. I stroke its nose.

"You're the only person I like here," I tell it.

"Don't you like Thomas?" says Robin.

"No," I say. "What's he doing taking us here? Why couldn't he just leave us where we were?"

"He offered!" says Robin. "And we said yes."

"Yeh," I say. "Well, I wish we hadn't! What sort of person takes someone else's children home with them anyway?"

"I think. . ." says Robin. "I think he was just . . . just riding, you know? Being sad. And then . . . he wanted to help us. Why not?"

"Maybe he's mad," I say. "Or dangerous! Did you think of that?"

But I don't really believe it. I don't like Thomas, but I do trust him, oddly enough. I don't think he's going to hurt us.

Nobody seems to expect us to do any housework, so after we've looked into every room in the house we seem to be allowed just to go out in the city and wander around – without even an errand to do, like fetching water or buying bread! Probably this is a very stupid thing to do. Probably coming here at all was a very stupid thing to do. If the miasma is anywhere, it's certainly here, in these city walls. The whole of York reeks with the stench of it. Maggie huddles up close to me, gripping on to my hand.

"Where are we going?"

"We aren't going anywhere," I say, as patiently as I can. "We're just walking. Look at the houses, Mag. Look at that one – who do you think lives there?"

Mag barely glances at the house.

"Why's that man lying there?"

The man is slumped up against the side of the houses, foul and bloated with death. A pair of wild pigs are snuffling bloody-nosed at the corpse. I feel my stomach rise inside me.

"He's sleeping, Mag, don't look at him."

I pull her over to the other side of the road. Ned studies the man with a practised air.

"He's been dead for days, I reckon. Look how swollen he is."

"Ned, don't!"

I can hear the shrillness in my voice. I sound like Agnes Harelip. Even the rub of Maggie's skin against mine irritates me. I pull my hand out of hers. She wails, and I stamp off down the street away from her.

What's happened to me? What's happened to that other Isabel, the funny one, who liked mummer's songs and bread with honeycomb, the one Robin blew kisses at and said was the cleverest girl in the village? Am I going to spend the rest of my life crying over kind words and little sisters with high voices?

I feel a sudden flash of sympathy for Agnes, always grumbling and fussing about everything. Maybe she used to be a bonny little girl too. Maybe she's as confused by the angry old woman she turned into as I am.

No! I'm not going to turn into Agnes! Not if the pestilence kills Robin and everyone I love, I still won't.

Robin is at my elbow.

"Hey," he says. "Hey. Isabel."

I bury my face blindly into his new wool cote, and he puts his arms around me.

"I'm sorry," I tell the grey wool. "I'm sorry."

"It's all right. Hey. It's fine."

"What's wrong with Isabel?" says Mag. She's standing a respectful distance from me, as though I'm about to explode on her.

"She's just sad," says Robin. He pulls back and looks at me, his old ploughboy face under his mop of brown hair. "What do you want to do?"

I jam the heel of my hand into my eyes, rubbing furiously at them. I never was the sort of girl who cried over nothing. Since Edward died I don't seem to do anything else.

"Let's go to the minster," I say, instead.

The minster dominates the city, huge and unimaginably solid. The only thing that's nearly as big is the castle, which stands apart from the rest of the city: four towers and four walls of stone. There's a prison there, Father told me once, and a mint where King Edward's money is pressed. Ned wants to go and look, but I tell him to whist. I want to see the minster.

The steeple is so tall, it's hard to lose our way, though we take a windy route, through dark, narrow streets. The smell is worse here – blood and death and excrement and animals. Animals are everywhere – wild chickens pecking at the dirt, even a dead horse lying on its side crawling with flies and rats. I think there must be more animals here than humans, because the city itself is eerily silent. Now and then I see a shadowy face at a window, and in one of the squares we come across a beggar mumbling to himself, but mostly there's nobody.

"Is everyone dead?" Maggie whispers.

"No," says Robin. "They all left – remember them all coming past Ingleforn?" I think about the poor folk, the servants and beggars and shopkeepers, with nowhere to run to. And I think about the rich folk too, finding the villages closed to them and perhaps the pestilence coming upon them on the open road and their friends leaving them there to die.

I'm in a mind to hate everything in York, but I can't hate the minster. Nobody could. It must have taken many, many craftsmen's lives to finish – the first builders' great-great-grandchildren must still have been toiling away at it long after their fathers were dead.

There are wooden scaffolds built up around one side of the entrance, but no sign of any workmen. The big wooden doors open easily enough, though, and we creep inside. Once upon a couple of months ago, I would have thought that nothing could hurt us in here, but now I'm not so sure. I'm starting to wonder how powerful God really is. Unless the sickness really does come from Him, and he wants all this suffering to happen. If so, if he wants us dead, then even these thick abbey walls won't protect us.

You don't really understand the size of the minster until

you're inside it. From the outside, it just looks like a fell, or a small hill, but inside it's bigger than any building I've ever seen. Sir Edmund's manor house could fit inside it four or five times over and still have room to wriggle. I have never, ever seen anything as wonderful as this.

The walls and the roof are made of pale stone, with great columns rising up and into the roof. The windows are made of stained glass, like the windows in our church at home, but much bigger and grander. It's like the inside of a king's palace, or an angel's house. It's like the inside of God.

It's grander than the hills back home, grander than the manor house, bigger than a wedding feast, or a sunset, or a new baby. Sunsets and fells are *supposed* to be grand; they're God reminding you how powerful He is. This is something else. Because it wasn't made by God. It was made by us. Men and women, believing in God, believing in their children and grandchildren, trusting that God's will would somehow be done after they were gone.

How could they do it? How could they even imagine it was possible?

It's so big we have to crane our heads back to see the roof, so big that the walls just stretch on up and up and up above us. I'm close to tears again. It's like the underbelly of a mountain. It's like heaven.

"Did people make this?" says Maggie.

"People just like you, Mag," says Robin.

People just like us. I understand what people mean now about churches being sanctuary. I never want to leave here. I pull away from the others and walk down the centre of the cathedral, tipping my head back to look up at the roof. Behind me, Mag and Ned are looking at the windows, trying to work out what the story is. Robin is looking for St William's shrine, but I'm not interested in dead saints. I get to the altar and bow my head. I want to remember this – this feeling like my soul is getting bigger, growing inside me until its almost too big to contain.

God, I pray silently, inside my head. Maybe you do want to destroy everything in the world. Maybe this is the end of everything. But oh, please God, if it isn't, let me survive it. Let Robin and Ned and Margaret survive it too. Because if men can build a place like this, with only faith and bare hands, then I can do anything. I can get my farmland back. I can farm it myself, with Robin, as a free man and woman. I can live in this strange city, in a dead girl's clothes. I can build a new world out of the old.

Compared to this big minster, these are tiny things.

Compared to this big minster, these are easy.

33. *The Other Family*

I'm in the kitchen watching Watt – the cook – gut a hare. Watt has a beard as coarse and black as horse's hair and a narrow, clever face like a scribe or a bailiff. His knife cuts through the dead skin as quickly and skilfully as Alice's would back home. Some things are the same the world over.

Watt is telling me about the pestilence in York.

"When it first came," he says, slicing the knife along the belly of the hare, "so many people left the city! Lines and lines of carts, all along all the roads out, people with animals and furniture and children piled up on top of each other. It got so you couldn't hire a cart for less than 1d a day, sometimes more."

"I know," I say. "We saw them come past our village. We didn't let them in."

"Aye," says Watt. "Well, that's what Thomas said. 'The villagers won't thank us for bringing the sickness to their children,' he said. 'And I'd rather die in my own bed than a stranger's.' And Juliana – that's the mistress – she said the same. They did talk about sending the children out of the city but somehow it kept getting put off, and then it was too late."

"How many children were there?" I say, though I know what the answer is. There were three.

"Three," says Watt, drawing the knife along the inside of the hare's skin. "William – he's the one that Robin takes after. I knew as soon as I saw him why the master wanted you. And Lucie: they were twins, about Robin's age. Then Edith. She was in her ninth year, ever such a bonny little thing."

Watt sucks his teeth at the sadness of a bonny little thing like Edith dying in the pestilence, then starts to whistle as he turns the hare out of its skin. That's interesting, about Robin. It explains why Thomas is so much more interested in him than he is in the rest of us. I thought it was just because he was a boy, or perhaps because the little ones are so small, and I'm so unfriendly.

"Didn't you want to leave too?" I ask, but Watt laughs.

"Me!" he says. "What would I do riding north with a cart? How would I eat? I'm only grateful my master didn't turn us all away. The poor can't run, and if they can't work, they can't eat."

I know all about this too. All the servants with no work because their masters left – all the men with no work because no one wants houses built or roofs thatched or rats killed or bread baked – all the hat-makers and tailors and furriers and cordwainers – because who wants shoes and hats and gowns now?

"What do they do?" I say, leaning forward on to my elbows. Watt plunges his hands into the water bucket, rinsing the blood and the gore from his skin.

"Well," he says, "they drive the dead-carts, don't they? And they dig the graves. They nurse the sick. They pray for their souls."

For the first time in my life, I have nothing to do.

Thomas sees no one, except for the people he meets through work. I don't see how he can have much work since the ships have stopped coming in with his wine, but Thomas is like Father; he makes work even when there isn't any. The taverns are the only business that don't seem to have suffered from the pestilence – like in Ingleforn, the people here are making merry while they can. Thomas has a whole string of taverns which order his wine, and Ralph goes out every morning in his ox-cart taking the barrels of wine around the city. I think Thomas has stolen some of the trade of those merchants who have fled or died. And he's teaching Robin how to write, and how to tally the numbers of barrels sold and money made in his big account books. Robin is better at sums than he is at writing, though he still pulls terrible faces over his work.

Thomas often takes Robin on his errands, though whether it's because he's training Robin to take over as his apprentice or his son, which is what Robin thinks, or because he's lonely and if he doesn't think too hard he can pretend Robin is his dead son, or because he's a kind man who wants us to be happy, I don't know. Perhaps it's all three.

"He'd take you too, if you asked," says Robin, in this not-because-he-wants-you-but-because-he-feels-sorry-for-you voice. I don't want him to take me. I don't want to start liking him, and I don't care whether he likes me or not. I don't want to stand around listening to boring old men talking about wine barrels and taxes and wine and death, death, death, death, death.

There's nothing for me to do. I'm not allowed to help in the kitchen or to help with the pig or the horses or the chickens. I'm not even supposed to sweep my own chamber. Probably when the world isn't ending, there would have been other people to see – other girls my age to talk to – probably Thomas's wife, Juliana, would have known what I was supposed to be doing and made sure that I was. But now nobody goes out and nobody sees each other and there's nothing. I don't even have a maid to talk to. Ralph's wife, Johanna, comes and ties me into my gowns in the mornings and helps me undress at night, but she doesn't stay during the day. She's a washerwoman – she does all the washing for the house as well. She's not interested in talking to me, and she slapped Mag once for babbling. I nearly slapped her back, but Mag was clinging to my skirts and wailing, and by the time I'd stopped her crying, Johanna had gone.

Lucie and Edith's chamber is full of fine things that sneer at me. There are their books I can't read. The parchment and quill pen for the letters they wrote to their father when he was away. Lucie's fine embroidery that I could never, ever finish. The threads are made of real silk. When I'm feeling particularly sad, I take the embroidery down and stroke it, feeling the softness of it, the realness of the violets and lilies and roses sewn into the cloth. It will never be finished now.

In the parlour, there's a loom like Alice's, but bigger, and finer. It belonged to Juliana. Sometimes – when Robin and Thomas are out – I go and pull the shuttle through the warp. Weaving is at least something I can do. But I always give up after a row or two. What's the point? Who is this cloth being made for, anyway?

Other times, I wander through the house, touching things,

opening drawers, peering into coffers. Why not? This is our house, isn't it? Once, I found a chest in Thomas's room with seven locks and seven keys like the chest in the tithing barn. The keys were hidden in a cubbyhole in Thomas's writing desk, and when I opened the chest, it was full of jewellery: silver bangles and golden lockets and jewelled pendants. I could have taken any of them out, and I bet Thomas wouldn't have noticed. I didn't, though. I put them all back.

Often, I just lie on my bed in Lucie and Edith's chamber and don't move for hours. I watch the dust falling and the light dimming around me, and I listen to the church bells ringing in the hours. I watch the way my pale hair falls over my arm, and I think about Alice and Richard and Father and Edward, and Geoffrey, in his cloister or his coffin. I wonder if he's still alive. Does he wonder about us too, or does he count us among the dead? Perhaps he's looking for us in Ingleforn, and nobody can tell him where we are. Thomas told Joan where we were going when we took the animals to her house, but perhaps she's dead too. My mind is pulled back and forth between my duty to Geoffrey and my duty to Maggie and Ned. Probably Geoffrey is dead too.

My thoughts move so slowly, like dust motes falling through sunlight. Sometimes, I close my eyes for a moment and when I open them, dusk is here.

Evenings are the only time I really see Thomas, besides meals. We sit together in the little wood-panelled parlour, shutting the door against the horrors happening in the streets and houses around us.

Thomas and Robin play chess. The chess pieces are made of carved ivory. They're much finer than Robin's mother's wooden pieces at home. Thomas plays with Ned sometimes too, taking one of his prime ministers off the board to give Ned a chance. He also has a backgammon set, which Ned and Robin like to play, all sprawled out across the floor. Ned has his dice from home as well, and he and Mag play raffle and hazard. And Mag plays with the dice by herself, throwing them up into the air and scooting them across the floor. My little sister is getting more peculiar by the day. Thomas doesn't let Mag and Ned play ball in the parlour, but she has a set of little wooden dolls all about the size of my thumb, which used to belong to Edith, and which keep her busy.

I sit on my chair and spin, because that's what I would have done at home, and because my old wooden spindle brings a little bit of Alice into this awkward parlour-space. I have Alice's spindle too upstairs, with the teethmarks in the wood where Edward used to chew it. It's mine; I won't let Maggie touch it.

Thomas mostly likes to read in the evenings, which means we have to listen to whatever he's reading. Most of his books are in French, or Latin, or Greek, so he translates as he goes along. Sometimes it works and sometimes it doesn't. He reads us the beginning of *The Iliad*, which mostly seems to be people killing each other, or arguing, or sulking. Ned likes it because of all the blood. Robin pretends to like it because Thomas does, and Maggie doesn't really understand it. I can feel the poetry straining behind his stumbling translation, which quickens me and twists up my frustration into a hard little knot at the same time. I hate it when he's reading it, but when he finishes I'm sorry almost at once.

"Would you like to learn to write?" says Geoffrey – I mean, Thomas. "You could look at Lucie's books, perhaps. I could teach you if you wanted."

"I can write," I say. I write my name in the air. I S A B A L, the way Geoffrey taught me.

"Or embroider, perhaps?" says Thomas. "I don't know – maybe Ralph would know someone—"

I don't want to do any of these things. I want to go home. But I don't have a home any more, and we ought to be grateful.

Probably what I should be doing is looking after Maggie and Ned. But they seem all right. They're out all day anyway, playing with the other children in the streets around Thomas's house. There are lots of children in York without fathers and mothers now. You see them begging on the streets, or driving the dead-carts, the older ones. Thomas doesn't like that Maggie and Ned play with these children, but he can't stop them.

"Maybe we should get a woman to look after them," he says.

"Why?" says Robin. "They're not infants."

"I suppose so." Thomas doesn't seem to know much about children. I wonder who looked after his own. "I should find a tutor for you and Ned," he says, vaguely. "It's so hard, with everyone gone. When this is over, perhaps. . ."

I know I ought to care about where Mag and Ned go, but I can't. I'm glad when they go. It means I don't have to watch them. Sometimes they come and stand at the end of my bed, watching me.

"There's a lady in the street who says she can cure the pestilence," says Ned.

"She can't," I say, without moving.

"She's selling dried toads," says Ned. "For two farthings. You rub them on the sores, and then they go away. And there's a man selling holy water and bits of saints. Fingerbones, and blood in a bottle. I told him about our St Bede, and he said he had some of St Bede's blood! If you wear it round your neck, it protects you!"

"No, it doesn't," I say, remembering Alice. "He's telling lies, Ned. It's just chicken bones."

Ned looks disappointed. They stand there at the end of my bed like the wooden husband and wife in the abbey clock. Then Ned says, "There's a magician who can tell you if you're going to die in the next year or not. Three farthings, he costs. You can ask him any question and he'll give you the answer. Mag and I asked him if Geoffrey was alive, and he said he was, but he was in *grave danger*. Which proves it!"

"Oh, go away!" I shout. "Leave me alone! Where did you get the farthings to pay magicians, anyway?"

Mag and Ned flinch back, as though they expect me to hit them.

"We're not going to tell you!" says Ned. "We would have done, but we're not going to now!" And he grabs Mag's arm and pulls her out of the chamber behind him.

I don't care where they get their stupid money from. Probably they stole it. I don't care.

Look after Ned and Margaret, Father said. Well, he didn't look after us, did he? He died, and left us here, all alone in a strange city. So why should I look after them?

I don't see what point there is in worrying about what's going to happen next. We're all going to die soon anyway. It's going to be plague, then earthquakes and rains of fire like they have every Saturday in Castille and Aragon, then lizards and elephants and rains of frogs and whatever else God wants to torment us with. Sometimes, lying in Lucie and Edith's chamber, I almost want it to happen. Anything would be better than this . . . this nothing. This waiting.

Thomas doesn't believe in God. I never met anyone before who didn't, but he doesn't. There's a dark little chapel in the corner of his house, with high, pointed windows and paintings of the saints on the walls and a little altar at the front. When I asked him why we never heard mass there, he said, "I can't ask a priest to come here, while the pestilence is in the city." But if he really wanted to pray, he'd go to church. He doesn't come to mass on Sundays. We go with Ralph and Watt and his son Stephen. Sundays are the only time when there's anything like a crowd on the streets. No one – except Thomas – wants to risk offending God now.

Robin comes into my chamber with his brown hair all tangled by the wind and stands at the foot of my bed.

"Thomas says he'll take us to France, if we want!" he says.

The world is ending, and he's like the boy who won the wrestling match.

"I thought everyone was dead in France," I say.

Robin frowns. "Some people must be left." He pulls at the bobbles on the blanket with his long, fretful fingers.

"Why don't you like Thomas?" he says. "What's wrong with here?"

He must know.

"*Everything's* wrong with here," I say. It comes out in a wail. "This whole city is dying . . . it's horrible . . . How can you be happy here? There isn't . . . there isn't anything for me to do. I don't want to be a merchant's wife. I want. . ." I stop, trying to line up in my head exactly what I *do* want, to say it so that he'll understand. "I want my own land," I say. "Our land. We left it for Joan, all that land that Father worked so hard over, and now the barley is just dying in the fields. And I want my own people back. I don't know how to be Thomas's daughter.

I don't want to be. I want to *grow* things. Grow things and be married to you."

Robin is still frowning over the blanket.

"All I ever wanted," he says slowly, "is to leave our village. To see ships and the sea – and London – and Avignon, where the Pope lives, and Spain where the grapes come from—"

"Everyone's dead in London," I say.

"You don't know that! They said everyone was dead in York, too!"

"Well, and aren't they? Everyone's dying, anyway—" Another bell starts tolling outside the window. "See?" I say. "Who wants to go to Avignon and look at dead people?"

"I do!" says Robin. "I don't believe everyone is dead. I want to go and see all those places. There'll still be sun shining, won't there, and elephants and dragons, and—"

"There's no such thing as dragons," I say. "And what will you do in France? You don't even speak French! And what about the people in our village? Geoffrey and Will Thatcher and Joan and the monks and Amabel Dyer and—"

"Amabel Dyer's dead," says Robin. "And so are the monks."

I'd forgotten Amabel Dyer was dead.

"What about me?" I say. "What about what I want?"

"Why should I care?" says Robin. "If you don't care about me?"

Because we're family. But we're not family. We probably aren't even really married. And he's right – he doesn't have to do anything I want.

I slide off the bed and out of the chamber, ignoring the hurt look on his face. I stumble down the stairs, clenching my lip to stop the tears falling. Maybe I'll just go and keep going. Back home – but the terror rises in my throat at the thought of home, our empty house, the horrible bed where Father and Alice died. Maybe I don't have any home any more. When I die, nobody will know my name. I'll be buried in a pestilence pit without a headstone and there'll be nobody to say the masses for my soul. I might not even be buried with Ned and Mag, if we die on different days. I wonder if we'll be able to find each other, on the Day of Judgement. And how will I ever find Father and Alice again, when I'm buried so far away from home?

At the foot of the stairs, I nearly fall over Maggie and Ned. They're bent over a king's hoard – two bracelets with what look like real gems, some silver plate, a chess set with carved ivory pieces. In amongst the shining things are bits of junk – a wooden doll in a blue woollen gown and a knife like Robin's in a leather scabbard worked with brass. Ned starts when he sees me, and makes as though to hide the things, but it's too late.

"What are those?"

"Nothing." Then, when he sees my face: "They're Thomas's. He gave them to us."

The idea of Thomas giving them bracelets of gold is absurd. They must be Juliana's.

"You stole them, didn't you?"

Ned looks taken aback. Mag says, "It's not stealing! Not if everyone's dead!"

It takes me a moment to realize what she's saying.

"You got these things from dead people's houses? You're stealing from the dead?"

Ned shrinks back against the wall.

"It's not stealing!" he says. "They don't belong to anyone!"

"I don't care about who they belong to!" I shout. "You're

going into pestilence houses! They're full of bad air! Is that how you want to thank Thomas – by bringing the pestilence back here?"

Ned turns away from me, digging his chin down into his shoulder, twisting himself around and away as though he's trying to bury himself into the wall.

"Thomas can't get the pestilence," he mutters. "All his family died and he didn't catch it."

"Well, I can!" I shout. "And you can too, and so can Mag and Robin! And we can all get hanged – for a stupid bit of plate!"

I kick the heap across the floor. Mag squeals and runs for the doll. It's just a bit of carved wood with wool hair, but she clutches it to her chest, shielding it from my anger, as though I'm going to make her take it back.

"Do you want Mag to get hanged for stealing?" I shout. "Do you?"

Ned is pressed up against the wall. He's shaking his head mutely from side to side. I look at him, and suddenly I feel ashamed. This is my Ned, poor red-haired lonely little Ned, in his old clothes while we're all dressed like princes and princesses, his white face wobbling between aggression and tears. I want to comfort him, but I'm not sure how. Alice would shake him and wallop him and then hold him while he cried. I'm not sure if he'd let me even hold him.

I put my arms around him. He pulls back at first and then he collapses against me. I rock him gently, forward and back.

"I want to go home," he says.

"I know," I say. "I do too."

Maggie comes and stands beside me, watching Ned critically.

"Ned's crying," she says.

"He can if he wants to."

"He's supposed to be a big boy," she says.

"Big boys can cry," I say, but I'm not sure if she believes me.

After I find Mag and Ned stealing, something changes. The borders of our croft shift. At first it was me and Mag and Ned and Robin. Then Thomas came along and wanted to join his house on to the edges. But the lines have moved again, and now it's Mag and Ned and me in one village, and Thomas and Robin in another across the water. Robin and I are like Tristan and Iseult, loving each other even though he belongs to one village and I belong to another.

Without saying anything to each other, Mag and Ned and I are starting a campaign to get home. So far it's just a campaign of glances and mutterings and promises, but soon it will be more. What we'll do and who we'll live with when we get there, I haven't worked out yet, but surely someone will want us? We've got nearly a virgate of land between us. Someone must have daughters they want to marry to Ned, or sons who'll be willing to farm Mags' portion for her. I can believe that everyone in France is dead, but I can't believe that everyone in our village is.

Ned still takes things. There's a whole gang of them – children from the streets around where Thomas lives – who steal things, and worse. They sit on the steps in the square at the end of our street and play games and drink ale and play and fight and share their loot. Mostly they're little ones Ned's age or a little older, but there are some as old as Robin, and one or two that are nearly men. I don't think those ones go into the houses, though. I think they just buy the better prizes from the little ones, or pick them casually from the cobbles and carry them off. Ned and Maggie have a whole dragon's treasure trove for the two of them to dress up in and play at kings and queens with. I wallop them if I find them, but they still do it. I'm not sure if Thomas knows. I suspect he wouldn't approve, but if not then surely it's his job to stop them? I can hardly blame them for running a bit wild. At home we were always busy – digging, building, making, growing. Here? There's nothing. No wonder they're bored.

"What are they like?" I ask Ned. "The empty houses?"

He shrugs. "Empty. Cold. Dark."

If it wasn't for Robin, I'd leave tomorrow. Tell Thomas we've changed our mind and we want to go home. But Robin won't go.

"He's already lost one family. I'm not taking his second one away from him."

"We're not a real family. He hardly even notices if Mag and Ned are there!"

"He notices if I'm there."

That's true. He does.

"He's going to take me to France," Robin says. "He promised."

"I know."

"France, Isabel!"

And I watch as the spaces grow between our village and his, and there's nothing I can do to stop them.

34. Matilda Alone

Dinner is one of the few things I like about Thomas's house. We eat in the hall: Thomas and us at the high table on the dais, and his household at two lower tables laid out against the adjoining walls. There's a flat stone hearth in the centre of the floor, but all the cooking is done in the kitchens, and it's still too warm to light the fire for warmth.

Usually, of course, there'd be all the men who work in Thomas's warehouse as well, and I think there were other servants who died – Juliana and the girls must have had a maidservant, and perhaps a woman to look after Edith. The hall has a mournful feel about it, half-empty, as though we're guests at a party to which no one has come, and must continue the festive atmosphere as though the others had never been invited.

The food is wonderful, though. Nearly as good as the food at St Mary's. Stewed beef with cinnamon and saffron, civey of hare, chicken with almond and rice for the meat days, and for the fast days, pike, and haddock in ale, and salmon, and all sorts of good things.

When we come in from the parlour today, there's a woman

sitting at the high table beside Thomas. She's an older woman, about Father's age perhaps, and her face is hung with wrinkles. The corners of her mouth pull down and the skin is loose and greyish, with the softness that worn skin takes on when it gets old. She's dressed in a gown made of dark red cloth – it looks like silk – and she's wearing a widow's veil, much more elaborate than the veils you see women wearing in our village. She looks at us with interest.

"And who are these, Thomas?"

Thomas gives her what I always think of as his secret-amused smile, the one that makes me think he's laughing at some joke that only he can see.

"This is Robin," he says. "And Isabel and Edward and Margaret."

"I don't want to know what their names are!" she says. "I want to know what they're doing here! Where did you find them – in a haystack?"

Ned sputters. Thomas very nearly did find us in a haystack, after all.

"I found them on the road," says Thomas mildly. "And now I've given them a bed. That's all, Matilda."

Matilda looks down her nose at Ned, who is still in his old green hose and stained russet tunic.

"Yes," she says. "Well. What you do is your own business, Thomas. Although I'd be wary of the eldest one, if I were you. He looks old enough to make a sow's ear out of a serious undertaking. And talking of which – have you heard the news from London?"

"Nothing recent," says Thomas. He nods at us to sit down, and they go off into a complicated grown-up discussion of trade winds and ships beached in unhelpful places, and various officials Matilda has apparently managed to persuade to let ships sail on when they oughtn't to have. I expect Thomas to be angry about this – he's the one who's so keen on people staying where they are, I can't see that he'd be happy about a fleet of ships sailing pestilence and death around the world – but he merely nods and steers the conversation on to the price of wine. I still can't see why he's having this conversation with a woman. Can women own ships?

Today is Friday, so it's a fast day, and no meat. There's creamed fish in almonds and ginger, followed by thick cherry and cream pottage. Ned and Mags grow bored of the conversation and start kicking each other under the table.

At last, Matilda announces that she wants to go to vespers, and we all have to stand up and take a formal leave-taking. She sticks her nose up in the air like we're something bad-smelling she's found on the bottom of her boot.

"Well," she says. "I trust you know what you're doing, Thomas."

"I very rarely do," says Thomas, with that smile again.

"Who's *she*?" says Ned, when she's gone. He screws up his face to show what he thinks of her. Thomas frowns. He hates rudeness.

"Her name is Matilda de Kyngesford," he says. "She's one of the wealthiest women in York."

"You mean her *husband* is wealthy," I say, but Thomas shakes his head.

"Matilda is a holy widow, Isabel. After her husband died, she vowed before the bishop to live in chastity for the rest of her life and serve God."

"Like a nun?" says Robin, but Thomas laughs.

"No, not very like a nun." His hand plays with his knife.

"Robin, I'll need someone to keep a tally at this meeting tomorrow. Do you think—?"

I pull the conversation back to Matilda.

"But—" I say. "Matilda. She's a *woman*, but she's a merchant?"

"And a very successful one, too." Thomas turns his attention back to me reluctantly – aren't-I-his-daughter? The one he's supposed to be having a conversation with! – "They say," – he smiles – "that she only took vows to prevent her father making another match for her. If so, it was a shrewd decision. She's very well-respected here in the town. Now, Robin—" And they're back to tallies and wine barrels and all the other dull things that Robin pretends like he's interested in just because Thomas is talking about them.

When we get up to go into the parlour, I catch hold of his sleeve.

"That woman."

"What about her?"

"She's a merchant – like Thomas!"

"So?"

"So she's a woman, doing whatever she wants to. Which means I can too. I can farm Father's land – our land – without having to marry you, or get someone else to farm it for me like your mother did! I can do it myself!"

Robin bites his lip. He doesn't know I'm going to run away. He doesn't want to be a farmer. He wants to stay here with Thomas. Travel to Castille and France and the Indes on one of his ships, bring back wine and silk and spices and other wonderful things. I drop my hand.

"We're supposed to be married," he says, and there's a tightness to his face and his voice. "Don't you remember? You made a vow to me like Matilda did to the bishop. You can't run away now!"

I look at Robin in his clothes that still don't fit him properly, and I see a gaol cell. I see a life in Lucie's too-big gowns, adding my clumsy stitches to her fine embroidery while the Isabel I want to be is dying inside, like a plant shut away without sunlight or air. I see a husband on the other side of the world, sailing to Africa without me.

"Will you hold me to a promise I don't want to keep?" I say.

Robin's eyes falter.

"No," he says. "Of course not."

I think of Geoffrey and his books. *He to whom God has given knowledge. . .* Your hands and your heart are gifts from God. Turning aside from that . . . it's like throwing yourself away.

And yet Robin is supposed to be my family. He's more like home than anything else I have.

And I'm going to leave him anyway.

"I'm sorry, Robin," I say, and I follow after Maggie and Ned, leaving him there in the hall, alone.

35. *Hue and Cry*

So it's decided. We're going home, Mag, Ned and I. I don't know how, because we don't have horses, and I wouldn't know how to ride one even if we did, and we don't know how to get there, and even if we did we'd have to walk the whole way alone, because there aren't any caravans going north any more.

At least Ned has plenty of money.

We ought to go soon. It's got to be dangerous staying in this city, where even the bells have stopped ringing. Father wouldn't let me go to the abbey, and he wouldn't let me come to the house to say goodbye, so he certainly wouldn't be happy if he knew I'd brought Ned and Mags to this city of death.

Though I'm starting to wonder if the sickness might be ending. There are fewer dead-carts rattling through the streets, and fewer bodies in the gutters. The smithy opposite our house has opened again, for the first time since I've been here. The smith was working at his anvil as I passed.

And if it's ending here, surely it must have ended in Ingleforn?

I'd go tomorrow if it wasn't for Robin.

If I wasn't so frightened of what I might find at Ingleforn.

If it wasn't for Thomas.

He's starting to notice us more, me and Ned and Mag – started to remember that we're real people and not just Robin's entourage. I wonder how much of the calm, polite, distant Thomas that we see is the real Thomas, and what he's really thinking about – below that mask. He's starting to listen to us when we tell him things. He talked to Mag for most of dinner yesterday. She was telling him about Alice and Father and Geoffrey and Richard and Edward – and he listened and nodded and asked questions in the right places.

"I didn't know you had so many brothers," he said to me when she'd finished. "You were a big family."

"Geoffrey might still be alive," I told him. "We don't know."

"I could send Ralph to the abbey to find out if you like," Thomas said, and something jumped inside me before I could stop it.

"Yes!" I said, and when he smiled, "I mean, please. Yes, please."

"It may be a while before I can spare him," said Thomas. "And there may not be anyone there to send an answer. Any survivors have very probably moved on by now."

"I know," I said, and I realized that I probably wouldn't be there when the answer came anyway.

I tell Ned and Maggie before we go to bed.

"We're going to go home soon. I'm planning it."

"How?" says Ned.

"We're going to walk. On the road to Felton. And when we get lost, we'll ask directions to Felton. And then when we get to Felton, we'll ask for Great Riding, and once we get to Great

Riding, I can find our way from there. That's how you do it. Alice told me. They got all the way to Duresme like that. Mag, listen to me. Stop playing with that." I take her doll out of her arms, and for once she doesn't scream at me.

"Are we going to Richard?" she says.

"Richard's dead," I tell her. I told her before, but she can't seem to remember it.

"Then who are we going to?" says Ned. He pulls a horrified face, tongue stuck out, eyeballs bulging. "Not Agnes?"

"I don't know who we'll go to," I say. "But not Agnes."

"I'd rather be dead," says Ned.

It's a cold night. Michaelmas will be here soon. Thomas's man lights the fire in the hall for the first time since we've got here. The smoke pours upwards and settles in a curtain of grey mist below the roof, the same way that the smoke from our little hearth-fire does at home.

Watt and his boy Stephen bring in the food. It's a whole salmon on a bed of green stuff, with rice and saffron and almonds. I'll miss the food when I'm gone.

As Watt puts the salmon down on the table, he says, "My cousin Muriel's come back to York. She's looking for work, if there is any."

Thomas holds out his goblet for wine.

"Are people coming back to York now?" he says.

Watt nods. "There are more people in the streets every day."

Could the sickness really be ending? For the first time in many days, I can almost believe it.

After supper, Thomas goes down into the warehouse to write up the day's accounts. Ned and Mag slip out of the hall and off outside. I know that I ought to stop them, but I let them go. I need to talk to Robin, and that's going to be easier without their noise and games and demanding voices.

Robin's in the parlour, practising writing on one of Thomas's wax tablets. He's had a lot of lessons with Thomas, but he hasn't got much further than learning the letters, as far as I can tell. Today, he's writing X Y Z X Y Z X Y Z with a polished stick of wood in the wax.

I point to the X. I know that one.

"That's ten," I say.

"And ecks."

I frown. "Geoffrey said ten. What's ecks? Ecks doesn't mean anything."

"It's not supposed to mean anything," says Robin. "It's just . . . itself. It's—"

"We're leaving," I say. "Tomorrow."

He stares. "Where? Why?"

"Home. Because. We can't stay here."

He fiddles with the bit of wood.

"I can't go with you," he says. "You know that, don't you?"

I hadn't. Not until that moment.

"We need you," I say.

He smiles at me, a little sadly.

"Not you," he says. "You don't need anyone."

"I need you," I say, and I feel the tears rising as I say it. I come and sit beside him on the bench and put my arms around him, breathing in his new, leathery scent, of ink and ale and William's clothes. My Robin.

I'm so tired of saying goodbye.

His pale face is bent, his thick hair falling in his eyes. I take his cheeks in my hands and I kiss him on the mouth, the way I did to Will that day under the trees. I want him to know that

I love him. I want him to come with us. *I'm your family now.* What good is family if they always leave you?

He kisses me back with an intensity that surprises me. All these months we've been living together, we've never kissed once, and now he kisses me like this. I close my eyes and lose myself in his lips and mouth, tongue against my tongue, lips against lips, warm and wet and fierce and urgent. I don't know if I'm saying goodbye or remaking our marriage contract, but at this moment I don't care about anything except this.

Somewhere outside, a bell is ringing. Another funeral. Except we don't have those any more, do we? And this isn't a passing-bell – it's frantic, urgent, wild.

I lean into Robin, sending the bell's urgency into my kisses, but Robin pulls away.

"It's the hue and cry!"

Below, Watt is shouting.

"The hue and cry! The hue and cry!"

The windows in Robin's chamber are made of cloth, waxed stiff with oil. We can't see out. I grab his hand and we clatter down the stairs together. My heart is beating like a bird in a cage. What's just happened? Is Robin coming, or have we just said goodbye forever?

Watt is by the door looking out.

"It's that young gang from the street," he shouts, and my belly clenches and the hairs rise all down my arms. The gang in the street. That's Ned and Mag. I'll die if anything happens to them, I think, and the thought surprises me, it's so clear and certain, like water, or the noise of a bell. I'll die.

"Hey!"

The gang are running down the street, pelting past us. Little lads smaller than Ned, boys as tall as Richard. A child falls down in the mud in front of us and starts to cry, but Watt ignores her. He runs off after a long-legged girl with her hair flying behind her. Robin starts after him, but I grab his arm.

"Don't! Don't go!"

He struggles out of my grip.

"It's the hue and cry, Isabel."

"*Don't*," I say. "It's Ned's gang," and he looks at me in astonishment.

There are other men in the street now. There's the baker from down the road, and Thomas's man, Ralph, and the constable. Watt has the long-legged girl in his arms. She's kicking and struggling, but he won't let her go. The baker is chasing after two of the bigger boys, but they're running faster than he is, and he won't catch them. The bells are still ringing, and more folk are coming out into the street, more people than I knew even still lived in York. Everything is happening so fast. My head is dizzy with terror and the confusion.

And now I see Ned. He's running so fast that he's catching the bigger boys up, but his cote is bulging with things that shouldn't be there, and as the bailiff – a man who knows Thomas to nod at and to exchange the time of day – comes haring round the corner, Ned loses his hold on the cote and the things all tumble out – plate and jewellery and a beaver-skin hat like Thomas's. He stumbles over the plates and the constable grabs his arm. Ned is fighting like a cat, or a wolf – not that I've ever seen a wolf, but Father has, in Scotland – kicking and struggling, all teeth and elbows and knees, but the constable is stronger, and he pulls Ned's arms behind his back. Ned sees us on the step and he starts to shriek.

"Isabel! Isabel!"

I run across the street. Robin follows, Thomas's set of wax

tablets with their X Y Zs still clacking together in his hand.

"Let him go!" I shout. "He's just a little boy! Leave him alone!"

"Not so little as all that," says the bailiff. He kicks at the plate on the floor with his boot. "You'll hang for this, my lad."

I remember the sheep thief, a leper back home, that Father said would hang for theft, and the panic swells up and threatens to overwhelm me.

"Please!" I shout. "Please! Our father's a merchant – he lives just there. Stop it! Please! He'll give you anything you want if you just stop it!"

Ned is still kicking, but there's a hopeless quality to it now, as though he knows it's no good.

The hubbub and the confusion are dying down. The men are coming back to the bailiff with their captives. The long-legged girl stands with her hair falling over her face. The two older boys are swearing and cursing. The little girl who was crying in the street is watching with her finger in her mouth. The men ignore her. I wonder where Maggie is.

Watt makes his way across the street to where we're standing. He sucks his teeth when he sees Ned.

"Eh," he says. "That's Master Thomas's lad, that is."

"He could be King Edward's lad for all I care," says the bailiff. "He's a thief."

"He won't hang," I say, "will he? Not a little lad like Ned?"

"That's for the assizes to decide," says the bailiff. He gives Ned a shake, not ungently. "Caught you red-handed now, lad, haven't we?" he says.

I want to go with Ned to the castle, but Robin pulls me away.

"Don't, Isabel," he says. "You can't help him now. We need to find Thomas, he'll know what to do. And what will Mag do if she comes back home and finds us gone?"

But Mag has already appeared, a long, dirty mark down the front of her gown and a dazed expression on her face.

"They were chasing us!" she says, indignant.

"We saw," says Robin. He tugs on my arm. "Isabel. Come on. Let's go and find Thomas. Thomas will know what to do." And despite myself, I allow myself to believe him.

Thomas is sitting at his table in the little scriptorium in the warehouse. There's parchment and ink on the table, but the page is blank, and the inkhorn is shut. He's staring off into the distance at something I can't see.

"Thomas," I say. "Thomas—" And he turns as though from a great distance to look at me.

I wonder how real I am to Thomas. Am I more or less real than those ghostly girls in their silks, for instance? Does he care about me at all?

He listens to what Robin tells him, and rubs his hands across his face.

"Why does every decision I make turn out so badly?" he asks, and I know he's thinking about his children, who he didn't send out to the country like all the other rich children in York. He did that to save the villages like ours, I know. But how much difference did it really make? The miasma kept on coming, blown north on the winds.

"This didn't turn out badly!" says Robin. "Thomas, please. It didn't. Coming here was the best thing that's ever happened to me!"

"Was it?" says Thomas, with that sad smile. "Is that what Isabel thinks?"

He looks at me, and I shake my head from side to side so that the tears fall out of my eyes and spill down my cheeks.

"No," says Thomas. "I didn't think so. I'm sorry, Isabel. This is all my fault."

"It's not!" says Robin. "It isn't – is it, Isabel? Tell him!"

The tears are still rolling down my cheeks.

"You shouldn't have brought us here," I say fiercely. "I'm not your daughter! Robin isn't your son!"

"Isabel—" says Robin.

"It's all right," says Thomas. He puts his hand on Robin's shoulder. "I thought..." he says. "I wanted ... I don't know what I wanted. To make right some of my wrongs. To make something good out of all this mess. To..."

To bring back my children, I think. Because surely that's what this is all about, isn't it?

"You have to do something!" I say. "Ned's going to *die* – and it's all your fault – you have to make them stop!"

"Isabel!" says Robin, again. "This isn't Thomas's fault! It's ours – for not looking after Ned and Mag properly – for—"

Our fault, he says, but he means mine. Ned and Mag were never his responsibility.

I can't seem to breathe properly, or to make the world come into focus. Everything is very bright and slightly unreal.

"It's all right, Robin," says Thomas. "Don't be angry." He stands up. "I will make this right," he says to me. "I promise."

And for the first time since we came here, I believe him.

We light all the candles in the house and sit together in the cold little parlour. Summer is nearly over. Autumn's coming.

"It's a crying shame," says Watt, but nobody answers, so he shakes his head again and goes upstairs with Stephen.

It's nearly midnight when Ned comes home. There's a cut

across his forehead and dirt in his hair and the streaky marks of tears across his cheeks.

Thomas isn't there.

"He went right into the castle," says Ned wonderingly. "He told that man that he'd made me steal those things. That he'd made me join that gang. They took him away and locked him up in the bottom of the deepest, darkest dungeon, and they let me go."

BOOK THREE

HOME

Flee from the throng and dwell with truth,
Let your own things suffice, though
they be small. . .
Savour no more than what behoves you.
Rule yourself well, that others may
learn from you,
And do not doubt it, the truth shall set you free.

Geoffrey Chaucer
Fourteenth Century

36. Thomas Again

Ned sold the ivory chess set to the tinker with the stall by the church. Robin took the coins to the baker and the cheesemaker and the alewife to buy the bread and the hard, yellow cheese and the flagon of ale. Watt used to make all of our cheeses and brew all our ale, but he's gone now, working with his brother in a manor in the south. He offered to take us with him – "Half the manor died, Isabel, they're desperate for hands" – but we wouldn't go. Not until the assizes were over.

I don't know where Ralph went. We woke up one morning and he was gone. So were the best cooking pots and the silver plate and the horses and the gowns from Juliana's wardrobe.

"He just stole Thomas's things!" says Robin, but I find myself unable to care. What does it matter if Ralph has Thomas's cooking pots? We have more important things to worry about now.

Thomas must have real money – coin – somewhere in the house, but I've never found it and I don't like to ask him where. That's his business. There's enough wine and stuff from Ned and Maggie's shining horde to feed us until the assizes come round, and if anyone deserves Ned's wealth, it's Thomas.

Maggie and I wrap the food up into a bundle with some clean linen and one of the leather books from Thomas's library. Ned I leave to mind Mag and the fire, and to make sure the animals are fed and the pig doesn't get in the herbs. Ned only came to see Thomas once at the castle. He shrunk himself small into my skirts, and looked at the floor, and wouldn't say anything bigger than "Yeh". If something more than "Yeh" was needed, he shrugged, and turned his face away. Thomas didn't seem to mind.

"Tell Ned it doesn't matter," he says. "I'm not angry. Tell him."

Life is beginning to come back to York. There are children in the house opposite, two little girls in fur-tipped mantles who gaze at Robin and me with interest. At the end of the street, there's a man with a tray of pastries over his shoulder, calling, "Meat pies! Meat pies! Get them while they're hot!" Robin and I buy one each and one for Thomas.

"Did you used to live here before the pestilence?" I ask him, and he nods, turning over our coins with his grubby fingers.

"Took the family to my brother John's when the pestilence came. The Good Lord took John, and his son too, and now my brother Roger says the farm belongs to him, and we're to be off back here where we came from."

"Is it really over, do you think?" says Robin, and the pie-man shrugs.

"Nothing ever ends," he says, and he hefts his pie-tray back on to his shoulder, calling, "Meat pies! Meat pies! Lovely meat pies!"

I wrap Thomas's pie in my bundle and we're off down through the streets to the castle. York Castle stands a little apart from the city, its four round towers visible as we come out of the streets. It belongs to King Edward, Father said, but he hasn't been to York for as long as Watt can remember. Now it's a gaol, and a mint, and a garrison-house for his soldiers, and a bed for the night if he ever travels north again.

The pestilence was very bad in the castle, particularly in the gaol, Watt said.

"The Lord's wrath was strong against those sinners." But I've been in that gaol, where the ordinary prisoners are kept, and the stench is strong enough there even without the pestilence, so it's no wonder so many people died. Plenty of people die there of ordinary sicknesses too, the flux and the styche and who knows what else.

This time last year, there was a garrison of soldiers guarding the prisoners and the mint, which is somewhere in one of the towers. Most of the soldiers are dead now, but there's one on the door who nods at us and opens up the little person-door inside the big cart-door to let us in.

Inside the castle walls there's the courtyard, with a well in the middle, and the stocks, and some chickens, and a pig nosing at the gutters. The courtyard is almost deserted. The whole world is half-empty, like a flood plain after the waters have receded, back to wherever it is floods come from. We pick our way around the bottom of the walls until we come to another door in another tower. The guard here is new and takes a little longer over us, asking us who we are and who we've come to visit. We show him our bundle and he nods and lets us inside.

The ordinary prisoners are kept at the bottom of the tower,

waiting for the assizes when their cases will be tried. The judges are travelling north on that long road from London, stopping in all the cities to try all the poor wretches in the gaols, to set them free or condemn them to death. They were due two months ago, but with the pestilence everything is knocked out of shape, and who knows when they'll get here now. There aren't many prisoners left. Those that didn't die of the pestilence have escaped through the great holes in the wall where the spring river flooded into the gaol and nobody thought to mend it. All that's left now are a couple of cripples and a mad woman who tells furious tales to the stones in the wall. And Thomas.

Thomas has a room of his own in the tower, with a bed and a wooden table and a chair and a little window. He's sitting at the table reading one of his books when the guard lets us in. He smiles when he sees Robin, or perhaps me as well, I'm not sure.

"There you are! I wasn't sure if you were coming today."

We leave money with the guards, so Thomas is always fed even if we can't come. But Robin comes nearly every day, and usually I do too.

"We brought you a new book," says Robin. "I couldn't read what it was, though."

Thomas takes the book from Robin and smiles.

"Come," he says, holding out his hand to Robin, "how much can you remember from last time?" And Robin pulls out his wax tablets, and the two of them are off again into their world of wax and wood and paper and black ink-spiders.

I go to the window and look out. From here you can see the bright snake of the river, winding through the city and out of the city walls. You can see the thatched roofs of the houses, and though it's too far away to see the people in the streets, there's an ox-cart full of straw coming into the castle and a man exercising a horse in the courtyard below.

Beyond the city walls, the patchwork of farmland starts, green fields for the animals, brown fields for the ploughing and here and there a yellowish field where the crop has been abandoned. There's a team of oxen pulling a plough over a bare field, and the sight of it tugs at my heart. I wonder what's happening in Ingleforn. They'll have started the ploughing there now. I wonder what's happened to our land, if anyone's ploughing it, or if the crops have been left to rot and sink back into the land. There's value in that too. Next year, the soil will be richer, the yield higher.

The birds are gathering on the battlements of the castle, circling in great flocks over my head. They're itching to leave, to take off to wherever it is birds come from and go back to. I'm itching to leave too. Somewhere along that road, Father's land – my land – is waiting to be ploughed. But we can't go before the assizes, before Thomas's case is tried. We all know that.

I turn back to look at Robin and Thomas. A bed, a chair, a table, a candlestick and a window. It's not much. But Thomas doesn't look unhappy. His head is bent over the book, his long finger marking the words for Robin to follow. Robin's face is earnest, but if his wits are like mine, I can see why the letters don't take. I can't hold a thought in my head for longer than it takes to walk down the stairs to the kitchen. I forget important things – the name of the baker in Ingleforn, how many brothers and sisters Alice had, and how many of them are still alive. I used to worry about it, when we first came here, but now I don't. I don't worry about anything, very much. I do the things I need to do – make the pottage, brew the ale, wash the clothes, bring the food and water to Thomas here – the rest I let float on by. The pestilence seems to be almost gone, and soon the assizes will be over too. And then we'll be moving on.

Robin has given up on the reading lesson and is trying to persuade Thomas to escape again.

"The ordinary prison has great holes in the wall where the floods came through last year," he says. "All you'd need to do is stop paying for this room and you could just climb out – nobody would care. There's only one guard left now in the prison anyway – all the rest died in the pestilence. We could get everything ready for you – couldn't we, Isabel? It wouldn't be hard." His face is pained. I can see how much he hates this. And so do I, sort of – that so many, many people died and we couldn't stop it happening, and that this man just sits and waits for the hangman to come. Because he will be hanged. What else will they do to a man who insists on confessing?

"Enough," says Thomas. He puts his hand on Robin's arm and smiles at him, that oddly distant smile that seems to have no connection to the rest of the world. "I don't want to make trouble for you and your family," he says. "And that's an end to it."

Robin's face is pulled out of shape with his unhappiness. I can see why. They might send some men after Thomas, but it won't be many. There are too few soldiers left and too many important things that need doing now – graves to dig, disputes to be settled, offices and titles to fill. One looter won't cause too much unquiet, with all the thievery that's been going unpunished these last months.

I don't think Thomas wants to run, is the truth. I think he wants to go back to his family, his wife and his children. He likes Robin – you can see how much he likes him – but I don't think he's enough to keep him here. It's worth fighting to stay alive if you've got brothers and sisters who need you, or a wife and a family. But I can see how dying like this might be sweet, if you're Thomas and you don't have anything left to live for.

Thomas is putting his books away, which means it's time for us to go.

"Isabel—" he says, and there's something in his voice that tugs at my attention.

"What are you going to do with your family?" he says. "After the assizes?"

Robin glances at me. It takes me a moment to catch my wits. I've got used to taking charge of my family since Thomas went, and I don't like the reminder that Thomas is still supposed to be our father. I say, with more force than I'd intended, "We're going back home. We've got land – good land. Someone will want us, if only for our land."

Thomas nods his head a couple of times.

"Do you need money – for the journey?"

I haven't liked to tell him that Ralph has fled with most of his precious things.

"We'll be all right," I say, instead, and he nods his head.

"God be with you," he says, and I feel like a door has been shut, leaving us out in the cold, leaving me alone with the family to care for again.

But this time I'm not frightened. This time, I know we're going to be all right.

37. Robin by Moonlight

The crowd in the square are strangely quiet. They wait at the edges and the walls, whispering and watching the wooden scaffold, which has been built against the window of the tavern. People *are* coming back. Across the square are two ladies in silks, whispering on the church steps while their maids scratch their noses and tug their fingers through their hair. The bodies are going from the streets, and the shutters on the houses are beginning to open. But it's a strange, sad, quiet ghost of a city.

I thought I'd hate the people staring, but this is worse. Like Thomas's death isn't exciting enough even to draw a crowd.

The world isn't helping. It's a miserable day, a pale, washed-out grey sky, the sun sitting low and sullen above the rooftops. The people look small and worn. We're a ruined world, the wasteland Noah saw when the flood waters melted away and left him with a muddy, empty wilderness to forge into a new nation.

When it happens, it happens without ceremony. The executioner leads Thomas up to the scaffold. His hands are tied. Thomas is standing very straight. The four of us are huddled against the wall, away from the others. Robin stirs and stands forward. I follow. I want him to know that we're here, even if those other children aren't, William and Lucie and Edith. I don't want him to be alone when he dies.

Thomas's eyes are moving around the square. They catch ours and settle. He nods, but doesn't smile.

They put the hood over his head. They put the noose around his neck. Maggie cries out, catching her breath in distress, and buries her head in my mantle. I put my arm around her shoulders and look across at Ned. His face is pale, his eyes vivid in the whiteness. His spiky red hair needs cutting. His eyes are watching Thomas. He's not going to look away. Neither is Robin. Neither am I.

Thomas drops. Ned flinches. Somehow I'd expected it to be dignified – Thomas is so dignified, and he's a martyr, like the holy saints. But there's no dignity in this death. He jerks and dances on the rope like a man in a fit, like a butchered pig. Ned is trembling, his hand up to his mouth. Magsy whimpers into my stomach. The crowd is quiet.

At last he's still.

They cut him down. That seems to be all. No one wants to linger. The people are moving off already. A woman passing us shakes her head.

"Haven't we had enough death already?" she says. "You'd think they'd be tired of it."

Ned is crying. His lips are shaking.

"I'm sorry. . ." he says. "Sorry . . . I'm sorry. I'm sorry."

I put my around his shoulders.

"I know, Nedkin," I say. "I'm sorry too."

Robin's face is soft with sleeplessness and sadness.

"He wanted to die," he says, and I wonder if he's right.

Thomas's house is empty. None of the fires are lit, or the candles. Outside, the rain is falling, rat-a-tap-tapping against the wooden shutters. I light the beeswax candles and we all climb into my bed together, the way we used to in our solar at home. This bed is softer than our old bed, and the mattress is stuffed with feathers, but the feeling is the same, of being together in a warm, cosy heap, like a litter of piglets or a nest of baby chicks.

"What do you think those girls would say if they found me and Robin in here?" says Ned, and he giggles.

"They'd say, 'Get that smelly villein out of my bed!'" I say.

"We're not smelly!" says Mags.

"We might not even be villeins any more," I realize.

"Doesn't mean they'd marry you," Robin says, and Maggie squeals.

"Poor girls," I say. "We shouldn't laugh."

"Poor Father and Alice and Richard," says Ned.

"And baby Edward!" says Mags.

"And Mother and Thomas," says Robin quietly.

And Geoffrey, I think, but I don't say it out loud.

I used to be afraid of going home, of knowing, but I'm not any more. Not knowing is worse.

In the dark chamber, we're silent, remembering the ghosts of our dead. I wonder how long they'll travel so close to us. Maybe for ever. That's a sad thought and a happy one, both.

"No one else is going to die, are they?" says Mags, burrowing her forehead into my stomach.

"No," says Robin. "No one else is going to die."

*

In the middle of the night, I get out of bed and go into the hall. We've left the shutters open in the corridor, and the moonlight shines on to the wall, silvery-white and eerie and beautiful. I stand at the window and look out at the town. So many people have died. Why were we left alive? What am I supposed to do with all of this life, this bounty I've been given? What can I do that's better than what Alice or Edward would have done?

There's a noise behind me. It's Robin, his face silvery-quiet in the moonlight.

"Hey, Robin," I say, and he comes and puts his arms around me.

"I'm your family now," he says, and he kisses me, the way he did on the night of the hue and cry.

The moon is high in the sky. The stars are out. Robin is in my arms, and we're kissing, mouth against mouth, heart against heart. We're kissing with all the life that we have and the dead do not. Because we're alive. Because so many people are dead. Because it's so good to feel something after so long feeling nothing at all.

In the moonlight, here in the hallway, it's hard to tell where my body ends and his begins.

I pull my mouth apart from his, and look at him, there so close to me that I can feel his breath on my cheek. I trace the shape of his face with my finger, the line of his nose, his cheek, his mouth.

"Let's have lots of children," Robin whispers. "Lots and lots."

"Let's have a cherry tree and a beehive."

"Let's get our animals back from Joan."

"Let's be free."

"I love you," I whisper, and I wonder if I mean it.

We're woken the next morning by the sound of fists. Hard, urgent fists banging at the door downstairs, hands and feet and fists and fear. A constable's bang, or a sheriff's, authority knocking. We try to ignore it, but whoever is banging won't go away.

"I didn't do anything!" says Ned.

"Don't answer it," says Robin. But it doesn't work. Whoever it is knows we're here. Maybe it's Thomas's family – maybe he has brothers and sisters, or cousins somewhere, who are coming back to claim what's rightfully theirs.

"Don't worry," I tell Ned. "I'm not going to let them take anyone else away."

I take out my knife. Robin takes Thomas's sword. Ned – desperate not to be left out – picks up the broom and Mag follows with the candlestick, bobbing a little on the soles of her feet with excitement. I wonder about telling her to stay upstairs, then change my mind. Whatever we're doing now, we're doing together.

We creep down the stairs. The fists are still banging on the door outside, loud and urgent.

"We're coming!" I call through the door. The banging stops.

I tug at the bolts, cold in the morning air.

"Ready?" I whisper. The others nod.

I open the door.

Richard is standing on the doorsill.

38. *Alive*

We sit round the table in the kitchen for hours, drinking stale ale from Thomas's wine goblets and eating meat pies from the pie man's stall.

"You're alive," says Richard. "All of you. Even Robin!"

"You can't kill me," says Robin, but his smile is quiet. He's not the same laughing boy who trod on my toes at Midsummer Eve. But then, am I the same Isabel?

"They said you were sick," I say.

"I was," says Richard. "And then I got better. And I came to find you."

"I didn't know that could happen," I say. "I thought you were dead."

"I didn't know what had happened to you," says Richard. And we're quiet, thinking of all the things that might have happened to us and didn't, and of all the things that did.

"Do you know what happened to Geoffrey?" I ask, but Richard shakes his head.

"There were a lot of deaths up at the abbey," he says. "Some people say all the monks died . . . some say there were a few left who went to a monastery in Felton. I know the abbot died. They shut the place up. I didn't like to go up there, Isabel, I'm sorry. And Geoffrey wouldn't have wanted me, even if he was still alive." But that isn't true. Geoffrey wouldn't have wanted to come home, but he would have wanted to see us, to know if we were alive. But if he was alive, wouldn't he have come to the village himself?

"You have a niece," says Richard quickly, seeing my frown. "She's called Sarah. A red-haired niece!"

It's like he doesn't care about Geoffrey at all. He's more interested in Joan's horrible baby.

"A baby!" says Mag. "Another new baby!"

Richard is looking at me expectantly. I'm supposed to be pleased, I know.

"What's going to happen now?" I say, instead.

"You're coming home, of course," says Richard.

39. *The Star*

We pack up all of our things on to old Stumpy. We leave Thomas's fine clothes behind – they won't be much use when we have to work for our living again. Ned takes Thomas's chess set and Margaret takes the wooden doll that they stole from some dead child. Robin takes his wax tablets and three of Thomas's big leather books. I take nothing except some bread and cheese and the salt pork from the kitchen. Everything else I need, I can find at home.

When I go up to find Robin, he's standing in Juliana's chamber. Open on the bed is the jewellery chest full of gold and silver – a golden necklace set with green stones, a ring dazzling with diamonds, a bangle set in the shape of a serpent eating its own tail. Robin holds up a necklace made of chains of silver.

"Look what I found."

I come over and let the necklace fall through my fingers. The jewels here must be worth more than Father's lands and house and everything he owned.

"It was under the bed," says Robin. "Ralph must have missed

it. Thomas wanted you and Maggie to have them. He told me so, ages ago." He picks up the serpent bangle and hands it to me. I slip my wrist through it. The serpent's eyes are set with rubies and all the scales are marked along its back. I look across at him and see that there are tears in his eyes. I wonder if this is what Thomas was trying to give us, back in the castle. There's a prince's ransom here. He can't have wanted it to go to the City of York.

"Why did he do it, Robin?" I ask, tears blinding my own eyes. "Did he go out looking for children to bring home?"

Robin shakes his head.

"I'm sure he didn't," he says. "I don't think he had any plan at all. I think ... well, I think I reminded him of William – you know" – I nod – "and I think he was lonely, and it seemed like a good idea at the time. I don't think he ever really knew what to do with us, once he had us."

He touches the serpent with his long finger.

"He was a good man, Isabel," he says.

"I know," I say. I put my finger on top of Robin's, and press it into the serpent's scalloped back.

"You should wear it," he says, but I shake my head.

"We'll buy good land with it. And oxen and bees and a pig and some geese for Maggie to play with. It won't be wasted."

Robin nods, but the tears roll out of his eyes and down his cheeks. I reach out and touch them with the back of my hand. Robin lost two families in less than two months, and then Thomas came and gave him everything he ever wanted. And now he's gone too.

"You've still got me," I say. "Robin. I'm still here. We're your family now, remember?" He nods and rubs against my cheek, but doesn't answer. "I'm not going to leave you," I say. "I promise. And it's time to go."

It's a dull, grey, misty day. All of the joy and gladness of yesterday has gone. We walk, trying not to notice the dead crops in the fields, the dead animals. Trying not to wonder what we'll find in Ingleforn when we return.

We sleep in the same inn that Thomas brought us to on our way here. It looks the same as last time – the long, smoky room with the tallow candles and the dirty straw on the earth floor. There are more people here than there were last time, although the room is still half-empty.

"People are getting braver," Richard says. "They're moving around again – leaving their old villages and looking for work."

The talk at the long table and the fire is all about land and work. Lord Hugh is offering three and a half pence a day to anyone who'll work his land. Lady Christina is offering three and three quarters. Lord Randolph only offers two pence and a farthing, the skinflint.

My father gave his labourers two pence a day and a bed in the barn, and they were grateful. Things are different now, it seems.

"We can ask for what we want," a big, red-faced man by the fire says. "If they won't give it to us, we'll go elsewhere, and they know it."

The old man opposite is nodding. "It's our world now," he says. "If we want it. They need us now." He turns and glares at Richard. "Make the most of it, lad!" he says. "It won't last. All this good land for sale! And the beasts! They say the gentry have so many heriot beasts, they can't give them away."

"I'd heard that too," says Richard. He perches on the end of one of the benches and leans forward. "I want good land," he says. "I can pay – plough land first, and pasture afterwards. I'm not afraid to work, but I want to go as a free man – and my brothers and sisters with me."

"Ahh." The other men lean forward too. "I heard St Helen's were selling good land – did you hear that, Harry?"

"Everyone is selling land!" snorts the old man. "But you wouldn't want to farm St Helen's – little mucky bits of earth and stone. Lady Christina – that's who you want to go to. She—"

Richard lifts his mug to his lips. To Richard this is the promised land of milk and grain. And I can't complain too much – isn't this what I've always wanted too? But there's something indecent in Richard's eagerness. I know he's lost people too – Father and little Edward and all the other people in Ingleforn that I haven't dared ask about yet. But something inside me rages at the idea that something – anything – good can come out of this. It's too soon. It's not fair.

I can see that Robin feels the same, or something like it. He sits hunched up on his bench, pushing at his pottage with his spoon. Magsy is tugging at his arm.

"Can you tear my bread for me? Robin? *Robin!* My bread's too hard."

Robin pulls his sleeve away.

"Not *now*, Mag!"

Magsy's face crumples. I can see her making up her mind to start wailing. I lean over the table.

"Here, Mag, whist. Look, there you go. Eat that and be quiet."

Maggie's lip is still wobbling. "I'm not hungry," she says, pushing my hand away. I want to tip the bowl over her head, but I don't. I break the rest of the bread into Mag-sized pieces and drop them into the pottage.

"Dolly's hungry even if you aren't – why don't you give them to her, eh?"

"No, she's not," says Mag sulkily, but she's not going to cry, and that's all I care about right now.

At least I don't have to worry about Ned eating. He's finished his bowl and half of Robin's bread, and he's eying up Mags's bowl with a calculating expression.

"Are we going back to Ingleforn?" he says. "Or are we going somewhere else?"

"We have to go home to pick up Joan and the baby," I say. "But then Richard's going to buy some new land somewhere. We're going to be free men and women. We won't have to work the lord's land any more. What do you think of that?"

Ned shrugs, but he looks pleased. "When I grow up," he announces. "I'm going to be the reeve like Gilbert. I'm going to have the biggest strip in the village – and servants to plough it all for me."

He looks so determined. Sturdy, wiry little Ned, chewing on Maggie's bread with his red hair spiked up and his face red and white with the cold.

"I believe you," I say, and I do.

The bar is getting busier as the night begins to draw in. Richard turns away from his friends by the fire and orders us all another mug of ale.

"Is there still pestilence in Ingleforn?" says Ned. He tips the top of his ale mug up slowly so the ale trickles down his throat. All you can see over the rim are his round blue eyes.

"Some..." says Richard. "Much less than there was. It's going – I promise."

But people are still dying. I feel my throat tighten.

"How do you know?" says Robin. He's scowling at the tabletop. "I bet it hasn't gone – not really. That's not how sickness works – it goes, and then it comes back."

"If that's true, there isn't much we can do about it," says Richard, far too cheerfully. I want to hit him.

Robin's face darkens. "I'm going to bed," he says, pushing his end of the bench back, jolting Magsy so that she drops her spoon in her lap with a surprised "Oh!"

Robin doesn't stop. His face is red. He's left most of his pottage in the bowl. I know I ought to go after him – make sure he's all right – but I'm so fed up with all this sadness and anger that I let him go.

A little band has set up in the corner of the room – a fiddle player and a drummer and a horn player. They're good. Ned bats his spoon on the table in time. It's getting dark. The girl who served the ale comes along and lights the rushlights along the walls. Magsy climbs under the table and on to my lap. She's a warm, heavy weight against my stomach. I hold her without moving, listening to the music, watching the shadows on the wall rise and dance as people move across the fire and the rushlights, thinking how fragile all this is. Here one day and gone the next.

It's late when we go up to bed. Robin is asleep at one end of the long room, in a bed with a red-faced woman and her child. The only beds left are right at the other end. Richard takes Ned in with him, and Mag and I have to share with a skinny little girl who scratches at her flea bites even in her sleep.

It takes me a long time to fall asleep. The long room is

warm and dark and stinks of ale and sweat and stale rushes. Whenever anyone goes to the latrine, you can hear them cursing and stumbling down the aisle between the beds.

When I do sleep, I dream about our little house, with the hearth-fire smoking and the lavender and rosemary drying from the beams, and Stumpy and Gilbert Pig sleeping behind their wattle wall. I dream about Alice, holding Edward and crooning to him as she bends over the cooking pot. I dream about the chickens scratching in the straw, and the rustle from the birds nesting in the thatch, and Ned kicking a ball against the wall, calling, "One, two, I'm with you! Two, three, you're with me!"

I wonder if this dream is going to carry on coming back for the rest of my life. I wonder if I will ever forget them, if one day I'll ever be glad – like Richard is – that they went and left us this bright, empty world for our own.

I wake to the sunlight shining through the narrow windows, and the sound of someone – I think it's a child – screaming hysterically at the other end of the sleeping room. Around me, people are waking up: complaining, grumbling, blinking in the sunlight.

I sit up. A small huddle has gathered around the child, who looks a little older than Mag. One of the women is holding her arms down, but she's struggling to get free, kicking with her bare heels at the woman's shins. Then another woman says, "She's dead!" and it falls in one of the silences between the child drawing her breath and beginning to scream, so that the whole sleeping chamber is suddenly still, even the little girl, who hiccups and shudders in the stranger's arms.

"Is it . . .?" someone says, but of course it must be; what else can kill so silently and so suddenly? You go to bed alive and you wake up dead. I expect panic, folk gathering together their things and fleeing, but no one seems even surprised. You live with death for so long that another body is just that – a dead weight to be disposed of somehow. We've all walked among the dead for too long to be frightened any more. Only to the dead woman and her child, who has begun to scream again, does this matter now.

"We should get going," says Richard. "We've a long way to go today."

"I'll tell Robin," I say.

I pull on my clothes and shoes and make my way down the sleeping chamber towards Robin's bed. All around me, people are muttering in low voices. The group around the little girl whisper to each other, and look across at the child. They're wondering what to do with her, probably. Does she have a father somewhere, or other family? As I get closer, I see that it's the child who was in Robin's bed. The woman is lying flabby and white on the bed like a plucked chicken, the fingers of the big hand hanging down from the bed turning black with the sinking blood. Her mouth is half open, but her eyes are closed. Her skin is white and plucked and faintly horrible.

Robin is lying curled up on his side beside her. He looks asleep. His hands are neatly clasped under his chin and his eyes are closed. I wonder how he has managed to sleep through the screaming and shouting. I touch his arm to wake him, and I know. His skin is cold. He's dead.

One of the women from the huddle is watching me. She comes over to the bed now.

"Was he a friend of yours?"

I nod.

"And the little girl?"

"I don't know her." I swallow. I want to shake Robin, to try and wake him somehow, but I don't dare with this bright-eyed woman watching me so intently.

"Pity." The woman doesn't turn away. "Something will have to be done with her." I don't answer. She shrugs. "And you'll have to do something with him," she says, nodding to Robin. I nod again. If I open my mouth, I'm either going to cry or hit her.

"Well then," says the woman. But she doesn't stop watching me.

I crouch beside Robin, and stroke his arm awkwardly. It's very cold. His face already has the parchment look of dead skin. His black hair is loose and hangs over his forehead. The world seems to swim in and out of focus. My hand shakes, violently, on the bed, and my teeth start to chatter. *I knew*, I think. *I knew this would happen. I knew that nothing could be trusted, that nothing would hold.* But in truth, I didn't know. I thought I was safe. I thought it was over.

Nothing is ever over, I think, with a sudden certainty, and a sudden sadness. And I know, sitting there by Robin's bed, that after today I will never feel safe again. I will never be able to love simple and sure and sweet without remembering this moment, and being afraid. I stand up, sick of it all, and go back to Richard and the others, to tell them that we can't go home just yet.

255

40. Goodbyes

There's no church for another three miles. We bury Robin and the body of the dead woman in the pasture at the back of the inn, where the landlord's cows graze and the horses are let loose to flick their tails and pull at the thick, tussocky grass. There's a big oak tree and a hedge of hawthorne and brambles. Cow parsley and thistles grow in the ditches. The pasture slopes down to a beck with a ford and rushing water. It's evening, and the sunlight sends long shadows stretching out across the grass. The sky is peach and pink and pale orange over the hills, the long clouds coloured like the inside of an oyster shell. It's quiet and cool and still.

There's no one at the graveside except for Richard and us, and the landlord's man, who helped dig the graves – the landlord moved the bodies to the cow-byre, he was so desperate to get them out of his house – and the woman's little girl, whose name is Beatrice. Beatrice is seven. She had a father and two brothers, who are dead as well. She and her mother were travelling to Felton, where her uncle lives. Later, I give one of Juliana's golden bracelets to a carter at the inn, to take her with him as far as Felton. Richard looks disapproving – how much land could that bracelet buy? – but I don't care. I think of Juliana, whose little girls were killed. I think about Robin, with nowhere to go, and Alice, with all of those children who weren't hers. I try not to think about what will happen to this child if her uncle is dead.

Beatrice spent most of the morning screaming, but she's quiet now. She sucks on a bit of bread and honeycomb and holds on to Mags's hand.

The men carry the bodies to the grave-mouth on a tabletop from the inn. They're wrapped in winding sheets, so I can't even see Robin's face. I'm glad.

There isn't a priest, and nobody heard Robin's confession, but I don't believe he's going to hell. I refuse to believe it. I don't want anything to do with a God who would send Robin to hell.

The men lower the bodies awkwardly into the grave, one on top of the other. It's clumsy, and the hole is too small, but at least it's not a plague pit.

"Do you want to say something?" says Richard, to me.

Yes, I think, but my mind won't work, my voice is stuck, my words won't come. What can I say that will make sense of this? I look at Ned and Mag, and they're silent too. Neither of them is crying. Richard shrugs, and begins to shovel the earth back over the bodies. *Wait*, I want to say, but I don't. Wait for what?

Later, when the others are finished, I want to stay here awhile, but Richard looks astonished.

"Who will look after Mag and Ned?" he says. And so I have to go.

*

The next morning, we leave for Ingleforn. I wonder if I will ever come here again. I wonder how long anyone will remember the two bodies in the cow pasture.

I think about what I would have liked to have said by the graveside, if I'd been brave enough.

I love you.

There was never anyone like you in all the world.

I would have been happy, married to you. We would have made a good family.

I'll never forget you.

But the words sound cheap, and inadequate. All over England, people like Beatrice and I are standing by gravemouths, saying the same things to those they have lost.

I love you.

I'll never forget you.

There was never anyone like you, in all the world.

41. *From a Grave-Mouth*

It's evening when we come back home. Richard has a lamp on a pole, which sends long shadows swinging over the wattle walls of the houses. Even in the darkness, I know what everything is, where everything is. That's the well. That's Emma Baker's oven. Those are Sir John's beehives, all in a row. That's the forge, and those are the stocks. It even smells the same as it always did: wet grass and pig dung and straw and earth. The air is cleaner here, wetter, richer.

We're home.

I don't care.

We aren't going back home, though. We spend the night in Joan and Richard's little house, which looks just like it always did, except that now there's a crumpled little red-faced person sleeping in a cradle by the hearth. Joan – who Alice always said gave up half her wits when she got married – comes running to the door when we knock and flings her arms around Richard.

"You came back!" she says, and then she sees the rest of us crowding in behind him.

"You found them!" And it's all kisses and caresses, without so much as a "how-was-the-journey?"

And there's the baby by the hearth. A baby girl, a frail little thing, not half as sturdy as Edward was. My eye keeps shifting towards her and then away, as though I'm frightened to look. Edward used to lie just like that – his tiny eyelashes and tinier fingernails and his serious sleeping face. I sit hunched by the fire, my hand on Mag's back for comfort, but she wriggles away to admire the baby. Richard gives me an odd look, as though he expects me to be celebrating. But the village is a place of empty houses and unploughed fields, and the baby scares me, and my heart can't seem to understand that Robin is dead – I keep expecting him to be here, in this room – and I'm going to have to go to the abbey and find out what happened to Geoffrey, and I don't know why, but Joan's neat little one-room house just makes me want to cry.

"You're an auntie now, Isabel," Joan says, and I clench my lips tight together and don't say a word.

We're leaving soon. Joan's sister married a tanner in Kirby Felton, and she's found a house for us to stay in while we're looking for land to buy. Richard's eyes gleam as he talks about pasture land and wheat fields and all the heriot animals, and the beasts with no owners that the new lords are desperate to get rid of. I feel empty.

I thought everything would be all right if we just got home, but maybe nothing will ever be right again.

I used to think I'd spend the rest of my life in this village, but now I'm glad to be leaving. Ingleforn is a strange, half-deserted place. The empty houses watch me with empty eyes, and everywhere I go I see reminders of the dead: the empty forge, shut up and unworked, the pigs and chickens wandering half-wild and ownerless through the village, slowly vanishing as villager after villager claims them for the pot, the houses with the shutters closed tight against the wind, the gardens already hazy with uncut grass and weeds. Sir Edmund is dead in his house in London, and a new boy heir is coming, a cousin from Duresme, so the rumours say. Church on Sunday is half-empty, and there's a new priest that I don't know, who's giving the mass to our church and the church at Great Riding. He says the mass without stumbling, unlike poor Simon, and the congregation listen dully and dutifully before wandering away to talk of other things, as always.

After church, Will Thatcher comes over to speak to me. He's gotten taller than ever just in the weeks that I've been gone – he's not a boy any more, he's nearly a man. Maybe I'm a woman.

"I'm glad to see you," he says, more directly than I remember, and with little of his old shyness. "I thought I'd never see you again."

I clench my arms tight across my chest. I don't have anything to say to him. I don't have anything to say to anyone. *I don't want to live in this world any more*, I think, very clearly, and I'm so startled by the thought that I blink. Is that true? Really?

"We're not staying," I tell Will, dully. "Richard's wanting us to move to better land," and he nods.

"I'll be gone soon too," he says. "The new lord – he's looking for men to garrison his castle down south. Most of his troops were killed in the pestilence. I'll not stay here."

I wonder if he remembers that kiss. I wonder if he'll miss

me, in his new castle with the new lord, who doesn't look like he's going to stay in Ingleforn any more than Sir Edmund did.

He shifts from one foot to another, the way he used to, then he says, "I'm going to be married too. To Maude Baker."

"Oh!" I blink at him. Then I say, "I'm glad, Will, really." Though I'm not. Maude Baker is lumpen and fish-eyed and stupid. She's still scared of rats and spiders and moths, even though she's a great girl of almost twenty.

"I hope – I hope you'll be happy," I say to Will, and this I do mean. He nods his head up and down a few times and says, "You too, Isabel. You too."

Nobody seems to know what happened at St Mary's. Joan thought all the monks died of the pestilence. Richard thought that a few had survived but they'd packed up all their holy books and taken them to the priory at Felton. The new priest, when I asked, said he thought there were a few monks left, "but they're leaving soon, I think, before the winter comes."

On the last day before we leave, I go up to the abbey. It's cold. Autumn's here. The abbey sits as it always does in the dip in the road, low and quiet under the white-grey sky. The big wooden doors are closed. I bang on them with my fist, but nobody comes. Weeds are growing out of the cracks between the stones, and in the chapel, one of the beautiful coloured glass windows has been smashed wide open against the rain. It should be sad, and it is, but mixed up with the sadness is the calmness and the sense of peace that always surrounds my abbey, and that old, tugging sense of home that Geoffrey always raises up in me.

There's a tree that I used to climb when I wanted to visit

him and didn't want the monks to know. It's still there up against the orchard wall. It's easier to climb than I remember. I must be getting taller. Little green-and-brown specks of bark and moss come off on my hands and my skirts, but I don't mind. This gown is too short for me anyway. I need a new one. I must remember to ask Joan about Alice's loom. More work for the long winter that's coming.

There's no one in the orchard, but there are noises coming from the gardens, someone whistling, and a thud, like metal on stone. I follow the sounds, noticing all the signs of decay, the dead leaves beginning to fall, dirty and unswept in the earth and the mud, the withered heads of the leeks in the herb garden. I'm filled with a great weariness, a heaviness. I wonder if it will ever really leave me. There's so much that needs to be done, here and everywhere, and I'm so tired.

The monk is in the field behind the graveyard. He's digging a grave. He's knee-deep in the earth, and it's slow going. The earth is stony, and he's forever stopping to dig out the stones with his spade. He looks cheerful enough, though. His hood is down and he's whistling.

He doesn't stop working as I come up to him, though he must have heard me.

"Where are the monks?" I say, a little too loudly.

The monk gives a bark of a laugh.

"Where's everyone?"

It takes me a moment to realize.

"They're dead? All of them?"

"Well, I'm here, aren't I?" The monk digs his spade into the ground and throws the load of earth back over his shoulder. "But yes, there's me – and poor Brother John – and that's the last of us."

I'm silent. I'd expected this, but somehow I *hadn't* expected it. I feel the way you feel after you lay down a load that was too heavy ever to pick up in the first place – weak and shaky and breathless. The monk glances at me, but he doesn't say anything. He goes back to digging the grave. I'm silent, watching. The day smells of wet grass and wet earth. My hands are stained with bark from the tree, and there's a green smudge all down the front of my gown. My feet are wet. My brother is dead. Shadows from the branches of the tree fall across the monk's face, shadow-brown, then white, then shadow-brown. Water is running in the brook, the last of the apples are ripening in the trees around me, and my brother is dead.

"Were you?" I say bitterly to the monk.

"Was I what?"

"Sleeping with devils. Is that why God killed you all? Was it worth it?" My voice rises. The monk carries on digging.

"If they were, they never invited me along. Pity. My bed got awful cold, those long nights."

"It's not funny!" I say shrilly. The monk looks up.

"No," he says, "I don't suppose it is."

I scuff the toe of my shoe in the mud at the edge of the grave. It's good, thick earth, soft and crumbly and full of worms and the white, wriggly roots of grass.

"I hate God," I tell the monk. He ignores me. He looks like Alice, lips clenched, getting on with her weaving while Mag has a screaming fit.

"I don't believe in God," I say instead. I'm not sure this is true – can you have a world without God? – but at least it makes the monk look at me.

"If you don't, you're not the only one. I've had boys from

Ingleforn throwing stones at the windows all last week. As if there isn't enough sorrow in this world already."

"How can you still believe in Him?" I say. "After all this. . ." And I swing my arm around in a gesture that's supposed to include the graves, and the empty abbey, and York with the corpses lying in the street, and Alice and Father and Edward in the grave with the rats, and Thomas swinging from the gibbet in the square.

The monk is quiet. The spade lifts the earth out of the grave and drops it on to the grass with a *splat*. It's strangely comforting, like being out in the fields with my father. My father is dead. My brother is dead.

"You know," says the monk, "I was a child in the Great Famine. Did you ever hear about that?"

I did. Lots of people in the village remember the famine, when the rains came like they did last harvest and all the crops were ruined. Father lost a grandmother, and a baby cousin, and a little sister smaller than Mag.

"And then their parents cut them up and put them in the pot!" Dirty Nick used to say, his teeth white in his red mouth, his long, grimy face screwed up as his muscles worked under the skin. But Father says no, they didn't eat his little sister, they buried her in the churchyard under the east window. But Will Thatcher says he's heard that people ate each other too.

"People are funny souls," says the monk. "They chop down the trees above their houses and wonder why the floods come. They eat all their barley and then wonder why their children are starving. They look at the Signs in Europe – the pestilence and the rains of fire and the plagues of frogs – and they say, 'That won't touch me. That can't come here.'"

"There was a man I knew in York," I say. "Watt. He said the people in France thought the pestilence was coming for the heathens, until it came to France. And then the people in England through it was coming for the French, until it came to England. And then the Scots rejoiced and thought it was coming for the English. . ."

"And now it's in Scotland," says the monk, and he spits. I nod. Now it's in Scotland.

"No one thinks disaster is coming to them," he says. "But it does. And it will. It came to Jesus, and it came to the Israelites and the Egyptians. Four hundred – five hundred – six hundred years from now, men and women will still be chopping down the trees and eating all the barley and hoping Providence will save them. But disasters will come to them too, all the same. And this has been a cruel trouble, I know, more sorrow than we ever thought we'd have to carry. But look! You're still here and so am I, and I've got a new abbey to shape and you've got land to work, I wager."

"We're going away," I say. "Before the new lord comes home. My brother Richard says nobody will care if we're villeins or free, so long as we've hands that can plough the fields. We're going to be rich, he says."

"Aye," says the monk. He throws up another spadeful of earth. "He mightn't be wrong, either." He looks up at me. "You should be grateful, my girl!"

I crouch down in the wet grass, ducking my head so I don't have to look at him, there in his grave. I remember the Bible story about the lilies in the field, who need not plough or weave or bake or sow, because of the grace of God who knows and loves them all.

"I'm scared of the baby," I say, through my hair.

"Scared of the baby!" The monk laughs. "A big girl like you! You can weather the end of the world, but you're scared of a baby!"

He's right. I'm a fool. But the truth is, the end of the world is easy to weather, if you don't expect to survive it. If all you have to do is wrap your mantle tight around yourself and live another day. Anyone can do that, I reckon. After Alice died, I never really thought I'd do anything but die too.

Living is harder than dying. I think of Joan's baby, Sarah. I don't want to live in a house with a baby and not love it, but I can't love Sarah without remembering Edward, and I'm not sure that I'm brave enough to remember all the people I have to remember, and carry all the grief I have to bear.

"Maybe I'll come with you to the other abbey," I say, to the blades of grass. "Maybe I'll be a nun instead. Nuns don't have to think, do they?"

"All the time," says the monk. "All the time." He stops in the hole and rubs at his forehead with his muddy hand. "Come," he says. "You don't look like a coward to me."

I hunch up my shoulders and crouch forward until my face is nearly touching the wet grass. I'm Isabel. I'm not a coward. But just for now I'm going to lie here and let my fingers soak up the droplets of water clinging to the underside of the grass and remember what it felt like to feel completely at home, and completely safe.

"What am I going to do?" I say to the grass and the little black ant which is climbing up a dandelion. It's an ant-mountain, that dandelion, but he's going to climb it anyway. I know what the answer is, and I'm not surprised when the monk gives it.

"You're going to live," he says. "What else are you going to do?"

Finis

Richard is proud of his new land, and he wants to show it off. He holds Joan's hand as she clambers over the earth, baby Sarah in a length of cloth strung over her shoulder. Sarah is beginning to take an interest in the world. She holds her head up and her blue eyes watch everything. Her hair is beginning to grow: fine, coppery-red strands, like Ned's.

"I thought we'd have rye all along here," Richard is saying. "And I want to try beans too – Father never had much luck with beans, but I think here—" Joan's face is cocked up to his, like Sarah's. She isn't at all interested in rye, but in the way his mouth twists as he speaks, the miracle of him being here, and happy, and alive.

The earth is hard with the winter cold. The sky above us is heavy and grey. Frost glitters on the weeds and the briar. It's going to take a lot of work to plant all this earth, and tend it, without the hired labour we could rely on in Ingleforn, but it's good work, purposeful work. Making something out of nothing – the best sort of work that there is. If I half-close my eyes, I can see what this field might look like, full of rye and beans and oats, and whatever else Richard thinks we should try.

"We could really make something here," Richard is saying to Joan, his eyes bright and proud. And he's right. We really could.

He to whom God has given knowledge, and the gift of speaking eloquently, must not keep silent nor conceal the gift, but he must willingly display it.

The woman who wrote those words was an abbess and a poet, and the poems that she wrote are still read and sung a hundred years after she died. Emma the baker's wife is as good a baker as John ever was. She was still baking bread when we came back to Ingleforn, she and her daughter. She baked us three flat loaves with the end of last year's rye.

We didn't stay long in Ingleforn. At Lady Christina's, Richard heard, they were paying three or four pennies to anyone who would help with the ploughing and the sowing for the year ahead. We were just labourers, paid hands, but no one asked too many questions about where we'd come from, and we were paid as free men and women. Sir Edmund's heir is a boy from Duresme with no more idea of who his villeins are than I have of how to build a cathedral. Gilbert Reeve is dead, and no one has the heart to come chasing after us.

"So are we free then?" I ask Richard. He shrugs.

"As close as makes no difference. No one's ever going to make us work for them again, and that's all that matters."

It's a fine thing to be free. At first, everything is so strange and grey and topsy-turvy that I can't make sense of what it is we have. But when winter comes, I look around and see that here we are, in our own little house, with our own land, and

Joan's little girl crying by the hearth. And every day, Richard and Ned and I are out in the fields, learning the lie of the land and the depth of the soil and the places where good crops will grow almost without tending and those where poor crops struggle up even with all the care we can give them. Richard was right to move us. This is good land. It will reward all the work we can give it.

Soon spring will be here again. A new harvest. A new year.

"The world is getting bigger, Isabel!" Richard says. "Look at all these people, coming here, living as free men. Look at the land we have!" He chucks baby Sarah under the chin. "What sort of world are you going to live in, eh?"

Richard is already a richer man than Father ever was. He's talking about using Thomas's money to buy some of the animals that no one has a use for, to make some gold for us until I'm old enough to run a farm for myself. Sheep need fewer hands to rear than barley does.

Joan grumbles. "If you wanted to be a shepherd, why did you buy all this plough land?" But Ned likes the idea of tending sheep instead of working on the land.

It's a strange thing, surviving, living when so many of the people you love are dead. Not everyone here can stand it. There was a woman who hanged herself over the winter, and a man who went mad and started talking to the leaves on the trees, calling them by the names of his children. Mostly what I feel isn't so much sadness as a great tenderness, as though the smallest knock would bruise me, as though a careless word would destroy me.

But my monk in the monastery was right. When you have to work, you work. When you have to live, you live.

Once I thought that the whole world was going to drown,

that no one would survive. But now the flood waters have passed and here we are, like Noah and Mrs Noah in the mystery play, standing on the top of a mountain, looking out at a new world and the land that is ours.

The Black Death was the single biggest catastrophe in historical memory. The exact number of casualties is unknown, but was probably somewhere between a third and a half of Europe. Certainly, the population of Europe halved between the beginning and the end of the fourteenth century. The Black Death was not responsible for all this destruction – the Great Famine of 1315-1316, the Hundred Years' War and the abysmal state of medieval medicine were all factors, but the Black Death was by far the largest. To put those figures into context, the First World War – the worst disaster Britain has suffered in living memory – killed around 1.55% of the British population. The most recent estimates put the victims of the Black Death at around 45%. The American government used records from the Black Death as a reference point when planning its response to a nuclear winter.

The Black Death – referred to at the time as the pestilence, *le morte bleu* or the Great Mortality – is believed to be a combination of three diseases: bubonic plague, pneumatic plague and septicaemic plague. Bubonic plague is the disease one imagines on hearing the word *plague* – black buboes in the groin and armpit, red markings, fever. Pneumatic plague is what happens when bubonic plague combines with pneumonia and the patient starts spitting blood – this form of plague is highly contagious. Septicaemic plague is perhaps the most frightening of the three – the patient appears perfectly healthy one minute, and is dead the next. In *All Fall Down*, Edward dies of bubonic plague, Simon of pneumatic and Robin of septicaemic.

Robin was right to wonder whether the pestilence had truly vanished. It would return to Britain in many incarnations over the next three hundred years, finally burning itself out in the Great Plague of London in 1666. Bubonic plague still exists today, although in a much less virulent form. Isabel would experience a second outbreak thirteen years after the events of *All Fall Down*, in which around 15% of the British population were killed, and again eight years later, in which around 10% died. Cruelly, the second incarnation mainly attacked children who had been born after the Black Death, and therefore did not have whatever genetic protection had enabled their parents to survive. It was known as the Children's Plague.

As a teenager, I was fascinated by apocalypse novels. I was born at the end of the Cold War, and – morbid child that I was – loved to read imaginings of nuclear holocaust, as well as depictions of plague, war and attacks by walking plants. I wanted to write about the Black Death because this was a very real apocalypse event. People living through it genuinely expected the world to end. And yet, in real life, this apocalypse behaved very differently to those in John Wyndham novels. Lack of food was not a problem for medieval peasants – in fact, many peasants had enough to eat for the first time in their lives. And society – although it was stretched to the very limits of endurance – survived. The dead were eventually buried. Orphans were eventually taken care of. The parish registers of 1348 and 1349 are full of neat lists of the dead. Wills and manor courts list the orderly succession of ownership as property passed from heir to heir – sometimes changing hands repeatedly in a matter of weeks.

Like the years after the First World War, the years after the Black Death were ones of great social change. Women like Emma Baker were allowed to take traditionally male professions for the first time, and many women thrived. Feudalism – the system under which Isabel's family were required to work for nothing on Sir Edmund's land – was severely weakened, as was the power of the church. Like Thomas, many medieval people were disinclined to blindly worship a God who had destroyed their entire family. Families like Isabel's went from a world where land was expensive and labour cheap to one where land was in abundant supply and labour hard to come by. Many – like Richard – grew very wealthy in the years that followed.

Today, we are so used to wealth and security that we forget the possibility of catastrophic suffering. Like the medieval English, we view disasters such as nuclear war or global warming as things which happen to foreigners, never to us. I wanted to write a book which showed that catastrophes have happened here, and could happen again. And I wanted to show that human beings have an astonishing ability to stand in the ruins of their world and to build it up again from the ashes.

Glossary

AGUE: Malaria. Common in marshy areas of medieval Britain.

ASSIZES: Courts administered by judges travelling through medieval England, trying all the criminals they encounter.

ASTROLABE: An instrument, consisting of a disc and a pointer, used to make astronomical measurements.

BUNTING: An affectionate name for a child, as in *Bye, baby bunting*.

CAMPBALL: An early version of football.

CORDWAINER: A shoemaker.

COTE: More properly called a cote-hardie, this is a close-fitting jacket with sleeves.

CROFT: The land surrounding a house. Like a garden, but used for agricultural purposes. Isabel's family grow herbs on their croft, and keep chickens. Her father also stores his ox-cart here.

DURESME: Durham.

FRANKLIN: A landowner of free but not noble birth.

FLUX: Diarrhoea, or any disease causing excessive flowing of blood.

HEARTH: A place for a fire, usually in the centre of a room and without a chimney. Isabel's family's hearth is a wrought-iron grate with a detachable hood. Thomas's hearth is a square of stone flags.

HERBS: A generic term for all vegetables. Medieval people believe that green vegetables are bad for you, and should be boiled thoroughly before eating.

HERIOT: A tax – usually a villein's best beast or most valuable possession – paid to the lord of the manor on his or her death.

HOOD: Medieval hoods are detachable. They cover the head and shoulders, and are often brightly coloured.

HOSE: Leggings worn by men instead of trousers and by women instead of stockings.

HUE AND CRY: The means by which the general alarm is raised to prevent a criminal escaping. Anyone hearing the hue and cry is required to stop whatever they are doing and assist in catching the fleeing criminal.

INFIRMARER: A monk in charge of the abbey's infirmary, or hospital.

JONGLEUR: A wandering entertainer, such as a minstrel or a juggler.

MANOR COURT: A court held several times a year to oversee the running of the manor. It deals with local crimes such as allowing animals to stray on to farmland or failing to turn up to work, and also records the transference of land. Fines and taxes are paid at the manor court.

MANTLE: A cloak.

MIASMA: A cloud of bad, pestilential air. Medieval people believe that diseases are carried in bad-smelling air, probably because some diseases – like the plague – cause the patient to smell, and because bad-smelling places such as cesspools are often unhealthy.

MUMMERS: A troupe of actors.

MURRAIN: A disease of cattle and sheep.

MYSTERY PLAY: Plays performed by the guilds, or mysteries, of a town at special occasions. Usually retellings of Biblical stories.

PALFREY: A horse, for riding.

PASTER NOSTER: Latin for Our Father, the Lord's Prayer.

POTTAGE: The staple food of the English peasantry. Most pottages contain oats, salt, meat stock and herbs, but – depending on what is in season – may also include peas, leeks, bacon, beans, cabbage, onions, garlic and other garden produce. Sweet pottages are also made from fruits such as cherries or blackcurrants.

QUINSY: A throat infection, still existing today.

REEVE: A lord's overseer on a manor. Usually one of the peasantry, a reeve has many responsibilities, including collecting rents, organizing the workers on the lord's fields and making sure that the villeins turn up for work.

SCRIPTORIUM: A room for writing.

SEXTON: A caretaker for a church and churchyard, often also a gravedigger and bell-ringer.

SOLAR: A room in a roof, an attic.

SPINDLE: A wooden spike, used for spinning wool. Spinning is woman's work in medieval England, as it can be done while minding a child, watching a pot or tending a fire.

Isabel uses a spindle and a distaff, a staff around which the unspun wool is wrapped while she spins.

STYCHE: A medieval disease, possibly a form of pneumonia.

TONSURE: Monks and priests in medieval England shave the top of their heads – or sometimes their entire head. This is called a tonsure.

TITHING BARN: Medieval law requires that one-tenth of a family's earnings are paid to the church in tithes. Since cash plays little part in a village economy, peasants literally hand over one-tenth of their eggs, corn, meat and other produce. These tithes are stored in a tithing barn.

TRISTAN AND ISEULT: A legend telling of the tragic love between Cornish knight Tristan and Irish princess Iseult. In some versions, Tristan is one of King Arthur's knights.

VIRGATE: Because all ploughs are pulled by great teams of oxen, all medieval fields are large – around seven to twelve hundred acres each. The fields are divided into strips, which are farmed by individual families. A virgate is around twenty to thirty acres of land, and for every virgate he owns a villager is required to contribute two oxen to the communal plough.

WATTLE: A wall or fence made from upright rods with twigs or sticks interlaced between them. Medieval fences are often made of wattle, and the walls of the houses in Isabel's village are wattle-and-daub – wattle daubed over with mud and left to dry. This means that peasant houses are very easy to build and to extend as families grow.

Acknowledgements

Thanks go to Phil Hoggart, for telling me about the Black Death in such a way that made me want to write about it (and for all those other strange and fascinating things that I'm going to write books about one day.) Thanks also to the good people at Cosmeston Medieval Village for knowing the answers to the important questions that history books never address, such as "Would medieval brothers and sisters sleep in the same bed?" and "Did medieval peasants have hen houses?"

Much gratitude to all the many hard-working and creative people who sat in coffee shops and attics and police stations, writing novels and comic strips and PhDs beside me while I worked on this book – Tara Button, Tom Nicholls, Susie Day, Pita Harris, Victoria Still, Carrie Comfort, Emily Hunka, Sarah McIntyre and everyone at the Fleece Station. Thanks for the authorly understanding, and for reminding me that Spider Solitaire really doesn't count as writing.

Thanks to the wonderfully-named Jessica Metheringham-Owlett, for her generous donation to the Firefly Project (http://fireflybosnia.org/), as part of a silent auction to win the dedication space in this book.

Thanks as ever to my editor, Marion Lloyd, for making me happy with editorial suggestions such as "Can we have some more gore?" and my agents – the much-missed Rosemary Canter and the wonderfully efficient Jodie Marsh. And to my dear boyfriend – now husband – Tom Nicholls, world-class provider of hugs, internet, screwdrivers, financial advice, and plausible reasons why the book I'm halfway through writing probably isn't nearly as bad as I think it is.

Read the heartbreaking opening chapters
of Sally Nicholls' award-winning

WAYS TO LIVE FOREVER

This is my book, started 7th January,
finished 12th April. It is a collection
of lists, stories, pictures, questions
and facts.
It is also my story.

LIST NO 1 FIVE FACTS ABOUT ME

1. My name is Sam.

2. I am eleven years old.

3. I collect stories and fantastic facts.

4. I have leukaemia.

5. By the time you read this,
   I will probably be dead.

A BOOK ABOUT US

Today was our first day back at school after the Christmas holidays.

We have school three days a week – on Mondays, Wednesdays and Fridays, in the living room. There are only two pupils – me and Felix. Felix doesn't care about learning anything.

"What's the point of being ill if you have to do maths?" he said, the first time he came to school at my house. Mrs Willis, who's our teacher, didn't argue. She doesn't fuss if Felix doesn't do any work. She just lets him sit there, leaning back in his chair and telling me what's wrong with whatever I'm doing.

"That's not how you spell ammonium! We never spelt

ammonium like that at my school!"

"There's a planet called Hercules – isn't there, Mrs Willis?"

"What're you doing *that* for?"

Felix only comes to school to see me and to give his mum a break.

Nowadays, Mrs Willis thinks up ploys to interest him. You know the sort of thing; making volcanoes that really erupt, cooking Roman food, making fire with a magnifying glass.

Only my mum didn't like that one, because we accidentally burnt a hole in the dining table.

Sort of accidentally-on-purpose.

Today, though, Mrs Willis said, "How about you do some writing?" and we both groaned, because we'd been hoping for more fire, or possibly an explosion. Mrs Willis said, "Oh, come on, now. I thought you might like to write something about yourselves. I know you both like reading."

Felix looked up. He was playing with two of my Warhammer orcs, advancing them on each other and going "Grrrrah!" under his breath.

"Only 'cause there's nothing else to do in hospital," he said.

Me and Felix are both experts at being in hospital. That's where we met, last year.

I didn't see what reading had to do with writing about me and I said, "Books are just about kids saving the world or getting beaten up at school. You wouldn't write about us."

"Maybe not you," said Felix. He pressed his hand to his

forehead and flopped back in his chair. "The tragic story of Sam McQueen. A poor, frail child! Struggling bravely through *terrible* suffering and hospitals with no televisions!"

I made vomiting noises. Felix stretched his hand – the one that wasn't pressed to his forehead – out to me.

"Goodbye – goodbye – dear friends—" he said, and collapsed against his chair making choking sounds.

Mrs Willis said, "No dying at the table, Felix." But you could tell she wasn't really angry. She said, "I'd like you both to have a go now, please. Tell me something about yourself. You don't have to write a whole book by lunchtime."

So that's what we're doing. Well, I am. Felix isn't doing it properly. He's written: "My name is Felix Stranger and", and then he stopped. Mrs Willis didn't make him write any more. But I'm on page three already.

School's nearly over now, anyway. It's very quiet. Mrs Willis is pretending to do her marking and really reading *70 Things To Do With Fire* under the table. Felix is leading my orcs in a stealth attack on the pot plant. Columbus, the cat, is watching with yellow eyes.

Next door, in the kitchen, Mum is stirring the soup, which is lunch. Dad is in Middlesbrough, being a solicitor. My sister Ella is at school. Real school. Thomas Street Primary.

Any minute now – there it is! There's the doorbell. Felix's mum is here. School is over.

WHY I LIKE FACTS

I like facts. I like *knowing* things. Grown-ups never understand this. You ask them something like, "Can I have a new bike for Christmas?" and they give you a waffly answer, like, "Why don't you see how you feel nearer Christmas?" Or you might ask your doctor, "How long do I have to stay in hospital?" and he'll say something like, "Let's wait and see how you get on", which is doctor-speak for "I don't know".

I don't have to go into hospital ever again. Dr Bill promised. I have to go to clinic – that's it. If I get really sick, I can stay at home.

That's because I'm going to die.

Probably.

Going to die is the biggest waffly thing of all. No one will tell you anything. You ask them questions and they cough and change the subject.

If I grow up, I'm going to be a scientist. Not the sort that mixes chemicals together, but the sort that investigates UFOs and ghosts and things like that. I'm going to go to haunted houses and do tests and prove whether or not poltergeists and aliens and Loch Ness monsters really exist. I'm very good at finding things out. I'm going to find out the answers to all the questions that nobody answers.

All of them.

My sister Ella went back to school today too. She and Mum had
a huge fight this morning about it. She doesn't get why I stay at
home all day and she doesn't.

"Sam doesn't go to school!" she said to Mum. "You don't go to
work!"

"I have to look after Sam," Mum said.

"You do not," said Ella. "You just do ironing and plant things
and talk to Granny."

Which is true.

My mum named me Sam, after Samson in the Bible, and my
dad named Ella after his aunt. If they'd talked to each other a bit

more while they were doing it, they might not have ended up with kids called Sam 'n' Ella, but it's too late to change that now. I think Dad thinks it's funny, anyway.

Ella's eight. She has dark hair and bright, greeny-brown eyes, like those healing stones you buy in hippie shops. No one else in my family cares what they look like. Granny goes round in trousers with patches and padded waistcoats with pockets for pencils and seed packets and train tickets. And Mum's clothes are all about a hundred years old. But Ella always fusses about what she wears. She has a big box of nail varnish and all of Mum's make-up because Mum hardly ever wears it.

"Why don't you wear it?" says Ella. "*Why?*"

Ella always asks questions. Granny said she was born asking a question and it hasn't been answered yet.

"Was I?" said Ella, when she heard this. "What was it?"

We all laughed.

"Where am I?" said Mum.

"Who're these funny-looking people?" said Granny.

"What am I *doing* here?" said Dad. "I was supposed to be a princess!"

"Who'd make *you* a princess?" I said.

It's afternoon now and I'm still writing. I bet I could write a book. Easy. I was going to do some more after Felix went, but Maureen from Mum's church came round, so I had to be visited. She only left when Mum went to fetch Ella from school. I was thinking up

"Questions Nobody Answers" at the dining table when they came back. Ella ran straight over to me.

"What are you doing?"

"School stuff," I said. I curled my arm around the page. Ella came right up behind me and peered over my shoulder.

"*Ella*. I'm busy," I said. It was the wrong thing to say. She tugged on my arm.

"Let me *see*!"

"*Mum!*" I wailed. "Ella won't let me work!"

"Sam won't let me *see*!"

Mum was on the phone. She came through with it pressed against her chest.

"Kids! Behave! Ella, leave your brother alone."

I pulled a face at Ella. She flung herself on to the sofa.

"It's not fair! You always let him win!"

Ella and Mum *always* fight. And Ella always says it's not fair. I bet that's the only reason I win, because I don't throw baby tantrums like she does.

Mum put down the phone and went over to Ella. Ella shouted, "Go away!" and ran upstairs. Mum gave this big sigh. She came over to me. I closed my pad so she wouldn't see the writing.

"Secret, is it?" she said.

"It's for school." I held my pen over the closed pad. Mum sighed. She kissed the top of my head and went upstairs after Ella.

I waited until I was quite sure she was gone, then I picked up my pen and started writing again.

QUESTIONS NOBODY ANSWERS NO. 1

How do you know that you've died?

LOOK OUT FOR

CLOSE
YOUR
PRETTY EYES

THE NEXT BOOK FROM
SALLY NICHOLLS

COMING AUGUST 2013